THE WILL OF IMPERIUM

BOOK V OF THE
IMPERIAL CHRONICLES

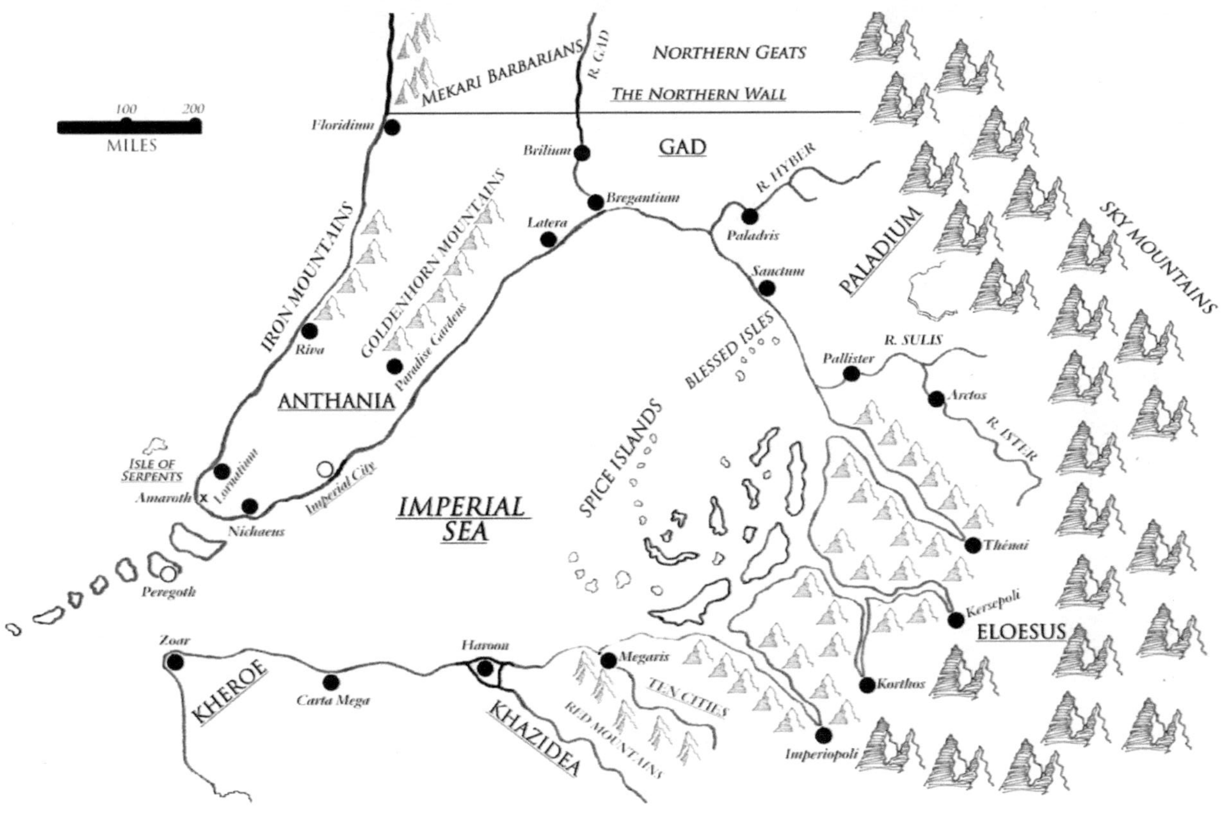

MILES
100
200
MEKARI BARBARIANS
R. GAD
NORTHERN GEATS
THE NORTHERN WALL
Floridium
Brilium
GAD
R. HYBER
Bregantium
Latera
Paladris
PALADIUM
SKY MOUNTAINS
IRON MOUNTAINS
GOLDENHORN MOUNTAINS
Sanctum
Riva
Paradise Gardens
BLESSED ISLES
R. SULIS
Pallister
ANTHANIA
Arctos
R. ISTER
ISLE OF SERPENTS
Lornatium
Imperial City
SPICE ISLANDS
Amaroth x
IMPERIAL SEA
Nichaeus
Thénai
Peregoth
Kersepoli
Zoar
Haroou
ELOESUS
KHEROE
Megaris
Carta Mega
KHAZIDEA
TEN CITIES
Korthos
RED MOUNTAINS
Imperiopoli

Imperial City

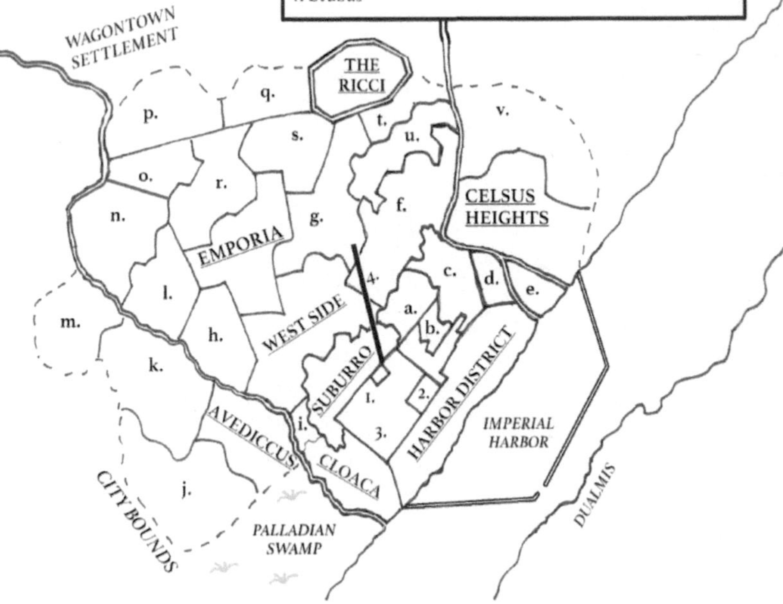

WARDS (LABELED)

a. Armory District
b. Kings Terrace
c. Maxima
d. Villa Regis
e. Bulus Wharf
f. Market District
g. Canyon Row
h. Newmarket
i. Mud Bottom
j. Meridia
k. Mystia
l. Villa Mares
m. Loud Surf
n. Perrine
o. Gaboline
p. West Limes
q. East Limes
r. Terrentian
s. Majorian Markets
t. The Strand
u. Meletus
v. Urubus

THE CITY: ITS SIGHTS AND WONDERS

City Bounds: *No legions may enter. It is the law.*
Wagontown Settlement: *A Haunt of Halflings.*
Dualmis: *An island across the sea.*
Imperial Harbor: *A wonder of the world.*
1. Imperial Square: *The Imperial Palace, the Council House and the Hippodrome, among other wonders.*
2. Campus: *The city's most ancient boundary.*
3. Imperial Arena: *Glory. Honor. Blood.*
4. Walk of Triumph: *See the nation's heroes and be amazed.*

PART ONE

I have worked furiously in the heat of my upper-story room. My son and all my friends are certain no one will read my "scribblings." But whether anyone besides me reads "The Imperial Chronicles" is not my prime concern. What has concerned me at all times is telling the tale of the nation I love, and getting to the very bottom of what ails it now.

I have finished writing of the time of trouble not long ago, when the Red Witch arrived from across the sea with her dark and barbarous religion. The faith of the One meant no wine or song — an unnatural and devilish philosophy if I had ever heard one.

Thus I begin the final words of the histories: "The coming years would test the courage of citizens and subject peoples, of legionaries and slaves, of the men and women of the Empire; and determine whether the nation chosen by Imperium would fulfill its calling: to rule over all the world."

Below in the streets, people begin to shout. Trumpets peal from the high towers — warnings of danger. I had penned the final words too soon—the tale is not over, yet.

"Invasion!" one man cries from below, in the street. "Get out! Run! Invasion, from beyond the sea!"

I fall back in my seat, overcome with terror, unable to bear what I heard. I shut my eyes and fall ill.

CHAPTER ONE:
THE SUMMONS

I.
CLAUDIO

Numa

Numa awoke in a place he didn't recognize, in a state of mind he didn't like, in a world that seemed in peril. The sky above, clear and blue, seemed within arm's reach; he was in a high mountain valley, near peaks still covered in snow.

And drums. There were loud drums pounding. In front of him lay a ruined temple with collapsed pillars… and a woman. A woman, naked, with a snake twined around her body. Numa gasped, suddenly out of breath and self-conscious, wanting to look at her but determined not to.

"Look at me, Claudio!" the woman boomed, and the spectral drums reached their fever pitch.

"I am not Claudio," Numa said, and finally allowed his gaze to fix on the nude woman. He gulped. "Wh-who are you?"

"I am Io," she responded. "I have always been Io. He is Hermas… he has always been Hermas." The snake flicked its forked tongue at the woman's words. Her white, sightless eyes indicated blindness, but Numa had no doubts she could see by a better vision than he. "And you," she continued, "*you* have always been Claudio."

Numa shook his head furiously. He had no doubts she meant Claudio-Valens Adamantus, the deified emperor. She could not be more wrong. "I am of no consequence, my good lady. I have no power, no wealth…"

"Neither did Claudio, when he rescued the Empire," she went

on. "Behold, I am Io, Oracle of Hylea, who sees all. 'Numa,' you are not dreaming. You are seeing visions of truth. A choice is before you, 'Numa,' and with your choice the fate of the Empire is decided. If you do as I ask, and journey to Mount Hylea to meet me in the flesh, then the Empire may be saved. If you refuse, the Empire will fall to the foreigners and those who aid them, and the free peoples of the Empire will be sold into bondage under the yoke of a dark foe."

"I—"

"Heed my words, Claudio! Journey to Mount Hylea or the Empire will fall."

II.
HARVEST HOME

Numa

Numa jerked out of bed. The morning light was filtering in through the window of his cottage. His thoughts turned to breakfast as he smelled bacon cooking in the other room. He remembered it was Harvest Home, the most joyful of days. And then he remembered the dream he'd had, and his stomach churned.

He scrambled to don his clothes, wondering just how in Varda the dream seemed so real—but he was certain it was only a dream, the product of his always desiring something better. Something better than Norriva, a tiny farming community just off the shore of the River Gad, where he and his ancestors had lived since before the Imperial invasion hundreds and hundreds of years ago.

"Get out of bed, you lazy oaf!" Mother squawked from the other room.

Days like these, he missed Father, who'd died when plague struck several years ago. It appeared, though Mother was plump and immobile and Numa stick-thin, they were made of sterner stuff than

Father.

Clothes donned, he entered the main hall, where indeed the bacon sat crackling on a pan, sizzling from the fire's heat. Mother had propped up a chair nearby. "Go make yourself useful, lazy boy! Go fetch some water, if you're wanting some boiled eggs."

But it was Mother who wanted boiled eggs, not Numa.

~

At the well, a commotion was apparent on the village green. A peddler had arrived in a great wagon, heavy-laden with valuables, but more importantly, with news of the outside world. The folk of Norriva swarmed him, eager to hear the latest morsels of gossip from Bregantium, perhaps even the faraway coastal cities Numa had never seen and likely never would.

Dropping the bucket by the well, he ran to hear what he could. The atmosphere in the crowd, however, had grown less excited and more—he noted anxiously—perturbed.

"What do you mean, my good man?" said Quintus, a bean farmer who lived nearby.

"I mean exactly what I said," the peddler replied in his coastland accent. "The Empire is under attack... foreigners have overrun Imperial City. There are lawgivers in the Imperial Palace."

"Lawgivers?" Numa shouted, and some in the crowd turned to gawk at him. "What do you mean, lawgivers? What are lawgivers?"

The peddler's eyes narrowed. "Ah, my good signore, the lawgivers are the most dreadful of all foes... they seek not just to conquer, but to take away all the things that bring mankind joy: wine, women, and song."

"Sounds good to me," said Alvus, the village priest.

At the words, the peddler's expression visibly darkened. "Then you will get what you deserve, my signore, when they come for you." He lifted up a dagger of steel. "You will need arms to defend yourselves and your families when the lawgivers come. This was made by the greatest smith in Imperial City, before he fell. Just twenty denara…"

Quietly, Numa lowered the bucket of water into the well, suddenly unsure about what he had been so certain of earlier. Perhaps he was wrong. Perhaps the dream from the oracle hadn't been a dream at all. Perhaps she was really calling him there.

"Oh, spare me!" Mother snapped when he told her. "You wouldn't last a day outside Norriva, you little fool. The southlands would eat you alive and spit you out."

A flash of anger shot up through Numa's veins, but he bit back a harsh reaction. *Mother is disabled, unable to fend for herself, and I shouldn't upset her.* Instead he plopped the bucket of water near her, grabbed a strip of bacon from the searing pan, and headed into his room.

Not long after he'd finished the tiny helping of meat, the door to his room opened, and he whipped around to identify the intruder.

His friend Appian stood there, blocking most of the entryway. He was tall and wide. A fat, handsome fool, the village girls called him, but Numa for some reason never considered Appian foolish.

"What's bothering you, friend?" Appian said.

"A dream."

"A dream? It must have been a very bad dream if it bothered you. I never thought you were superstitious."

"It wasn't a bad dream... I guess some might even think it's good."

Appian smiled. But as Numa told him of the oracle and the snake, his smile faded into a look of stunned silence.

"Oh, my, Numa. I don't think that is just a dream."

Numa narrowed his eyes.

"You aren't much of a reader, Numa," Appian said, "but I am."

It was true. Appian was the biggest bookworm in all Norriva – and though that didn't say much, his dozens of books were by far the largest collection Numa had ever seen.

"The Oracle of Hylea is a madwoman, some say," Appian explained. "But I don't think she is. We Imperials moved her from her old home in Eloesus... and her snake, Hermas, too. Gods, Numa, have you gotten into my books? Have you read about her?"

"No," Numa answered. "No, I haven't. I haven't at all."

"You did not dream a simple dream," Appian said. "You have to do what she said. You have to go to the mountain. The Empire—"

"I don't know how to get there."

"I will come with you." Appian looked serious.

"No," Numa said firmly. "I won't leave Norriva all because of a dream... risk death for something that might be foolishness."

"You're right," Appian said. "The dream must have been false... you don't have near the guts of Claudio."

Numa's shoulders sank as Appian turned to leave. Numa eyed the floor and thought on what Appian had said. When he shut his eyes, he saw the oracle's white, sightless eyes staring at him.

~

The day progressed and Harvest Home began in earnest. In big towns such as Brill and Bregantium, there would be firework displays and grand parties. Not in Norriva.

In Norriva they had stands lining the village green. Hilda, who called herself "everyone's grandmother," had set out dozens of apple pies and scores of cherry tarts. Bottles of wine and kegs of beer were piled high, and in the center of the green were a pile of pumpkins carved with faces.

Others Numa's age stood around the green in groups, not bothering to look at him, but surely discussing him. No one in Norriva liked Numa — no one except Appian. Sometimes Numa really did want to pack up his things and leave. But where would he go? To the Oracle, perhaps.

But there was Mother. There was always Mother. At age thirteen, Numa had noticed her health begin to decline. Whenever he thought she'd reached her nadir, her condition only worsened. Now, she couldn't even walk.

"Did y' hear, Silvia?" a village man said from nearby. "Th' southrons have invaded us. 'Tis only a matter of time afore we must worship Athra the Fire God, and set up a right temple in the middle o' the green."

"Fool's talk," Silvia snapped back.

"Not Athra." The voice of Shareeka boomed from behind Numa. "A god much worse, I'm afraid."

Numa turned to face him. The ratling stood a little over four feet tall, with an Imperial shortsword and an imposing presence to match, but the people of Norriva didn't think much of him. Even Mother didn't like Numa paling around with a ratling, though he was a veteran who'd fought in the legions of Claudian Adamantus. Shareeka was much too old, Mother said, and he's got a tail, and whiskers. Whiskers!

So many said ratlings spread disease, though neither Numa nor anyone in the village had any evidence. "A god much worse," Shareeka said again. "Mazda."

"Mazda," Numa repeated the foreign word.

"A god of tyranny and anger. A god of slavery and submission. A god who demands you hate all other gods."

"That doesn't sound like any god I know," Numa breathed.

"But I have seen Mazda and his followers. I fought the lawgivers in the war."

And Shareeka had the shortsword to prove it. Ratlings were too short to fight side-by-side in the legion with sword and shield, but the Imperial Army needed skulks and spies as much as any other nation. The weapon Shareeka bore had many scrapes and scratches, a leather handle and a rich gilded pommel. "Perhaps the Empire needs you, then," Numa muttered thoughtlessly, but the ratling's pink eyes sparkled with interest.

"Yes," the ratling answered. "Perhaps it does. But I shouldn't want to leave without my good friend Numa."

"I wouldn't want to tie you down." A trace of a smile formed on Numa's lips. "Norriva is no place for a war hero."

The ratling smiled in response. "Norriva is not the place for anyone who wasn't born in it."

Numa laughed. At that moment, the fact he'd been born in Norriva became a weight of shame on his shoulders.

He thought of the oracle, supremely wise in her madness. He wondered if she really called him — if he really should go. But he couldn't. He didn't have the means or the know-how to get there. And Mother would starve without him. *If it weren't for Mother…* That woman would be the end of him. But without her, he was nothing.

Seth, a cherry farmer who'd come all this way to town, strummed his lute to the fast-paced tune of "If I were an Adamantus…" as he sat perched on a beer barrel. The village girls scrambled to begin the annual harvest dance, and the boys ran out to join them. Numa ducked away, having learned long ago to avoid such occasions—they invariably ended with a hurt heart and wounded pride.

Appian nonetheless gathered the gumption to begin the dance. By the way the boys were lining up, it looked like Appian's partner would be Esmeralda, the village blacksmith's daughter. She was a cow of a woman and very sharp of tongue, but Numa had grown fonder of her lately—more often than not she stood up for the most despised in the village, and though the elders called her a *lupa* in the making, Numa's respect for her had only grown.

"Ah, my Numa," the voice of Shareeka purred from behind.

Numa whipped around, startled even though it was his friend speaking.

"I am sorry… your mother…"

"What are you talking about, Shareeka?" The ratling often skulked about his house.

"Come with me."

~

Mother lay still by the fire, a half-eaten boiled egg in her hand and a stein of ale in the other.

When Numa rested his hand on her cheek, the skin was cold to the touch. "Gods." He huffed. "Gods damn it."

"I am sorry, my signore."

When Shareeka said "signore" he sounded like a southerner, but the only true Imperials in Norriva were Appian and his family. "Gods, I never knew when it would happen," Numa said. "I never knew how I would feel." In truth, the fact he felt so gutted surprised him. He fought tears, warding them off like demons. *A man should never cry*—so his father had said, before his life was cut so prematurely short.

"I suppose we will have to go to the southlands together, my signore—you, me, and Appian. I think we will make a good team."

"Do not call me 'signore.'" He said it cuttingly, through nearly-clenched teeth. His words were true; what else did he have, here, without Mother? Through a watery film of tears, he eyed the ratling before him with a growing suspicion. *What are the chances*, he thought, *of her dying right now?* And how did Shareeka know of Numa's dream? Appian must have told him.

~

Numa did not cry at the funeral the following morning. As the village priest sang hymns to Terrena the Harvest Queen and a group of men lowered the coffin into its resting place, Numa managed to keep his turbulent emotions in check.

When Appian took his place near Numa, as the village priest went on and on about how everybody returns to the soil, Numa uttered the words he knew would change his life, but words that needed to be said: "I am leaving."

"And I am leaving with you," Appian replied without a moment's pause.

From behind them, Shareeka spoke, unexpectedly as always. "And I will show you both the way."

CHAPTER TWO:
THE PHILOSOPHER QUEEN

Cleon Adelphos, Vice Provost of the Thenoan Academy

Priscilla Marianus, by Cleon's estimation, was one of those few specimens that Nature rarely but invariably produced: supremely intelligent and gifted, a being who could argue with the most highly educated scholars and the most talented philosophers. Priscilla, he reflected as the other scholars joined him in the midst of the Council House, was undeniably a master of ideas, the most well-read and learned of anyone he'd met. A wonder, considering her Imperial heritage: a heritage she had scorned and disowned publicly in Thénai's lecture halls, yearning for the days when Imperial City was a backwater village of bandits and thugs and the philosophers of Eloesus reigned intellectually supreme.

Some found Cleon's doting on her "pathetic" and "unseemly" but how could he possibly not hold reverence for a woman who had single-handedly driven out the legions of Imperial City to create the new utopia? Certainly, they had to employ the use of foreigners—the lawgivers, whom the simple-minded Imperial citizens despised—but they, in the Academies' collective estimation, were a lesser evil in the grand scheme of things.

Priscilla entered the former Council House, and Cleon's fellow scholars stood up at rapt attention, holding a potent mixture of fear and reverence for the Provost of the Eloesian Academy. In her hands she clutched a thick tome, which she—assuming the Speaker of the Council's former position—set on the grand lectern and cleared her throat. "Scholars, philosophers, great thinkers and persons of impressive intellect, I will begin our meeting with a lovely quote from the philosopher Theiarchus: 'There is no cause or idea I would die for; I could be wrong.' A supremely wise statement. My friends, we truly live in the age of Thenoan Philosophy, where we are neither the pawns of the gods nor true free agents. The Empire's many imbalances and injustices need righting, and with the help of our friends the lawgivers we will finally achieve our utopia."

Cleon smiled at the woman, old and gray now yet still strong. *The lawgivers are our friends.* Sometimes it was hard to remember—they had made a great massacre in the streets and burnt down the taverns and ale-shops, murdered the brothel workers and imposed a new law over the few citizens that chose to remain. But there were no gods, and—as Priscilla so brilliantly put it—the Academies should not consider at any point the means of achieving their goal, but only the ends.

"Dear friends of mine, I bring before you a question of logic and philosophy. It may seem irrelevant to the task of dismantling and rebuilding we are focused on, but it isn't. The question is this: if the gods are good, and we do not live in the best possible world, then is the gods' absence positively, negatively, or neutrally true?"

Such wit, Cleon thought to himself, that he did not fully comprehend the question.

"In less civilized days, when the Empire was at its grandest, we would ask ourselves silly questions such as 'How many gods could fit on the point of a needle?'" The Council House echoed with laughter. "Now if the gods are good, and we do not live in the best possible world, then is the gods' absence positively, negatively, or neutrally true?"

The doors to the Council House opened and a man in lawgiver blacks strode in. Dangling from his belt was a curved saber inset with rubies. Priscilla had despised the ability of the Imperial citizens to wield weapons, and she in fact hated blades of all kinds, but the lawgivers refused to part with them, even in close quarters with her. On some matters there was no negotiation. "My good men," Umar, the Theomancer's highest-ranked field marshal, said. "The Imperial citizens who refused to obey the law have all been cleared out of the city. Many thousands have decided to call Mazda their lord. Thousands more have begun paying their tax as protected nonbelievers. The Theomancer has begun to mobilize his army to subdue the countryside."

For so long, Cleon noted with a grin, the Empire had thought its legions were invincible, a fighting force that simply could not be defeated. Yet in these men of the distant south the prideful Empire had found its match.

"Praise Mazda," Priscilla answered.

Words, Cleon noted, that she did not especially say with conviction, but words necessary to appease the lawgivers and enlist the Theomancer's aid.

Yet at them, Umar's dark eyes only narrowed. His few yellow teeth bared in a half-snarl. "Do not say words you do not mean, woman."

"But I do mean them." Priscilla spoke the word with a hint of fear, and took a step back.

Cleon wondered, occasionally, if these lawgivers saw past their ruse, if they knew the Academies were using them.

"The faith of Mazda is an ancient and venerable faith, much preferable to the former gods," Priscilla went on.

At the words Umar's lips perked into a slight smile; perhaps Priscilla had, at last, pleased him. "You will learn to revere Mazda and his Hand in time, my good woman."

And the frazzled Priscilla returned the grin with a radiant smile.

Perhaps, Cleon thought, *we all will.*

CHAPTER THREE:
THE BREGANTINE COURT

Emperor Secondo Janus the God

The massacre in Imperial City had been so sudden, only Secondo and a handful of Imperial Councilors escaped with their lives. Maximian, Marshal of the Guard, battled the lawgivers at the Imperial bedchamber as Secondo made his way through the secret door. He had heard Maximian's death-cry, and he would remember it for all time with a heavy weight of guilt.

At the official rendezvous point in times of disaster, Victory City—the former Eximenius—Secondo Janus had found only a few minor officials and four councilors waiting for him.

"Good gods, what has become of our nation?" Secondo Janus had exclaimed.

And the councilor Vitellian had said, "We can think about that later. Now, we must get you to safety. We must set up an interim government—"

"Where?" Secondo Janus had cried.

"Bregantium," another councilor had suggested, and in an instant it became their sole course of action.

For the first time, Secondo Janus had wished Imperial City had walls.

~

Yet now Secondo Janus rode on a ship toward Bregantium— a terrible thing, since Secondo had held a lifelong fear of the sea. A landlubber to the innermost sinew, he had barely held his panic in his youthful days in the military. When he returned from the south as a veteran, he had sworn an oath he'd never travel the sea again.

And yet now, staying on land is more terrifying than traveling by ship. So much of the past few days seemed a dizzying blur. The men in their black flowing robes, wielding scimitars, no doubt came from the far south, but they were not Fharese. "Gods," he cursed as he stared out into the bright blue sea.

"Your Undying Glory," Vitellian said from behind. "To defeat the lawgivers we must mobilize all our forces."

Secondo Janus turned to face him. Through all his trials and travails the youngest councilor had remained a dear friend. "The lawgivers." *Ah, now I remember.* Long ago, they had troubled the Fharese Kingdom, wishing to impose their unnatural law, before the padisha became their dearest ally. "How did they get here?"

"Treason," Vitellian said. "Though I do not know exactly who betrayed us. Yet I know we were betrayed; it is the only explanation. Our navy did not intercept them. Our allies in Kheroe did not warn us. This smells of something elaborate, a grand scheme of someone who knows all the Empire's inner workings, planned deliberately from inside."

"Then who?"

"I fear," Vitellian muttered as the ship dipped down from a high wave, "someone in the government. There was an element in the Council I have always feared."

Secondo clutched the railing to steady himself against the ship's rocking, and drew in a cold breath. "Who?"

"Crispus Servillius… and others."

"The very Speaker of the Council?"

"We should not act on a single man's suspicions… least of all me."

Vitellian was too modest. A wave of nausea seized Secondo. He retched over the railing but no bile came out. "Damned seasickness." Or was it fear?

"In Bregantium, we must form our plans."

"In Bregantium," Secondo breathed. "Yes, in Bregantium all our troubles will cease." Yet even Secondo knew his words were false, a reassurance to a terrified mind.

~

Neither storm nor pirate assailed them, and within four days' time they had reached—on the back of good winds—the capital of Gad. Here, the ravages of the lawgivers were nowhere to be seen: no burning buildings, no smashed statues or images. Yet the people of the city, wandering among the stone-paved streets, bore the signs of the crisis: hushed whispers, a hurried gait, and a growing sense that the Empire was doomed.

Seeing Secondo Janus the God, still wearing his silver Imperial Circlet, enter the city with a handful of Imperial Councilors and soldiers seemed to only worsen the mood of thickly-building unease. It seemed Secondo Janus was living proof of the Empire's doom, that the nation they loved would be subjected to the lawgivers and their onerous rule.

~

Tidus Arappo, governor of Gad, greeted Secondo Janus and his entourage at the Governor's Mansion. Its white limestone pillars and rosy brick walls, flanked at all sides by palmettos, no doubts had all the amenities any man would require. *In times of peace,* Secondo thought glumly, *the Governor's Mansion would have been such a nice place to stay.*

Tidus Arappo fell to his knees. "Your Undying Glory."

Vitellian took over; Secondo was too caught up in what might have been.

"Tidus," the Imperial Councilor said. "No doubt the news has reached you. Imperial City has been sacked, the first time in living memory. The first time in history, in that scale."

Arappo frowned. The governor of Gad wore clothes luxurious even in their simplicity: a tunic dyed deep navy blue, a belt of dark leather with a gold buckle, and a pair of breeches dyed forest green. His golden brown hair gave him the look of a native Getan, though the Arappos were an August family of Peregothian descent.

Though, Secondo thought, *there is so very much intermarriage.*

"I don't know what to say," Arappo said, and sighed. "Certainly I will do all I can…"

"I know you will," Vitellian said. "You are, after all, a patriot. We need a new base of operations for the Empire… a temporary capital, while we fight the lawgivers."

"Indeed," Arappo said. "Anything for the Empire… anything for the emperor." His chestnut eyes met Secondo's, and for a reason he did not understand they unnerved him.

Perhaps I am not fit to be an emperor after all.

CHAPTER FOUR:
THE WHITE ACACIA COURT

Astarthe, Queen of Haroon

Astarthe was not immune to the news. Another woman, another queen, might take advantage of the new calamity, and declare Khazidea a sovereign and independent nation, free of the Empire's overbearing grasp. But Astarthe was not that queen.

No, she had donned sackcloth and powdered her face with ash, drawn up the curtains to her private chamber and sobbed restlessly. No longer did she call the Red Palace the joyful White Lotus Court or the reflective Blue Lotus Court; no, she called it the White Acacia Court, after the flower garlands with which they buried the dead. A day had passed since she last left the place of her mourning, for the death of the Empire, the father of her son.

Worst of all was the aggressor. Few knew of her experience with the lawgivers. She'd been taken captive at a young age, and seen firsthand their grave oppression and dark-heartedness. She had seen the great darkness of their souls. Her caretaker, the Godling priest Issachar, and her own brother-husband Anakh, had both perished because of them.

"Why, Issa?" she prayed. "Why, my celestial mother? Why, Moon Goddess, would you place the free people of the Empire under the lawgivers' yoke?"

Someone pounded on the door.

"Leave me alone!" Astarthe snapped cuttingly.

Instead, whoever it was tried the door, finding it locked.

"Leave me alone!" Astarthe hissed, harsher than before.

"When crisis falls over the Fertile Land," the high-pitched eunuch voice of a Godling priest echoed through the door, "the queen must lead her people. '*Or Issa's tears will stop their flooding, and Atman's seeds will not bear fruit.*' The Fertile Land needs its ruler."

Astarthe could not respond as harshly to his words. *I am in mourning. I am in despair.* But her people needed her.

Still in the sackcloth garb and ash-powdered face of a mourner, she opened the door and entered the troubled Red Palace with the Godling priest by her side.

~

At the foot of the Red Throne, the members of the White Acacia Court had gathered: handmaids and Godling priests, and her son Adamantion.

"The queen mourns," said Midian, the Godling priest at her side. "And who shall blame her? But she must lead."

"Indeed I must," Astarthe muttered.

"The Empire is in its death throes," said Sinn, another Godling priest. "The capital city is a battlefield. The time has never been better to declare our independence from the barbarians' yoke, and have the true sister-queen reign in all her power."

Astarthe strove to tame the fire rising up inside her. "Is that what you want, Sinn? You wish the Empire to fall?"

Sinn looked uncertain of what to say.

"By Issa, the Moon Goddess, I should cast you outside the walls of Haroon and see you devoured by wild dogs."

Sinn backed away.

"We will lend the Empire all our support. We will do everything we can to preserve it. It does not matter if the lawgivers are stronger… we will fight them to our dying breath. I would be pleased to die a servant of Issa and the friend of the Empire. Would you say the same, Sinn?"

"Yes," Sinn answered, but he backed away, having the look of a frightened dog.

"There are five legions in Khazidea…"

"There is one," Sinn corrected her. "All four have left along the Imperial Road, heading east. The last remains at the edge of the

Desolation to stand guard over Fharas. The legate said he hopes we will remain loyal."

"And we will," Astarthe said firmly, "to our dying breath."

~

Late in the day, a messenger entered in the Red Palace, the rare occasion an adult male was let inside. Astarthe met him in the Red Throne room, having washed the ash from her face and donned her silken royal robes.

"Your Highness," he said, "I bring you news of the Fertile Land and beyond."

"Speak," Astarthe answered him.

"The Asa—"

At the word, time seemed to stop for Astarthe. The name of the nomads who lived in the Red Mountains hadn't been spoken in a long time, and then only in passing. For decades the brother-sister sovereigns of Khazidea had warred with them but never managed to completely extinguish the threat.

"—they have received an emissary of the lawgivers. They have agreed to follow the Law of Mazda, and serve the Theomancer. And you have no doubts heard that the Theomancer has declared war on you. He has called you immoral and wicked and all manner of names."

It dawned on Astarthe that perhaps the lawgivers remembered her. It had not been long since she was a young girl, held in captivity by the lawgivers yet broken from their control by the god Claudian Adamantus.

"Yet the Asa are our largest concern, I fear… they will cross the desert to ravage our lands, if they have not already."

"And there is no legion to protect us," Astarthe said. *Only two-hundred Anakhil, the laughing stock of the Imperial Army, and a few cohorts.*

"The four legions are busy in Eloesus," the messenger continued. "A sedition has begun there. It started in the Academies. Some scholar said he'd uncovered a long genealogy, and discovered the last remaining descendant of the King of Thénai. The false king Anastasios wants to create a new Thenoan Empire."

"The world has gone mad," Astarthe said, and wondered if she of all people—the sister-queen of Haroon—was the last remaining patriot.

"It has indeed," the messenger said. "Some say the Eloesians have never been truly happy under the Imperial yoke. King Anastasios promises freedom from 'tyranny.' Yet I am sure in a way he wants to bring in a new kind of tyranny."

Astarthe frowned and looked down. "Either way, we must act quickly. Warn all the peasants to take shelter—in Haroon, if possible. Send riders everywhere. By dusk, we will shut the gates. The Asa are bloodthirsty and vicious if the history books tell the truth."

"And if recent events have shown us…" Midian's high eunuch voice heralded his presence as he walked into the Red Chamber. "The Law of Mazda will make them even more barbaric and vile. 'Those born into the light, and yet choose darkness, are the darkest-hearted of all. Praise be to Atman the Progenitor, Lord of the Khazan.'"

Astarthe smiled grimly. "Ah, Midian, I can always depend on you to know the holy verses." She eyed the sandstone floor of the throne room. "Trials await us. Darkness awaits us. The Empire faces its most difficult test. But I… I will rise to the challenge, and defend it." She stood up from the Red Throne. "Long live the Empire!"

"Long live the Empire!" Midian shouted.

"Long live the Empire!" the messenger followed.

~

By nightfall, the horde of Asa had reached the border. The South Gate of Haroon closed just before.

CHAPTER FIVE:
THE ANCIENT WAY

Numa

All roads led to Imperial City, perhaps, but it took many days traveling dirt paths and poorly-kept roads before at last Numa, Appian, and Shareeka reached the Path of Tidus.

The ancient way, which served as a model for all the Imperial Roads that crisscrossed the Empire and shortened the distance between its many provinces, stretched many yards across, and its pavestones gleamed white in the bright late summer sun. Numa had never been here, nor had he ever thought he would. In truth, he never thought he'd ever travel to Brill, perhaps not even leave Norriva, let alone go on this fool's quest to the Oracle of Hylea.

"The Path of Tidus," Appian said. During the journey, he had been a human encyclopedia. "No one knows its origins exactly. It was here in 1 Y.E., when the first brick of Peregoth was laid. Do you know why it is called the Path of Tidus, Numa?"

"Of course I don't," Numa answered, and smiled faintly. "I'm an ignorant rustic from Norriva."

"As we all are," Appian said, and returned Numa's faint smile with a bright one. "Tidus, the third emperor, controlled all of Anthania. At last he followed the road, until he came to the Wall, which no Imperial had seen before. And he traveled the whole extent until he came to the northern capital—an assemblage of stick huts and crude dwellings, then, built along a river. We've called it the Path of Tidus ever since."

"Maybe," Shareeka laughed, "you should become a scholar, and teach in the Eloesian Academies."

"I am an Imperial, an Anthanian," Appian said. "Imperials are meant to rule, not study."

He is an Imperial, Numa thought, *and I am a barbarian Getan. So why would the oracle have such an interest in me? Why would she call me Claudio?* Yet at the end of it all, the dream could be meaningless—and the thought of that gutted him like nothing else. The thought of wasting his friends' efforts on some foolish vision. Of traveling to Mount Hylea, and realizing he had been right at first, when this journey began—that Numa was no one, nothing, just a simple rustic from Norriva.

He sighed in despair.

"Now our journey begins in earnest," Shareeka said. "Follow this path, and eventually you'll reach the gleaming domes and high apartment blocks of Imperial City. But that is not where we are going. The Path of Tidus will take us near Mount Hylea. Then, to the oracle."

A fool's journey, Numa wanted to say, but he kept his mouth closed.

They walked southward in the hot sun, and Numa's shoes became increasingly threadbare. Of all of them, only Shareeka had been on long journeys, and then with the security of the legion. Still, he was well prepared; he'd brought an Imperial Army shortsword, and a pair of daggers, as well as a pouch of gold libra Numa was certain he stole. Among the other things, Shareeka was rumored to be a thief and a pickpocket. Whenever someone lost an object of value, Shareeka received the blame first.

And Appian's parents—as carefree as they were well-to-do—consented to the journey, and even loaned him a family heirloom, an Imperial legate's shortsword. Its gold hilt was forged into the shape of a horse, the Appia family crest.

And Numa—the supposed conqueror, the second Claudio—had only a walking stick as a weapon, and a tiny kitchen knife he'd taken from home. *It is Appian who should have had the dream, not me.*

"The further south we go, the closer the enemy," Shareeka said ominously. "The lawgivers are a savage people, but they are strong. At some point, we'd best stray off the road."

Numa gulped. He told himself to stay strong, to keep his

courage, to strive to be like Claudio-Valens Adamantus even though he wasn't even a fraction of the legendary conqueror.

~

Night fell and the humid heat hardly eased. In the roadside inn Shareeka had found, a group of legionaries quite clearly drunk out of their minds played dice. The serving girls brought out meat pies to a party of travelers. The innkeeper, a pudgy man with thick brown hair and a grease-stained apron, sized them up as they entered. "Greetings," he said. "Welcome to the Looking Glass Inn. Where is your final destination? North, no doubt."

"No doubt?" Shareeka responded without answering the question.

"You aren't going south, are you? So many refugees fleeing Anthania I'm sad to say I've profited. The Empire's a lost cause, they say. The emperor has fled to Bregantium with the few councilors that survived—"

"*Bregantium?*" Appian said incredulously.

"Indeed," the innkeeper responded. "To the very land where no proper Imperial would think of visiting until now. To the land of us barbarian Getans, yes? And the East is in revolt."

"The East," Appian muttered the words like they were curses. "Useless philosophers and academes… We need a second Caro."

Numa recalled now-dim history lessons of Caro, the bloodthirsty grand legate who destroyed the old eastern world and brought it into submission.

"Indeed we do," the innkeeper said. "But there is no Caro without a legion, and the southron invaders have all but demolished the ones that dared fight 'em. It's either appeasement or death, some say. Others are hoping for a better life in the northlands… a life as a peasant is better than life under the lawgivers—if you can even call it that."

"Cowards," Appian muttered.

"Indeed," Numa voiced his agreement.

"You aren't going south, are you?" the innkeeper said.

"Yes," Numa answered firmly.

Shareeka snapped his gaze toward Numa; his beady pink eyes burned hot with anger.

Perhaps I shouldn't have said it. But what could this innkeeper possibly do?

"I wish you all the best," the innkeeper said. "But you are going to the graveyard of so many. Thousands have died."

"We are not changing our course," Shareeka snapped. "Now, come with me."

~

In their upper story room, Shareeka hissed all manner of curses at Numa. "There was no reason to tell the innkeeper anything about where we were going. True, he probably cannot and will not do us any harm, but you must make a habit of keeping that mouth shut."

Numa could not bring himself to say "sorry."

"And we need to get you a sword. I wouldn't trust a smith here, ignoramus that he probably is. But I won't have you unprotected. Here…" To Numa's surprise, Shareeka unclipped his sword and sheath from his belt, and handed it to him. "This belonged to me in the legion. It's a good sword, as good as all legionaries' swords are. It will serve you well."

Numa took it in his hands. "Ah… I… thank you, Shareeka. What about—?"

"Don't worry about me," Shareeka said. "My daggers will serve me perfectly well. After all, I am a sneak and a skulk, not a warrior like you wish to be."

But do I wish to be? "I don't know how to use it."

"Then we will practice," Shareeka said, "and soon you will learn how to fight with the best of us. I will make a Claudio out of you, yet."

The words comforted Numa somehow, to think that perhaps Shareeka believed in him, even if he himself didn't.

~

The Path of Tidus stretched for indeterminate distance, piercing through the north woods and cutting through hills, straight as a sunbeam. In the early mornings, while Appian packed up the tent, Shareeka sparred with Numa, using wooden practice swords and refusing to go easy on him. By the end of the week, Numa's hands and arms were covered with welts and black bruises. But day by day, morning by morning and night by night, Numa began to find his center and his balance. Any experienced legionary would no doubt cut him to pieces, but at least Numa could answer the most basic of stabs and slashes with parries, and make a few cuts of his own. His arms were thick and strong, forged in the strenuous labor of the lumbering trade, but he had not even begun to master the finesse that true swordsmanship required.

Five days down the Path of Tidus, and the refugees traveling north grew thicker. Shareeka said they had traveled a hundred and fifty miles, and Numa's sore, aching legs were proof. Yet the province of Anthania lay many miles distant, and Mount Hylea an even farther, impossible journey beyond the border. The milestones, placed at even lengths along the road, only worsened Numa's travel-soreness. To think that Imperial City lay as much as six-hundred miles away—six weeks of walking—would have been too much to bear, had it not been for the company he was in.

With Shareeka, the town pariah who knows his way around the world. And, of course, Appian, the sole Imperial in the group, the only one who had a passing chance of becoming the next Claudio. Perhaps if the Oracle of Hylea was mistaken, she would use Numa's friend, the noble scion of the line of Appia, instead.

~

Mile by mile, the storm of rumor grew: that the foreigners had completely overrun all of South Anthania, up to the Central Valley, spreading their dominion north. And the three friends rode together down the Empire's most ancient way, south into the gathering storm.

CHAPTER SIX:
A NEW EAST

Pontio Piraeus, Chief Lecturer

Pontio grinned as he watched the newly-declared "king" of Thénai, Anastasios, lifted high above the crowd on a litter. The simpleton even wore a diadem of knotted purple silk, in the fashion of the ancients, though he was in all likelihood the descendant of a commoner. Pontio would know; he had conjured up the long, illustrious line going back to the Eloesian king Arestides, and Tarchon the Conqueror. His goal—and the goal of Priscilla Marianus—was to merely begin a revolt, to loosen the Empire's grip while she did her work with the lawgivers abroad.

With the two crises combined, the Empire—great juggernaut of power that it was—would falter and collapse. Then, Pontio's leader Priscilla Marianus had already decided who she would execute: the former warmongers who slew hundreds of southrons and brought untold destruction upon that ancient and glorious civilization, to whom the Empire owed all its culture and knowledge; the simpletons who followed what she called "blind patriotism" and refused to repent; and lastly, she would execute the soldiers, and disband the Imperial Army altogether.

Yet now, all Pontio could do was laugh at the young fool Anastasios with his purple diadem and his trimmed philosopher's beard. The Eloesians cheered—the joyful cries of a people freed from their rude master.

"People of Eloesus!" Anastasios cried, reciting the words Pontio's fellow academes had fed him. "We stand at a crossroads! For many centuries before the Empire, while Peregoth was a village of stick huts beside a muddy river, the glory of our people outshone anyone else in the Middle Sea..."

Not the Imperial Sea, Pontio thought with a grin.

"We were friends to Fharas, and learned much at the feet of the padisha emperor. With Tarchon the Conqueror we laid hold of all the wealth of Khazidea, hundreds of years before the Empire! And now, my good subjects, we are free again! The legions will try their best to destroy our spirits, but they will undoubtedly fail. The ancient lion has awoken, and there shall be no silencing him. The Glory of the East begins anew today!"

Pontio had heard word that the legions stationed in Khazidea had begun their march down the Imperial Road. The ones that had foolishly left Eloesus, trusting in the submission of the populace, were in Gad now, with the cowardly emperor. Now, Pontio had no doubts the ancient sister-queen of Khazidea would assert her control over her ancient nation—but hers was a losing battle. Nazeer, leader of the lawgivers, had agreed to aid Priscila only if he could have Astarthe as a captive to do what he'd like to her—torture and humiliation in what was once Imperial Square.

"We will do everything in our power to cast off the Imperial yoke!" Anastasios continued. "We will invoke all the powers of heaven, yes, but also all the powers of hell! I have revoked the ban on black theurgy, and I intend to reinstate it as soon as the four approaching legions are decimated!"

The response to Pontio's other instruction was a bit more muffled. Though proud and wise Eloesians, free from Imperial superstitions, the ban on black theurgy was generally popular. Some truly believed black theurges used the powers of hell, though Pontio and his fellow academes had already proven that neither hell nor heaven existed.

"That is the last thing the Imperials would expect; and that is what they will get. It is what they deserve. Do not be afraid of black theurgy, my people; the superstition of heaven and hell is an Imperial fabrication, used to subdue its slaves."

The cheers were muted, but there were cheers—better than Pontio had expected. Such lines of logic were difficult for the unlearned, even Eloesians.

"Like Phadron the Liberator we will cast off the yoke of the oppressor, and ascend to greater glory."

That elicited a much louder roar from the audience. *Ironic,* Pontio thought—Anastasios, in the silk diadem and glittering golden bracelets of an ancient Eloesian king, preaching about Phadron the Liberator, who overthrew the original tyrants of Eloesus and established democracy. Yet those words, too, Pontio and the Thenoan Academy had fed him.

The city of Kersepoli had pledged allegiance to King Anastasios, and Korthos looked soon to follow. Of the great eastern cities, only Imperiopoli remained loyal to the emperor—a humble and loyal puppy, wanting nothing more than the love of its Imperial master. The citizens there had even offered their city as a launching ground, opening their gates to the legions as well as the despicable loyalists in Thénai and Kersepoli who had fled in the midst of the rebellion.

But here, in Thénai, to speak well of the Empire was to ask for a quick death. The mood had become palpable, almost sensational, and the zeal of the rebels uncontrollable—yet even the most fervent among them did not know the grand scheme of the Eloesian Academies and their fellow conspirers among August politicians. *They,* Pontio thought cynically, *are all tools, in the long run.*

"The glory of the East is not in soldiers and machines of war, in tools of oppression like the Empire!" Anastasios roared on. "Our glory is our wisdom! We are more than conquerors; we are citizens of the earth, of the greater world community, and always have been!"

Words fed to him by Pontio, but false words. Before the Empire asserted its control over the eastern world, Eloesian city-states and kings had pursued a constant scheme of expansion. The east's pillaging of Khazidea and establishment of colonies throughout the Middle Sea had only ended when the Empire—the much-feared Shadow in the West—asserted its dominance over the region.

"Now is the time to seize our glory!" Anastasios roared. "Thénai has declared its freedom! Korthos and Kersepoli will follow! Imperiopoli we will leave to the dogs!"

Imperiopoli had never been popular among the Eloesian old guard. *But still, they are all tools… pawns in a grander scheme.*

"Know, citizens of the world, you fight for freedom! *Freedom!*"

But they are all fools, Pontio thought with a grin. *They are all fools.*

CHAPTER SEVEN: DOOM'S DOOR

Emperor Secondo Janus the God

In the Governor's Mansion of Bregantium, where the new headquarters of the Imperial government now lay, Secondo Janus at last came to realize the Empire was doomed.

"The province of Eloesus is in full revolt," the messenger before him said. "Only Imperiopoli remains loyal. A Thenoan has named himself king. Anastasios…"

Another nail in the coffin. Secondo felt sick.

"Thénai has officially seceded. Korthos and Kersepoli refuse to pay taxes… they reject the authority of the governor. Only Imperiopoli is loyal. The Second Harak Legate has been named Grand Legate…. He is trying to reconquer Eloesus, but with all the legions gone from Khazidea it is likely the sister-queen of Haroon will secede as well."

"We should never have let the southron witch have the Red Throne again. Gods damn you, Claudian Adamantus. Perhaps the stuttering fool was just that—a stuttering fool—after all." At the news Secondo Janus' illness grew. As his mind raced, he pored through his options. He was wanted as a criminal in the Northern World; they would not accept him, not even as a common peasant. The kingdom of Fharas retained its ancient hatred. The last and best option was to grant these lawgivers permanent residency… to adopt their creed as a part of the Empire's many faiths. Some might call it defeat, but what else was there for Secondo? What other option for him didn't end in death?

"The greatest concern I have," Councilor Vitellian said, standing at Secondo's side, "is the occupation of Anthania. We *must* reclaim Imperial City. For strategic reasons, and for morale. With enough force…"

"More lawgivers come by sea every day," Secondo grumbled bitterly. "The Imperial Sea is a no-man's land, now. Piracy will no doubt return. The Empire is over, gods damn it. Can't you see, Vitellian?"

"Not good words for the emperor to say," Vitellian lectured him.

Secondo almost struck Vitellian, the man he had once considered the dearest of friends but now whom he had grown to hate. His sense of superiority was palpable at all times, a blatant hatred for how Secondo Janus—His Undying Glory—ruled the Empire. Yet Vitellian held a higher allegiance to abstract concepts—glory, honor, sacrifice—than he did to logic. And the truth of what was happening became clearer and clearer to Secondo every day: the Empire was unraveling, and sooner or later he would have to give in.

~

Three days passed in Bregantium. Riders came frequently, telling of the deadlock at the Anthanian border—that man-for-man the legions were better equipped and trained, but the lawgivers were innumerable. *An entire civilization,* Secondo thought, *mobilized for war.*

At dusk of the third day, a new kind of messenger arrived, riding through Bregantium's gate. When he arrived in Bregantium, he made his way immediately to the Governor's Mansion, and Secondo— finding his name, Malihl, odd—at once granted him access.

The man met Secondo Janus and the court in the makeshift throne room. Malihl had sharp features, with smooth brown skin and two piercing eyes. His black beard came to a sharp point, and he wore a black turban on his head. A golden ring pierced his nose. He smelled of perfume and richly-scented oils. At the sight of him, Vitellian drew back.

"Your Undying Glory," Malihl said, and dropped to one knee. *He is respectful,* Secondo noted.

"The Theomancer greets you and asks a blessing of Mazda upon you, that you will at last see the light as so many of your people have."

"You are a lawgiver," Secondo muttered, not surprised in the least but still a bit disappointed.

"That is what you call the community of the faithful, I understand," Malihl went on. "My good friend, we have heard that the Empire shows a great deal of tolerance for all gods…"

And Vitellian, Secondo thought, *would have me believe the lawgivers wish to take advantage of that.*

"…but we, the community of the faithful, serve a god supreme above your false images and idols, a god who abhors wine and beer and all unclean meats. He is Mazda the Supreme."

"Go away, enemy, before we strike you dead!" Vitellian hissed, the cur.

"Do not call him an enemy yet, Vitellian." Secondo's words elicited a growl.

Malihl's demeanor brightened; a brilliant white smile grew on his dark face. "The Theomancer does not wish for war. He has more loathsome opponents than the Empire to deal with. He will allow the Empire to remain, as long as it follows the Law of Mazda, and as long as you, Secondo Janus, King of the Empire, call the Supreme One your god."

"And I would reign as… king?" He would not belabor the difference between emperor and king. After all, Malihl and the Theomancer were offering him a position of supreme dignity, regardless of the title. What was the small matter of faith in Mazda, compared to that?

"Of course," Malihl purred. "The Theomancer would be delighted to let you serve as emperor, if you only revered the one supreme god. But you would have to come to Melchaddad, and announce your faith in him."

"Melchaddad," Secondo breathed. He intended it as a question rather than a statement.

"What you once called Imperial City is now the center of worship for the one supreme god."

"Then I will go with you to Melchaddad," Secondo Janus said.

"*Janus!*" Vitellian howled.

"The war is lost." Secondo at last said what was in his heart. "The Empire is doomed. It is time to honor Mazda and his holy law."

"*Give back your circlet, traitor!*"

"I don't think so," Secondo answered him and walked away coldly, in the presence of Malihl his new friend.

With a contingent of lawgivers on swift desert horses, led by Malihl, Secondo Janus left the confines of Bregantium wearing not Imperial purple, but lawgiver black.

Augusto Vitellian

In the Governor's Mansion, Vitellian and the five remaining councilors spent what they considered the darkest night yet of their lives, talking feverishly of how to reverse the tide of what by all estimation was a losing war.

"Secondo has betrayed us!" Councilor Valerio exclaimed hysterically. "I knew the Jani were bad, rotten to the core. They are not true patriots; they are not made of sterner stuff, like the Adamanti…"

"We must kill him," said Councilor Geta. "By the gods, we must sent soldiers to hunt him down and kill him, and pry that Imperial Circlet off his head."

"They ride on swift horses," Councilor Alba snapped. "We would never catch them, fool."

"If only the Adamanti were still alive…" Valerio sounded like he was weeping. "If only a descendant of Claudio the God were still here with us… Gods damn Claudian for becoming a celibate monk."

"There is a descendant of Claudo-Valens Adamantus still alive," Vitellian muttered, caught up in the memory. "He lives with the southron queen, Astarthe. She calls him Adamantion. Janus the Traitor had done his best to kill him."

"An enemy of Janus is a friend of mine," Valerio said. "And a descendant of Claudio-Valens has a god's blood in his veins."

"A journey of many days across the sea," Vitellian said. "Only one of us must go."

"Who better than you?" Valerio rested a hand on Vitellian's shoulder. "We will do our best to keep the nation under control while you are gone."

"I would not be surprised if the queen has rebelled, if she has me killed on sight," Vitellian said. "But what is the small risk of my life, for the sake of the Empire?"

Valerio smiled. "Indeed."

CHAPTER EIGHT:
ENEMY LINES

Numa

Four more days down the Path of Tidus, and dozens more bruises had formed all over Numa's skin. In the mornings and the evenings, he and Shareeka spent an hour or more sparring with wooden swords, honing Numa's poor skills. Numa had never won a fight.

At noon of the fourth day, a stump of a wooden sign greeted them. "Once," Shareeka began, "that would have welcomed us to Anthania. Now—*look out!*"

The thundering of hooves echoed through the air. Two black-garbed warriors appeared, wielding giant curved blades of steel. Numa leapt out of the way and drew his sword, nicking his left hand in the process. Shareeka tumbled under them as they rode by; Appian ducked and then leapt out of the way.

Both their slashes missed. "Unbelievers, no doubt!" one howled as they both wheeled their horses around.

One galloped toward Numa, curved blade pitched back. He held up his shortsword as a shield; against all his best efforts a cowardly whimper escaped him. Then a dagger stuck the rider in the chest.

Numa turned to look at Shareeka. The ratling, now with only one dagger, tumbled again under the rider. The rider turned around and galloped for him again, but Shareeka now had a perfect shot. He hurled the dagger, which whistled through the air before sticking the lawgiver in the chest.

Soon, both of them had fallen from their horses, bleeding on the ground.

"Nice work." Appian smiled.

Numa drew in deep breaths, too shocked by what he'd seen to speak any further.

A pained look formed on Shareeka's face as the horses galloped off-road, out of reach. He eyed the lawgivers, still in death spasms, blood pooling around their bodies. He tore the embedded daggers from their flesh. "We will leave them in the open air for the vultures, like trash. That, after all, is what they are."

Numa smiled at the words. "Indeed." He had heard nothing of the lawgivers to counter that statement.

~

They now traveled with a stronger determination than ever, yet in a less direct and more winding route. Pockets of civilization remained free of the lawgivers, especially this far north. But Mount Hylea lay south by the sea, deep in the heart of Imperial civilization, where the Law of Mazda now held sway.

CHAPTER NINE:
STRANGE SIGHTINGS

Ruz the Pious, Prison Warden

The tortured body of Maximian, or *Maksimun* as the native lawgivers called him—the former Marshal of the Imperial Guard—lay hanging in his prison cell. He had held firm to the end, refusing to honor Mazda and his prophets, cursing the supreme god to his last breath, and calling Ruz a cowardly "worm" for betraying his old faith. The words had stung Ruz, angered him deeply, and only caused him to torture Maximian even more, but the foolish Imperial Guard remained firm to his insults and his faith in the many gods.

Yet now, Ruz had access to Maximian's personal affects, a veritable fortune worth more than many kings' stores of wealth. Chief among him the adamant sword Maximian called *Imperium's Rebuke* but which Ruz would call *The Enforcer*. *The Enforcer*, that is, of Mazda's supreme law.

He headed to where he kept the blade, stowed with the rest of the prisoners' belongings. The guard there, dressed in black like Ruz, grew ashen-faced at the sight of him. Ruz scanned the room, seeing no sign of the blue adamant sword, which had rested plainly on the table just an hour ago. Ruz fixed his eyes on the guard and glared at him intensely. "Where is it?" Ruz growled. "Where did you put it?"

"My lord," the guard shriveled before him, "the most fearsome snake slithered in here, took it by the hilt, and I dared not disturb it. It was so large and fearsome and venomous."

"A snake? A *snake?*" Ruz roared. "How foolish do you think I am? I will torture you until you tell me where you hid it. Gods damn you!" He cursed himself for uttering the blasphemy, a relic of his prior life. "*Mazda* damn you!"

The guard ran but Ruz caught him in his hands. He would enjoy torturing the truth from his lips.

Secondo Janus

When Secondo awoke before dawn near the border of Anthania, the most priceless item in his possession was gone—the Imperial Circlet. The humble but masterfully-crafted work of silver was worth more than the semiprecious metal it was made out of. It was a symbol of rule—a symbol the Theomancer no doubt wanted, to show that the emperor had spurned the old gods for the new faith. He stood up in the rage, so suddenly the horses nickered in fear. "*Where is it?*"

The three-dozen lawgivers were all asleep, save for one—the man on the last watch of the night, a convert to the Law of Mazda. "My good emperor," he said, "as I was watching over everyone, a great snake came slithering in, and I was worried that if I disturbed it, it would strike me. He picked the Imperial Circlet from your head in its teeth and slithered away. And as it was passing it said to me, 'A coward does not deserve this.'"

Secondo's blood was nearly boiling by the time the fool finished his words. "A *talking snake?* How stupid do you think I am? And a coward! You *dare* call me a coward!"

"Not me," the watchman said. "The snake—"

Secondo grabbed his sword from its sheath, and rushed over to kill the insolent cretin where he sat.

CHAPTER TEN:
THE NATURE OF THE REBELLION

Tiverio Bellorus, Grand Legate

At the gates of Thénai the three legions stood, demanding the submission of the Eloesian rebels. Tiverio Bellorus had made it clear if they lay down their arms, the Empire would show utter mercy and kill not a single soul. Yet the self-proclaimed king, Anastasios, had sent word that they would never submit to the Imperial "dogs." And in response, Tiverio had demolished whatever materials he could find in the city sprawl outside the inner walls to begin the construction of siege engines. Tiverio wondered whether he would raze the city to the ground like the grand legate Caro did to Tharta before creating Imperiopoli.

Then the gates opened, revealing a great paradox. The rebel leader, Anastasios, was younger than Tiverio expected, a healthy and handsome young man wearing a diadem of tied purple silk like an ancient Eloesian conqueror; but behind him, the army that faced them was quite clearly amateur, scarcely armored and wielding mismatched swords, daggers and axes. *Does he intend to make some suicidal last stand,* Tiverio wondered. *Does he think he can create victory by adhering to some strange philosophical principle? Or is he just mad?*

The Imperial soldiers would cut into this motley assembly of common citizens like lambs for the slaughter. "Have you lost your mind, young man?" Tiverio shouted at him.

"Do not speak to a king so rudely!" Anastasios shouted back. "Tell me, do you surrender, Imperial dogs, and announce the sovereignty of the Thenoan Kingdom?"

"You are mad!" Tiverio shouted. "Of course we do not surrender! But if you put aside this madness now, young man, we will spare your and all the citizens' lives!"

"Very well!" Anastasios roared, and from the folds of his

purple cloak drew a gilded horn. He blew a resonant note.

And above the walls, ten men appeared. Tiverio gasped as they sprouted scarlet bat-like wings and floated down to land mere feet before the legion. They wore hooded cloaks of black and red, and obscuring their faces were scarlet-colored veils. In their right hands they held silver lanterns without fire; in their left, thin black poles.

Theurges, Tiverio recognized suddenly, but not the white-cloaked, green- or blue-veiled theurges he knew.

Fire tinged with shadow spewed from their hands. Legionaries went up in flame like they were oil-soaked torches. Tiverio turned and dashed away as panic overtook the legion. Yet the fire only spread, from one legionary to another. Above them, in the sky, a portal shimmered to reveal a world of fire and volcanoes with a yellow sky. The scent of sulfur grew thick in the air. Bats flew out from the portal—horned bats with blazing red eyes—as the fire continued to grow and spread, immolating all in its path.

The black theurges were cackling as the legionaries' deaths multiplied. A hellish bat swooped in near Tiverio as he ran in a panic; it latched on to a fellow soldier's chest and then tore out his throat in its needle-like teeth. Chaos and fire overtook the day, and more portals opened up. Soon the sky was darkened with legions of infernal bats.

This, he reflected at the verge of death, *is the nature of the Eloesian rebellion—desperate and unprincipled enough to traffic in the powers of hell, willing to abandon all honor to achieve some inexplicable end.*

CHAPTER ELEVEN:
THE BURNING OF KHAZIDEA

Astarthe, Queen of Haroon

Though the walls of Haroon were practically impregnable, and many thousands of Imperial soldiers stood watch over the Red City, Astarthe could not help a stab of despair when a farmer brought news.

"The Asa have swept into the Khazan Valley like a whirlwind." The trembling, thin figure exhaled the words. Doubtlessly, he had taken a ship into the city's harbor, for the Asa had encamped around it, preventing everyone from entering or leaving. "They have begun torching the farms and the fields. They told the people who entered my village that they must swear fealty to the god Mazda... those that didn't they beheaded."

"You poor thing," Astarthe muttered. "The ships we have will keep food coming. Rest yourself, signore, and trust in the Moon Goddess." The slight, thin man, despite his reddish Khazidean complexion, had turned white in splotches. "Most of all, signore, remain strong... strong for your country, and for your queen."

The man bowed deeply and turned to leave.

A request to Imperial City, sent weeks ago, had not been returned. The ship itself and the messenger had disappeared, and only recently did the news come to her from her allies across the desert in Kheroe that Imperial City was totally occupied by the enemy, that the Theomancer had taken up residence in the Imperial Palace, and a grand temple to Mazda was under construction just outside the city grounds. *I sent that messenger to die,* she thought with a shudder.

The farmer was walking out the door. "Remain strong for the Empire!" she called out after him.

Yet the Imperial government had been practically dissolved. In her youth, the lawgivers had held Astarthe captive, corrupted her brother into a young man who hated her. Though Claudian

Adamantus the God had prevailed against the Theomancer with the help of Fharas, the lawgivers had all but resurged, and treachery within the government's ranks could be the only explanation. How else could a vast fleet of ships sail undeterred through Imperial waters?

The Imperial Sea had lost its title… now it, too, was a battleground. *Perhaps,* she thought, *I am wrong… the Empire will fall, and the Law of Mazda will prevail across the land. Perhaps there are no gods, no eternal rules or principles, only strength and weakness, and shades of gray.*

At the thought she returned to her bedchamber, donned coarse, unspun black wool, and powdered her face with ashes. She draped a necklace of white acacia flowers around her neck, shut the door, drew the blinds, and cried.

~

A week later, as the situation outside the City of Issa deteriorated, Astarthe remained in her room, mourning. She had not eaten since she entered, and only left for small drinks of water. When Sinn pounded on her door, demanding that she speak with him, she cursed. "I am mourning the loss of my husband, the Empire…"

"Your husband beckons you!" Sinn shouted in reply.

"Do not torment a grieving widow," Astarthe growled, and the wellspring of tears came trickling down anew.

"I am not tormenting," Sinn said. "Your husband the Empire yet lives. Come and see."

Astarthe, weak with hunger, at last stood up. She opened the door and found Sinn standing there in his woman's robe, his expression beaming. She could not smile in return. She would not smile. She would never smile again.

~

An old man waited before the Red Throne, dressed in an Imperial-style white tunic and a purple Imperial sash. A warm smile was on his face—a warm smile that indicated a weary soul, a smile he offered as a gift of comfort to Astarthe. She recognized that graying hair, those dark eyes, and that aquiline nose.

"Councilor," she said. "I do not remember your name." Even now, she could not smile.

"I am not offended in the least," the councilor laughed. "I am Vitellian."

"You come from Imperial City? I thought—"

"Imperial City is lost, for now," Vitellian said, and for the first time his smile wore thin, briefly disappearing. "The emperor is gone to the other side."

Astarthe collapsed to her knees. "I am the last patriot."

"No… there are many—even a majority. But even if there weren't a majority, we must take up our nation's cause despite all obstacles. It is better to die fighting the lawgivers than live under them, no?"

"You are right," Astarthe said, and though a tear fell from her cheek, she forced herself up onto her feet. "Have you brought help?"

"All the available legions are fighting the lawgivers on the Anthanian border."

"They have gotten that far?" she gasped, thinking of all the millions of people under the lawgivers' sway.

"We need a strong leader, one who will command respect."

"Surely you don't expect the Queen of Haroon to be elected emperor," Astarthe scoffed. She would rise to the task, but it was the last thing she wanted.

"No," Vitellian answered as she expected. "We need one with the body and soul of adamant, stern of courage and commanding. We need a living god. We need—"

"Adamantion," Astarthe breathed.

Vitellian nodded.

The little boy came bolting in from the room, wearing the gold chains of an Anakhil and the striped cloth headdress of a brother-king. "Did somebody say my name?"

Even in such a desperate time, he was a child—simple, and eager to play.

"We tried this once," Astarthe said. The past remained with her, the injustices and crimes that had caused her to flee. "The emperor tried to murder my son. I will not let you harm him."

"The emperor who tried to murder your son is dead to us; he has joined with the lawgivers," Vitellian said. "I bring you a request from every member of the Imperial Council, begging that your son be crowned emperor."

"Why should I trust you?" Astarthe found herself saying. "You tried—"

"We did not. Secondo Janus the traitor did. Come with us."

"There are wild nomads outside the walls. My people—"

"The wild nomads will remain for now. The Empire needs you, Queen Astarthe, and your son. Some said I was a fool to come here, asking from a disenfranchised queen, plucked from her rightful throne—"

"I am not disenfranchised. I was not plucked by the Empire from my throne. I owe everything to the Empire."

"Yes, as I thought. You are a patriot." A broad smile grew across Vitellian's face. "My queen." He bowed. "The Empire needs you. Will you heed its call?"

"I will," Astarthe said, without a trace of hesitation this time. The Godling priest, Sinn, lurked in the corner.

"Prepare my things," she told him.

~

Before the sun had set, Astarthe had boarded the ship, and together with Adamantion, left north through choppy seas in the late summer heat, underneath a rare cloudy sky.

CHAPTER TWELVE:
NOT IN NORRIVA, ANYMORE

Numa

The summer heat beat oppressively down on Numa, Shareeka, and Appian as they made their way south. Numa's clothing, though light, was drenched with sweat as he traversed the back roads.

Here, in the hellishly dry Central Valley, the grass was a bright yellow color, such a far cry from the lush forests of Gad. And yet Numa did not miss it; the further away from the village of his birth, the further he had grown from his past. Now, he relished the fear and excitement that came with adventure. Now, he was fighting for something; before, he had been living for nothing.

A few days after they had crossed the Anthanian border, Shareeka said they were drawing near the Iron Mountains and beyond them, the sea. "The Empire once equipped its armies with the ore it found there… now, perhaps, the lawgivers are in control of the mines."

Numa grated his teeth at the thought. So far, only Shareeka had killed a lawgiver. One day soon, he hoped to change that.

That evening, the vague outline of mountains appeared across the rolling yellow hills. Twin aqueducts appeared as well—one, heading south as it carried the life-giving water to some city; the other, ending its journey close-by in a large un-walled town. All around it, fields of wheat—now cut—sprawled in every direction. The red tile roofs sparkled like bronze in the sun.

Together, Numa, Shareeka, and Appian made their way down the hill toward civilization.

In the fading twilight, the sound of pipes and lyres flooded through the stone-paved streets. In the center of the town square, a fountain bubbled with water—fed, no doubt, by the aqueduct. Overlooking the square was the largest inn Numa had ever seen—a towering, red-roofed building three stories tall. Above the door, its name was written in giant bold letters: "The Dancing Satyr."

The inn proved to be the source of the pipes and lyres, and underneath their fast-paced rhythm was the quick beat of drums. In the midst of the grand feasting hall, a group of legionaries sat around a long table. And there, rising above them, was a sight that turned Numa's stomach to knots—the very thing his mother had warned him about: a southern woman like what you'd see in the coastland cities, as loose of morals as she was beautiful.

Against the music, the woman performed an exotic dance on the table, letting her long raven hair flow wild as she pounded her feet to the beat. A thin, tight dress of scarlet cloth slowly but surely fell off as the legionaries cheered.

"Lucilla! Lucilla!" they cheered as at last a breast fell loose.

Numa, feeling his body respond, looked away in shame. Appian, at his side, stood transfixed. Far away—too far—Shareeka haggled with the innkeeper as the legionaries called out with delight.

"We aren't in Norriva anymore," Appian said, still transfixed.

"No," Numa said, and stalked off, trying to avoid the situation altogether.

"A Getan," the innkeeper said as Numa approached. "I know one when I see one." He was a fat man with balding black hair. "Do you not like the entertainment, my boy?"

"It's vulgar," Numa said simply. Shareeka turned to give him a damning look.

"Yes, yes, it is vulgar," the innkeeper went on. "But the brothers-in-arms seem to be enjoying it."

Numa nodded. "They do."

"So tell me," the innkeeper said as he counted the copper aesa and silver denara. "What brings a ratling and two Getans to Anthania?

Most importantly, where are you headed?"

Shareeka fixed his angry eyes on the innkeeper, giving Numa a bit of relief. "That is exactly none of your business, signore."

"Ah, the ratling has a tongue." The innkeeper smiled. "If you are going south, you will find a world at war. Foreigners have overtaken Imperial City, but there are battles in the streets every day, even there… the rebellion is alive and well, and growing."

"As it should be," Numa said.

The innkeeper's smile grew. "My good signores, your rooms are upstairs. We've gotten few travelers of late, so we have plenty of fine Korthian wine still left. I'll let you try it, on the house."

When Numa turned away from him, the woman's scarlet dress was on the table, and the woman herself was nude.

I have entered another world, Numa thought. *A world far from my provincial upbringing.* He wondered if he would survive it, or worse, learn to enjoy it.

"Come on, scatterbrain!" Shareeka snarled and jerked him out of his thoughts. "We're going to get settled."

"Don't talk with strangers," Shareeka said once they reached their private room. "Don't speak well of the rebels or against the lawgivers. We should keep our allegiance secret."

"I would rather say what I think and be honorable than live in safety as a coward."

Shareeka backhanded him across the face. "That attitude will get you killed."

Numa bared his teeth. He knew better than to fight Shareeka—though three-quarters Numa's height, he was twice the warrior still, even despite all they'd practiced.

"Guard your tongue from hereon out," Shareeka snarled, and turned to unload the rest of their belongings.

Numa headed back downstairs for Appian.

The tall young man sat at a table in the inn's main feasting hall, looking stylish as always in his tunic of sleek black wool. The sword buckled to his side made him look the part of a warrior, though Appian wasn't half one. His fingers were wrapped around a ceramic cup filled with wine. He looked disturbed.

"Appian," Numa said as he sat down.

"What I wouldn't give to bed that dancing *lupa*. But she gave the legionaries the cold shoulder, too… left as soon as the dance was through."

Numa found himself smiling at the words. "Appian the Bookworm, they called you in Norriva… Once you were only concerned about the emperor's honor. Now you are concerned about girls."

Appian's smile was faint, and vanished quickly. "The *lupa* is the least of my worries. Korthian wine isn't half as good as people say it is."

"What is really bothering you, Appian?"

Appian's dark eyes met his. "There were people here just a moment ago… lodgers on their way north to safety. They said Emperor Janus has defected, capitulated to the lawgivers. He is making his way to Imperial City for the terms of surrender."

The bottom dropped out of Numa. The stunned surprise lasted only a moment. From the surprise, the seed of anger soon built itself into a shaking, inconsolable rage. Somehow he managed to form coherent words, words he intended as wisdom: "In times like these, we must not despair. We must answer the abomination with anger… anger and violence. *Violence!*" He slammed his fist on the table. The ceramic cup fell over, spilling the red wine.

Numa expected a condemning look on Numa's face; instead, he saw respect, and agreement.

The innkeeper came rushing over with a rag cloth. "Ah, I am so glad I didn't set out a tablecloth. No slamming of fists… no matter how angry you are with each other. You looked like Claudio-Valens would look, if he saw the state of our nation."

"I…" He found himself unable to apologize. Yet somehow, the innkeeper's words provided small comfort.

~

The next day they left the city of Vida behind, walking further south, even as news reached them that the lawgivers were tightening their grip over the coastland cities, demanding they either pay crushing taxes or change their dearly-held faith… that collaborators in the Imperial Council and the Academies of Eloesus were joining with the invaders to build a temple to Mazda—the first of its kind in the Empire.

The Academies, Numa thought when he first heard the news, *have preached freedom and liberty, and argued tirelessly against moral laws.* It was unthinkable they would join with the barbarians, but as Numa pondered it, he realized the political and intellectual elite of the Empire shared a far deeper bond with the lawgivers than their diametrically opposed viewpoints would suggest: a deep vileness that permeated their innermost sinew. They were all bottom-feeding worms.

CHAPTER THIRTEEN: THE DEDICATION

Cleon Adelphos, Vice Provost of the Thenoan Academy

The temple to Mazda had just been finished outside the city precincts, a thing never seen before in the Empire. They had demolished a shrine to Imperium, against the angry heckling of the common citizens, and erected it despite a wave of rebel attacks.

In all, it impressed Cleon less than he would have thought, though it certainly was unique: a short thing, compared to the other buildings, no more than fifteen feet in height but several hundred feet in width, shaped into a box and colored pitch black. The High Theomancer called it a *kabakh,* and had explained to Cleon that such buildings were all replicas of the original *kabakh* in a far-away land, where the prophet had received his revelations.

Priscilla Marianus fidgeted at Cleon's side in the building summer heat, looking uncomfortable as she increasingly had in the past few weeks. Her out-of-place feeling was perfectly understandable: a man such as Cleon who did extensive business with the lawgivers would think that the hundreds of thousands of immigrants were all male. In truth, the lawgiver women never left their dwellings, and when they did, their faces were never shown.

In an increasingly male regime Priscilla stood alone, but she had not budged an inch from her position—there were troubles, yes, and reasons to complain, but her core goals had not changed. She would create a utopia free from control by the common citizen, and the lawgivers were the most effective and efficient way to enact it. Whatever complaints she had, Priscilla made clear, were minor in the long run, and could be resolved through reason and diplomacy.

"In the name of Mazda the giver of the Holy Law," the Theomancer shouted, "and in the name of his prophet whom we shall not name, I consecrate this *kabakh* as a source for our god's law to be enforced over all the earth. May all those who fight the Holy Law perish; may the lovers of images, and music, and dancing, and dogs, and wine, be slain before the armies of the upright, and condemned to the fires of eternal hell. Praise Mazda!"

"Praise Mazda!" Cleon, Priscilla, and the lawgivers shouted in unison, and dropped to their knees.

"From this new *kabakh*, the Law of Mazda will spread over the Empire, and soon all nations under the earth will live under its rule!" the Theomancer shouted.

"Praise Mazda!" they all shouted again, and at last stood up.

An arrow arced above head but missed narrowly. "Damned rebels," Cleon cursed. *And people wonder why we hate the common people. They do not answer argument with argument; they answer it with violence!*

"Bring me the rebel's head!" the Theomancer snapped.

Together, Cleon and Priscilla wandered the streets of Imperial City—now called Melchaddad—and the Provost of the Thenoan Academy had a more unnerved look on her face than usual. Her skin had paled. In a prior time, before the foreigners came, Cleon would have advised her to drink some wine for her health. Now all the wine bottles in the city were smashed, all the taverns and wine shops shut down or burned. Cleon wondered if the meals of spicy beef and unflavored water had at last gotten to her.

He grasped Priscilla's thin hand, and found it trembling. He still had the utmost respect for the philosopher queen of the Empire, possessed of such strong intellect that no one could argue with her and win. "What ails you, my signora?"

"Not now," she snapped.

~

In the Imperial Palace, now suitably alone, Priscilla Marianus and Cleon Adelphos wandered the halls, lined with busts of great statesmen. Now, their cold stone eyes were bashed out by the lawgivers. Once, grand paintings of the Themurian wilderness hung on the walls, but those had been ripped off and burned. It was a minor disappointment for Cleon, indeed. Who cared which set of untrue myths the stupid citizens of the Empire believe—the false tales of the gods, or the false stories of Mazda?

Eventually, they found themselves what once had been the Imperial court's private library. Still, shelves and shelves of books remained. Near the door were the histories—great lengthy tomes, records of the Empire's unjustness, added proof of its unfitness to exist in the wider community of nations.

Priscilla ran her hand over the spines of the books. "In my darkest moments," she said softly, "when I question what I have done, I only have to remember the Empire's sins. I only have to touch these books… these records of slavery and domination, of mass killings and unthinkable brutality. And then, I remember, whatever I brought to these shores cannot possibly be worse than what came before."

"Do not doubt yourself," Cleon purred.

"I do not. Most of these books are rubbish… blind patriotism at its worst." She turned and walked further down the library. They came to the far end of the room, where the books of plays sat on display. On the wall nearby, two masks hung—the white smiling face of comedy, and the black frowning face of tragedy. Priscilla was running her hands down the spines of the books. "One of the lecturers at the Academy told his students the Empire's art was better and more refined than that of Fharas. He said *that* is why the Fharese put on Eloesian plays rather than their own. Such ignorance."

One of Priscilla's most dearly-held points was that the Fharese enjoyed the Empire's entertainments for one reason alone—the Empire's crude domination. "And what did you do to that lecturer, my signora?"

"What any reasonable provost would do… I suspended him without pay and made it clear he was unwelcome in any of the Academies. It was far less than I wanted. I hope he is dead."

"He soon will be. The lawgivers do not like outspoken patriots."

"Outspoken," she breathed, and her knees trembled. Her eyes had moistened.

Footsteps echoed through the palace halls. Umar appeared at the doorway, scimitar in hand. Behind him stood the Theomancer in his black turban and square gray beard. "Priscilla," Umar said. "The most holy Theomancer and I have something to say."

Priscilla smiled, but her stance and the look in her eyes betrayed the fact that she didn't want to see them. "What is it, Your Holiness?"

"The Theomancer understands the terms of our arrival here," Umar said. "You shall be exempted from some of Mazda's laws as we spread it across your nation. But there is one thing he cannot bear."

"Anything," Priscilla said, and forced her smile to grow.

"It greatly irritates His Holiness you walk around with a naked face. He can tolerate your presence in the company of men as part of the agreement, but that one thing he cannot abide. Most women do not go outside in our land, and those that do are fully covered. We expect your face to be covered from hereon. If you refuse, you will receive lashes or worse. The rule starts now."

"I... I do not have—" she stammered.

"Then we will find you some proper clothing or wait—ah! Yes! This is perfect." Umar hurried across the room as Cleon watched, wondering what in Varda he was doing.

From the wall, Umar removed the black mask of tragedy. "You may wear this, Priscilla. If you do not, you will be scourged, or worse. Unlike the Imperials, we mean what we say."

Umar set the mask on her head.

It was all for a purpose, a greater goal of utopia, but something about the sight of her disturbed Cleon. The great sloping frown and crying eyes of the mask would be the face of Priscilla from now on. For indeterminate time, those who looked Priscilla's would see a sad, tragic clown, always weeping even when she was joyful. *And yet, I have not seen her joyful in a long, long time.*

"It suits you well, Priscilla," Umar said with a smile.

The Theomancer, behind him, laughed lightly. "Keep it on your face, my dear, or I will see to it that you are stoned. Now excuse us—we have a war to win, and an emperor to meet."

Umar and the Theomancer left. In the silence of the palace, Priscilla's low sob was the only sound Cleon heard. *It is all for a purpose,* he told himself. *These lawgivers are all tools in our hands… tools to build our utopia.*

CHAPTER FOURTEEN:
THE END OF KNOWLEDGE

Pontio Piraeus, Chief Lecturer

Pontio Piraeus had left all his books of geography and mathematics behind him, so hasty was his flight from Thénai. As disembodied voices howled in the wind, an infernal fog crept through the city streets, and sores formed on the citizens' faces—even Pontio's—he made the highest bid to an intrepid sailor, a king's ransom of fifteen gold libra, and demanded that he disembark at once, leaving the slovenly citizens behind. The lynchpin of "King" Anastasios' plan—the use of black theurges—had backfired, unleashed a power so destructive that Pontio wondered if Thénai would ever truly recover.

Yet riding above-deck on a swift merchant's ship, the wind blew in Pontio's face, and—though he had left his books of geography and mathematics in his upper floor study—he could not help but smile. Relief washed through Pontio as the winds blew them steadily westward in view of the rolling hills and jagged rocky mountains still lined with snow, and the olive groves which—in ancient days and now—made Thénai rich.

But Thénai is gone.

"Where to, Signor Pontio?"

"To Korthos," he said simply.

"To Korthos it is. Anywhere, for a rich man."

Pontio laughed lightly. The sailor, likely a poor simple fool, thought Pontio was abandoning the rebellion. He did not realize the rebellion itself was merely a distraction while Priscilla and Cleon did their work in the west.

After four days of fair sailing, the Thenoan Inlet opened up into the wider Imperial Sea—now, the Middle Sea. The ship rounded its edge, a low plain dense with habitation. Aqueducts, the only good thing the Empire had ever brought the world, carried water to the dense cluster of stone buildings and concrete apartment blocks. Beyond, the Imperial City shone a pure angelic blue, the same color as the cloudless sky. Yet the winter days of rain and darkness were coming soon, the days of choppy waters and churning seas. They stood at the cusp of summer. At the thought, Pontio shivered.

The ship turned and made its way southwest, flagging slightly against the wind. It was another five days before they turned again, into another inland water that belonged to Korthos and Kersepoli, and from there an agonizing seven days against the wind before they drew near Korthos.

Cedars and cypress trees lined the foothills of the inlet. One morning, when the captain said they were within hours of Korthos, Pontio was above-decks, feeling restless, when an arrow zipped by and tore a hole through the main sail.

"Brigands!" the captain shouted and yanked his sword from its sheath.

Pontio gasped and drew back, grasping the railing and, in the confusion of the moment, standing rigid and still.

In the midst of the green forest, chainmail sparkled in the sun. One stood outside the forest, Pontio realized, a man in a suit of scale armor, wearing a cape of royal blue, and a bow in his hands. He did not have the look of a brigand.

A horn pealed, echoing across the sea—a war horn, fine in its noise and timbre. *No, these are not brigands.* Nonetheless, Pontio rushed below-decks, trembling all over, having the urge to pray but resisting it.

The hours passed by slowly, but when the ship jolted as it was put into the dock and the shouting, noise, and smells of the city reached Pontio, he breathed a deep sigh of relief. Still dazed, without an aes to his name, Pontio left the darkness of the ship and walked out into the bright daylight and brilliant colors of Korthos.

Among the most ancient cities of the Empire, the crown jewel of Eloesus as some called it, Korthos lived up to all its hype. Leaving the innumerable ships docked in the harbor, he passed through the Sea Gate and traveled the steadily-ascending stone steps into the city proper. There, two towering bronze statues, blue in color, outdid the Colossus in Peregoth by far, forged into the shape of the twin gods of dusk and dawn.

Yet the colorful statues and gushing fountains all became a blur to him, an unwanted distraction as Pontio made his way to Academy Row, the seat of the new Korthian administration. Through the white-pillared halls of the Academy of Politics he wandered, still lined with busts and statues of democrats and monarchists and theorists of all types, he eventually found himself in the presence of Tychon, the second-in-command of the rebellion.

"Thénai is lost," he said without sparing a second.

"Thénai? Lost?" Tychon looked stunned. The news seemed to add a year to the already seventy-year-old man's life.

"Indeed."

"And here we are, worried about the machinations of Prince Basil…"

"Basil? Who? What are you talking about?"

"There is a rebellion against the Academies' rule, Pontio, even here, in the enlightened realm of Eloesus. Even people in Korthos leave our city to join them. They wear blue cloaks. They follow Prince Basil of Harkeon Keep."

"Blue cloaks," Pontio muttered. "I saw them—"

Tychon's expression turned bitter. "They call themselves the Free Eloesian Army. Free? Ha! They call themselves free, and they fight for the Empire."

"Rebellion? Against the Academies' rule? And good, full-blood Eloesians join them? Slaves, yearning for their master's domination?"

"That is not how they see it," Tychon sneered.

"This, then, is the end of knowledge!" Pontio cried. "The end of all reason, all good thought, all right purpose. A plague on their heads. We must crush them all… we must—"

"Our army dwindles. Few wish to fight for our cause. We must hire mercenaries. Or send for the lawgivers to protect us. With Thénai gone there is little hope… but we still have Korthos, and its walls are sound. Its people, however…"

Pontio sneered. *The people.* The people had always been the problem, from the beginning.

CHAPTER FIFTEEN:
FIRSTS

Numa

Down the road the trio walked—Numa, Appian, and Shareeka—as the world changed around them. Though the small clusters of population increased and drew closer together, there was an uncharacteristic silence Numa didn't expect. Many had left their homes—to escape, perhaps, or more likely to fight in the war that now consumed the Empire. Often, as they traveled the back roads far from the well-traversed Path of Tidus, columns of black smoke would appear in the horizon. Numa gathered that those who refused to honor Mazda or pay the tax on unbelievers were killed, their houses set aflame. Occasionally, Numa would spy an entire town destroyed, its once-stately buildings burned to a pile of gray ash, its walls thrown down to their foundations and the bodies of its citizens piled high in the center.

Seeing the choice before him—submission to slavery, or death—Numa knew what he would choose; but beyond all else, the sight instilled in him a growing rage, a rage that could not and would not be sated. Shareeka thought that some of their own countrymen had allowed these foreigners into the country, and that above all enraged Numa, enraged him until he could scarcely think.

Down a back road late one evening, as the sun set in gold-and-pink colors over the wheat fields, the pounding of hooves echoed through the air. Up ahead, two men dressed in lawgiver blacks rode forth, their faces hidden by hoods. Clipped to their belts were long, curved blades—scimitars—and Numa could sense their arrogance as they closed the distance between them.

"Three men, heading south," the lawgiver at the fore said in a southron accent. "Going to Melchaddad, perhaps? To offer a sacrifice at the *kabakh*, perhaps?"

"I have no idea what you are talking about," Numa sneered.

"We are going to Imperial City," Appian added.

Shareeka sighed.

"Imperial City?" the lawgiver continued, and Numa could hear his derisive smile. "You must have been gone a long time. It is now called Melchaddad… the seat of the Theomancer and of the Law of Mazda."

"I will never call Imperial City Melchaddad," Numa said and drew his sword.

Shareeka hissed some unintelligible curse.

The lawgiver lowered his hood, revealing a head of wild black hair and a tan face with harsh, angular features. "Such disrespect I have found before, in this unclean land… in the rebels who still plague Anthania, before their tortured cries echo through the air." His eyes narrowed. "Turn back. I am merciful, like Mazda the Supreme. You are not welcome down this road."

Numa glared at him. Shareeka began to turn, then Appian. He did not.

"I will count down from three. Three… two…"

Numa charged forward. The lawgiver's horse bucked onto its hind legs and whinnied; it hoofed Numa hard down onto the stone-paved road, and his eyes watered at the pain. Still clutching the hilt of his sword, he climbed to his feet and, failing to maintain his balance, almost toppled over; the lawgiver's scimitar came whistling toward his head and he ducked, falling forward and striking his knees on the ground. The lawgiver laughed.

Through tear-blurred vision, the other lawgiver had lowered his hood as well, preparing to fight. Numa wiped his eyes with his sleeve. The lawgiver had the olive complexion and graying brown hair of an Imperial. "Traitor!" he screamed.

Beside him, the southron lawgiver gasped for air, the hilt of a dagger sticking out from his chest. Numa could hear Appian's clumsy footsteps drawing near.

"Traitor!" Numa cried again, and charged the Imperial.

Within a second's time Numa had reached him and their blades kissed, sword against scimitar. Yet the Imperial traitor was old, with more silver than brown in his hair, and his scimitar blow betrayed his weak arms. Numa hacked furiously, hacking until he scarcely could breathe, losing himself in the wild rage.

Sometime in the midst of his fury he realized he was standing over a corpse, its black clothing shredded beyond repair, the road all around it dripping with blood, its flesh savaged and ripped open to the point of mutilation. Numa was dripping with sweat, and his clothes were sopping with blood. He fell to his knees in the midst of the damp liquid on the road, panting and desperately thirsty.

He wondered how much time had elapsed.

"Numa." Shareeka laid a hand on his shoulder. "I was about ready to kill you for what you did. But now we have horses. And lawgiver clothing."

"I will never wear the clothes of a lawgiver."

"Well, you shredded it beyond recognition, anyway. Here's to Numa's first kill."

Numa stood up, wet with blood and sweat, and turned to face Appian, who was regarding him with admiration.

"Poor Appian has the best sword of all of us," Shareeka said, "and not a single dead lawgiver to his name." The ratling laughed.

Appian smiled in return. "I am sure I will have some use, eventually."

"I am sure you will," Numa answered him, and grinned.

"Here's to dead lawgivers, and to a quicker journey," Shareeka continued.

"But there are only two horses," Numa observed.

Appian held both of them by the reins. "You and I can ride two-a-saddle. I am an excellent horseman, after all. I am of the Knightly Class, anyway… isn't that my calling?"

"A Knight's calling is to rule over others and tax them to starvation," Numa said with a grin.

Appian laughed. "Aye… that, and riding horses."

~

Riding their horses down the roads, they traveled a further distance in one day than they previously could have in two. Closer and closer they drew near their goal—to Mount Hylea where the oracle prophesied, to their destiny, or their doom.

CHAPTER SIXTEEN:
THE GOD ARRIVES

Astarthe, Queen of Haroon

After fifteen days out to sea on the cusp of winter, the sight of Bregantium sent waves of relief through Astarthe's body. The winds had begun to pick up, clouds became more frequent, and the water grew less and less placid. They sailed into Bregantium's breakwater and docked in the capital of Gad on the fourteenth day of Anthanos, just barely dodging the winter storms.

When Imperial officials visited Astarthe in Haroon, they spoke of Gad as a hopeless backwater from which nothing truly good could emerge. Their derision had been so severe that Astarthe—when she set out on this journey with Councilor Vitellian—expected to find a village of mud huts and dirt roads. Instead, she found something totally different: a large town with cobblestone streets, perhaps lacking the red-roofed houses of the south but beautiful in its own way.

The buildings surrounding the harbor, far from being crude stick-huts, were built of stone and mortar, longer than they were tall, with steep thatch roofs. When Astarthe's ship at last put into the dock, and she and her son Adamantion left its confines, she saw—despite the northern character of its buildings—Bregantium was a thoroughly Imperial town. Hundreds of legionaries surveyed the comings and goings of the ships, examining their cargoes for anything incriminating.

For the first time, Astarthe was not greeted with the pomp of a grand entourage. Instead, as she crossed the wooden docks toward the city proper, Adamantion in hand, a lone Imperial Councilor met her halfway. "I see Augusto has brought his cargo," he said.

Astarthe offered him a faint, weak smile, as much as she could offer in this dark time. "And your name, Signore?"

"Why, Lucius Alba, Signora Queen." He drew near, grabbed her hand, and kissed it. "I had my doubts that a southron could be a patriot, but I am glad to be proven wrong."

"I am a patriot, to the innermost fiber of my being, Signor Alba." Astarthe looked down at Adamantion—the true cargo that he wanted. A boy of seven, immature and playful like all children his age, but possessed of a god's blood. The thought that all the Empire's hopes rested on him unnerved her, and she drew in a cold breath.

"The grandson of Claudio-Valens Adamantus," Councilor Alba went on. "Who better to save the Empire?"

"Alba!" Councilor Vitellian shouted from behind her.

She turned to regard the man she had spent the last fortnight with, the man who had told her far more about the Empire's dire peril than she wished to know. *Oh, for the days when the Empire was strong, and the lawgivers were the last concern on anyone's mind.*

"She is more beautiful than the stories tell, Vitellian," Alba said. "I do wish you would have warned me."

Astarthe's smile was even weaker than the first. "Signores… shall we make our plans?"

Five councilors were all that remained of the Imperial government: Augusto Vitellian, Lucius Alba, Marco Geta, Niko Longus and Valerio Anderis.

"Twenty-five are gone," Vitellian said. "Some have certainly died."

"Or all?" Astarthe said faintly, her voice echoing through the small room in the Governor's Mansion that now served as the seat of government.

"Not all," Councilor Alba said, and at the words a shiver passed through Astarthe. "One is certainly not dead… Crispus Servillius is alive."

"You are certain, now?" Vitellian asked.

"It has become quite clear," Alba finished. "Moreover, Crispus Servillius may have been the architect. At the absolute minimum, he was a co-conspirator."

All the color had left Vitellian's face.

"Spies in the capital have also determined something else quite remarkable in your absence, Vitellian," Alba continued. "Two names: Priscilla Marianus and Cleon Adelphos."

"They are only vaguely familiar," Vitellian said.

Astarthe's mind raced with the possibility of treason in the uppermost echelon of the Empire. The thought sickened her.

"Priscilla Marianus was provost of all the Eloesian Academies," said an elderly councilor, one Astarthe recognized as Marco Geta. "Don't you remember? Councilor Servillius thought the world of her. He had a wing of his personal library dedicated to her books. We have reason to believe she, and her second-in-command Cleon Adelphos, were in league with Servillius, or perhaps led him. The transportation of the hundreds of thousands of lawgivers was only possible with the help of Servillius and certain other councilors..."

"But why?" Astarthe snapped. "Why would Priscilla want lawgivers in the Empire? They are the most oppressive group in the world. Why would the Academies—"

"The Academies believe their own ends justify any possible means," Councilor Geta continued. "They believe they are using the lawgivers as tools, but it will backfire... on them, and on the Empire."

"The Academies have long preached treason and sedition," hissed Vitellian, and for the first time the youngest of the councilors looked thoroughly disturbed. "I simply never thought it would come to this."

"And yet," Councilor Alba said, "we have reason to believe the conspiracy runs far deeper than Servillius. Certainly many in the Council have died, but our spies believe many are alive and aiding the lawgivers... Septimo Seánus, for one, and Jiacomo Lornodoris."

Valerio Anderis sighed. "And there is little we can do with this knowledge. We must make a plan. All our available legions are fighting at the Anthanian border. The sailing season ends very soon. We have the god with us, in this very mansion. We have thrown all our hope on the divine Claudio's grandson. So we must make use of it. We must send the last of the Imperial fleet and attack Imperial City at once. Perhaps, with the help of a god, we will prevail."

Their words twisted Astarthe's stomach to knots. "I will go with him. I will not go alone."

"You will not," Valerio commanded her. "You will stay with us."

"I—"

"You have shown yourself a true patriot. Now you must do your duty, Queen Astarthe. We need you here… you are valuable to us, and if something happens to the fleet and our hopes of divine help are dashed—"

"That is why I must go," Astarthe sobbed.

"No," Councilor Longus spoke for the first time. "That is why you must stay."

That night, which proved the eve of Adamantion's departure, Astarthe sacrificed a lamb in the mansion courtyard. She prayed to Issa, goddess of the moon, that her son might be spared. She prayed to Atman, lord of the sun, that if Adamantion died, that heaven would accept him. She consoled herself with the thought of Adamantion in the Fertile Land where the crops never failed. She thought of Adamantion in the presence of the Twin Gods, happy forever.

Then, hands stained by the lamb's sacrificial blood, she collapsed to her knees and wept inconsolably.

CHAPTER SEVENTEEN: THE GREAT BETRAYAL

Alexo Avidéo

Alexo had been a simple young man before the lawgivers came. He had been a street-rat, a parasite as some liked to call him, sleeping in alleys or with friends while subsisting on the free bread the Imperial government provided. He had spent all his days at the Imperial Arena, or when in the mood, at the theater to watch some bawdy comedy. Now, when the lawgivers came and imposed their unnatural laws over everyone, and canceled the program of free bread altogether, shut down the Imperial Arena for its "immorality" and all the theaters for their "encouragement of idolatry," then gone ahead and destroyed all the pretty statues and pictures in Imperial Square, then… *then,* Alexo had become a warrior.

In the now-silent streets of Imperial City—which the foreigners called "Melchaddad"—Alexo and his friends, the Five Patriots, had taken knives, daggers, and javelins from the abandoned guard posts and empty homes. At any opportunity, they stuck a dagger in a lawgiver's heart or tossed a javelin from a distance. Alexo's dear friend, Leptus, had been killed—beheaded by a scimitar—so there were only four of them left, but their gang was still the Five Patriots. Leptus remained with them in spirit.

In the abandoned apartment building which they had made their base, Alexo's friend Andrus spoke the words he had been fearing: "The emperor Janus has surrendered. The Empire's done for."

"If the lawgivers win, then it's not the Empire, anymore, then," Alexo's friend Masimo said. "Maybe we should head north… go to the faraway land. The one beyond the north wind, where the Elders live."

"That's just superstition," Pietro, the smallest of the group, said. "The Elders are as real as talking rabbits and green goblins."

"I know what I'm going to do," Alexo said. "The emperor is here, you say? Why, I'll kill him, yes I will."

"He's probably guarded," Andrus said.

"You'll die, the same as Leptus," Pietro snapped.

"So be it." Alexo smiled defiantly. "I'll go out in glory, and you three can live the rest of your lives with the lawgivers. It's not the Five Patriots anymore… just the Two."

~

Climbing had gotten easier since Alexo joined the rebellion. In Imperial Square, he climbed halfway up the Temple of Imperium with few handholds, and launched himself onto the outward-projecting terrace. A javelin in his right hand, he crouched in the shadows, and watched as the emperor, Secondo Janus, walked into the middle of the square.

A small crowd of a dozen people gathered on the square's outskirts. About a hundred lawgivers surrounded Janus. Few remained in Imperial City and those that did, paying the tax of the lawgivers, rarely left their homes. Those that joined the lawgivers wore all blacks like the rest.

The city overall had gone quiet, losing all its entertainment and color and joy. *And that is why I am here.*

Secondo looked tired, pale, and weary. And he did not wear the Imperial Circlet, something emperors never went without. Perhaps the lawgivers, too, thought that was idolatry.

From the direction of the Imperial Palace, a black-turbaned man Alexo recognized as the Theomancer marched out with a hundred lawgiver soldiers in his train. *Now,* Alexo thought, *is the best opportunity I will get.*

He pitched back his javelin, strode forward, and launched.

CHAPTER EIGHTEEN:
A NEW LAW FOR THE EMPIRE

Emperor Secondo Janus

Secondo Janus had never met the Theomancer before. He was observing the man's square gray beard and piercing grayish eyes, and the turban black as pitch, when something sharp grazed his mouth, drawing blood. Something large and wooden bounced and skipped across the pavestones. *A javelin!* Secondo cursed, and looked up from where it had come. A small shadow slinked away from the Temple of Imperium. The lawgivers who had escorted him called out and ran after the assassin with swords.

Secondo cursed. "This is what I get, for promoting stability! This is what I get, for ushering in a new peace!" He looked at the few Imperial citizens gathered to watch, who—despite their best attempts to put on a bold face—could not disguise the hatred in their eyes. "I am doing what every reasonable man would!" He turned toward them, sneering. "And you hangers-on, you people so dedicated to stopping a new law for the Empire, you are so proud of yourselves, so haughty and condemning! You view me as weak, don't you? Gods, I will teach you otherwise."

"Janus!" the Theomancer boomed, and Secondo pivoted to face him.

He dropped to his knees. "My domino."

"Where is the Imperial Circlet?" the Theomancer boomed again, his voice shaking with disappointment and anger. "Your approach is symbolic, and you deny me the ultimate symbol."

"I am sorry, my domino. It was misplaced." Misplaced, Secondo thought, was a better explanation than the one he had been given—that a magical snake took it.

"*Misplaced?*" the Theomancer roared. "It is no matter."

From the alley near the Temple of Imperium, the lawgivers

were dragging out the headless body of Secondo's assassin, still dressed in a roughspun poor man's tunic.

"Nonetheless I am glad you are here. Secondo, the Law of Mazda is strict and unyielding, and no one may resist it and prosper. Under the eye of Mazda there is no forgiveness. Do you agree?"

"Of course. Praise Mazda!" he shouted.

"Then I sentence you to die. With the Queen of the North, not long ago, you committed an act of adultery… Mazda does not forgive, and adultery is a grave sin."

Janus gasped, tried to stand up, but a forceful hand shoved him back down.

"My allies in the Imperial government have told me all about your sick perversion. Thus, I sentence you to death. In Hell, may you burn and never perish, O son of dogs and child of swine."

Janus let out a bitter scream and struggled as the Theomancer left him, as his henchmen approached with scimitars drawn. Deep down, he had expected the end to come for him soon, but never had he expected it to come like this.

CHAPTER NINETEEN: MOUNT HYLEA

Numa

From the city of Vida down the ambling roads, Numa had ridden seven days into the heart of the Empire, beside towns either burnt to smoking ruin or living under the heavy yoke of Mazda's law. Shareeka had made it quite clear that they would not stay in any inn, even though he had sewn together the lawgiver clothing, and now Shareeka and Appian blended in quite well.

Riding with Appian, Numa now played the part of a captive. Yet it was only on that seventh day, in the far south of Anthania, that a lawgiver passing by stopped them on the road.

"Where are you going, brother?" the man in lawgiver blacks said, his Imperial accent making it clear this was a convert.

Numa bit the sides of his mouth and looked down, doing his best to act the part of timid captive.

"Our business is our own, brother," Appian answered. "But if you must know—"

"—We are going to fight some rebels near Amaroth."

"Amaroth, yes?" the man answered. "The priestesses have paid off the Theomancer, for now."

Numa recalled Amaroth, the City of Love, the home of the priestesses of Amara.

"The Theomancer won't tolerate them for much longer, though. He doesn't like idolaters, not one bit."

Shareeka nodded, his face hidden behind the black hood.

"And who is this?" the man said.

"A prisoner," Shareeka answered. "He refuses to honor the Law of Mazda."

"With the pressure of taxes, he will convert… I assure it. That is what happened to me."

Numa's blood began to burn.

"Either way, the war is won. The last ships of the Imperial Navy came by, trying to destroy the lawgiver ships. We sank every last one of them."

"Good," Shareeka answered.

"Their last ships are gone, and we broke through Gad. Bregantium has the last of the government. When Bregantium falls, we'll all be under Mazda's law."

Go, Numa wanted to say, *go, before I draw my sword and kill him.*

"The captive of yours had best learn to accept it, or he will die."

I would rather die, than live like you.

"We must get going," Appian said and clucked. The horse took off, carrying Numa with him. Shareeka followed, a few seconds later.

Saddle-sore and exhausted, Numa was about done-in when, two days later, a wooden sign appeared: TO ISLE OF SERPENTS, MOUNT HYLEA, LORNATIUM AND THE OCEAN.

"Mount Hylea," he breathed, "now we will see if I am a madman."

"You *are* a madman," Appian said. "We already knew that."

Numa laughed despite himself, despite his exhaustion, despite his fears. *It is good,* he thought, *to be with friends, here, at the end of all things, at the end of the Empire and the nation that I love.*

An hour later, the high mountain peak of Hylea appeared, towering above them. Beyond Numa, near the ocean, the limestone buildings of Lornatium still stood, its people no doubt paying taxes as unbelievers.

Here, Numa thought, *my destiny lies.*

CHAPTER TWENTY:
SURROUNDED

Astarthe, Queen of Haroon

Beyond the waters of the harbor, an army of dhows and warships had begun to blockade Haroon. In early morning a low horn blew, and within an hour's time messenger came running into the governor's mansion with the news that Astarthe already knew in her heart: "My signores, the lawgivers have surrounded us."

The city of Bregantium had water enough, and food stores that would last them six months—Astarthe had been instrumental in ensuring so—but it was only a matter of time before it fell. The presence of lawgivers outside the walls could only mean one thing, that the legions had at last failed against the overwhelming numbers of lawgivers, and that the Empire was doomed. Astarthe wept, for her heart knew something else as well—something she dared not admit— that her son, Adamantion, was lost. She had felt his death days ago, but she had not admitted it to herself in her conscious mind.

In full view of Councilor Vitellian, she fell to her knees, buried her head in her hands, and wept uncontrollably.

CHAPTER TWENTY-ONE:
THE COMMON

Priscilla Marianus, Provost of the Thenoan Academy

The common folk of the Empire were the chief problem to the revolution, Priscilla knew. At every maneuvering of the Academies they resisted change, resisted the utopian designs the Thenoan philosophers set forth. Priscilla did not know why it surprised her that the common folk so hated the lawgivers, but somehow it did. Now, standing in the White Chamber but daring not sit on the throne where so many evil Imperial men had, she had just about reached her wit's end. For twenty days and twenty nights a woman had sat outside, begging for an audience with Priscilla. The common woman had covered her face in ashes and invoked all the gods—entities conjured up to comfort small minds—begging for a word.

At last, Priscilla screamed at the messenger: "Let her in! Yes, let her in! I can bear you no longer. Let her have a word with me. Perhaps she will surprise me with an intelligent comment."

When at last the common woman arrived, dressed in a roughspun woolen gown and covered in ashes, sobbing and pitiful, Priscilla realized she would not be pleasantly surprised.

The sobbing stopped however, when the woman looked up at her. "My domina, why are you wearing a mask?"

"Quiet!" Priscilla hissed. She had grown so accustomed to the tragic actor's mask that she had forgotten she was wearing it. "I have given you an audience, common woman, which is far more than you deserve. Now do not condescend to me. What ails you? Out with it!"

"My domina Priscilla, you have much influence over the lawgivers. I beg of you to save my daughter. The lawgivers have said she is not a virgin, and is unmarried, and now must be put to death.

Tomorrow at sunrise they will execute her."

Priscilla sighed. She knew, in her heart, how this common person felt. She understood, in a way, the anguish. But in true common fashion, this woman did not understand the Academies' grander goals, that these lawgivers were tools to advance the wider cause. "Good woman, I cannot bear your words," Priscilla said. "I have no way of fixing your problem. Leave me."

The woman fell to her knees, clasped her hands. "I beg of you. They are oppressing us."

"You are oppressing me!" Priscilla howled, perhaps a bit too harshly, but she had feelings too. "I have told you I cannot bear you. You are probably a blind patriot, aren't you? A lover of the Empire?"

"I… I don't understand… Please!"

"I have never felt so attacked in my life," Priscilla snapped. This common housewife was an excellent manipulator, trying to fill her with guilt. But Priscilla turned all that would-be guilt into anger. "Get out of here! Be thankful you have your own life."

"Please! I beg of you!"

Priscilla screamed. "Get out, before I have your head!"

Seconds after the common woman left, Priscilla stormed out of the White Chamber. Two lawgivers in blacks, with scimitars in their hands, stood guard. "Do not let the common into the White Chamber ever again!" she screamed.

One of the lawgivers pivoted and grabbed her, digging his fingers deep into her shoulders. She sensed his anger, and her own helplessness before his warrior strength. "Do not tell us what to do," he sneered in a thick lawgiver accent, "or we will end the charade prematurely."

Charade. Priscilla wondered what in Varda he meant.

"Do you understand, Mnester?"

The other lawgiver chuckled. At the name of the famed tragic actor, Priscilla flushed hot in embarrassment behind her mask. She turned and left the way she had come, followed by a chorus of laughter.

CHAPTER TWENTY-TWO:
DESTINY

Numa

In early morning he began the journey up Mount Hylea alone, and it wasn't until late afternoon before the dirt path reached its destination, a small valley near the summit. Before him lay a ruined temple, its pillars and limestone blocks in a heap amid the scraggly pines. The high mountain air was much cooler than below. A wind blew, cold yet refreshing, howling through the dale.

A drum began to beat, at first soft but growing louder and louder. Numa's eyes darted this way and that. He turned around and looked around the peak, but caught no sight of the drummer. All his doubts came to a fore—that he had come here for naught, that he was mad, or worse, a wishful dreamer.

"Claudio-Valens Adamantus!"

When he whipped around to face the voice, coming from the temple ruin, his eyes met the oracle—the very woman he had seen in the dream—naked despite the cold, a snake wrapped around her leg and chest. "Io," he said.

Her eyes were white and sightless, yet Numa sensed she could see all—in this world, and the next. "I knew Claudio-Valens would come. You have made a long journey, but a greater journey is ahead of you… the journey to return the Empire to greatness, to crush its enemies abroad—but most importantly, within."

"I want nothing more," he said, and truthfully.

"Two gifts I have for you… one, taken from a man unworthy of it, who, in trying to preserve his life, has found his death and eternal flame. Another, taken from a man worthy, a courageous lion-heart who proclaimed the Empire's virtues to his dying breath. He has gone on to glory… but still, he is not as worthy of it as you."

"What are you talking about?"

"Look down!"

Somehow he had missed the two objects lying at his feet. One, a sword of bluish metal—*adamant!*—and the other, the intricate silverwork of the Imperial Circlet. "Gods!" he cursed.

"God... that is what you are, Claudio-Valens Adamantus."

"I am not Claudio. I am not even an Imperial—"

"Quiet, devil!" the oracle hissed. "You are Claudio, and you are an Imperial! What is an Imperial? An Imperial is a citizen... a thing not determined by birth or blood. May Mira damn you to hell if you ever claim you are not Claudio again."

"I am Claudio," Numa said, and for the first time he believed it.

"The sword... grab it!"

He stooped down, grasped the weapon by its fine leather handle. It was heavy but not prohibitively so. He knew a little about adamant—that a hair, falling on its blade, was split in half, and that the blade before him would shatter all other metals besides adamant.

"It is called *Imperium's Rebuke.* And with it you shall punish the Empire's enemies. You shall cut to pieces those who hate the Empire. It shall spill so much traitors' blood the world itself will be soaked. By the power of Mira, the Trifold Mother, and by Imperium, the Spirit of Empire, I bless your weapon with accuracy and strength."

"And the other?"

The oracle laughed. "Do not play the fool, Claudio-Valens. You know what it is. The Imperial Circlet lies before you... grab it, and lay it on your head."

"That is blasphemy," Numa said, but his voice trailed off at the anger he sensed. When he looked up the oracle's eyes blazed with fury. He stooped over, grabbed the cold silver, and laid it on his head.

"Now, I proclaim you emperor... emperor and god, Ruler of the Six Nations and soon seven. What I began with the first Claudio, you—the second Claudio—must complete."

"Complete? What?"

"Long ago I told the emperor that he must marry a whore...

against all the laws of the Empire he obeyed. What began as such a small crime, you must take to its fullest extent. But do not look at me, Numa, and expect me to tell you what to do; for it is in your heart."

"I don't understand..."

"You do not have to understand, for it is in your heart... destiny shimmers all about you, child."

The pounding drums reached a pinnacle of volume. The oracle twisted this way and that, and the snake tightened its grip on her.

"Mira!" the oracle howled. "Mira and all the gods, they light my path." She tossed her black hair this way and that, consumed by the intoxicating rhythm.

Numa drew back a step.

Soon the oracle was dancing on air, her body floating an inch above the ground. Her white, sightless eyes flashed like blue lightning. "The words of Mira, Queen of Light, and of Brecko, Lord of Ecstasy. The voice of the gods themselves..." Her voice was a peal of thunder. "Go, Claudio-Valens, who calls himself Numa... go east to the seashore. The last ship sails for Carta Mega. There, in the city of Melkior, you must find the most precious gift of all... her name is Eudora."

Numa drew back another step. The wind howled and light seeped away from the mountain meadow. Lightning flashed. The oracle was growling like a bear. Her sightless white eyes took on a new look of hunger as she licked her teeth.

"Go!" she roared. "Run, Claudio-Valens Adamantus, before I eat your flesh!"

PART TWO

In bed, I lay awake, unable to sleep, consumed by the dream.

The walls of Bregantium are surrounded; the war-horns blow at constant intervals. The chants of the lawgivers even now rise above the silence of the town.

I had hoped the Empire would prevail, but its enemies are too great, the traitors far too many. I had hoped our nation would rise again, but now I know that we will fail.

In the daylight and the midnight hours, I curse Imperium, unable to sleep, consumed by the dream.

CHAPTER TWENTY-THREE: THE FERTILE LAND

Astarthe, Queen of Haroon

In the shrine of Amara, Astarthe honored a different god, but the beings of light were forgiving, and Astarthe was sure the Lady of Love did not mind. She lit a candle, her body smeared with mourners' ash, and asked the goddess Issa why she had allowed Astarthe's son to die.

The wick burned in the silence of the private shrine, causing the silver figurine before it to glisten. Outside the walls of the Governor's Mansion, Astarthe knew well what worry had consumed the citizens. But here, in the shrine of Amara, Astarthe could only feel guilt… guilt, and anger.

She stormed away, cursing Issa. She ran from Amara's shrine and down the winding halls, all the way to her private room, where she slammed the door and began to weep. She had thought all her tears were spent, but now the innocent face of Adamantion, lost in battle, was fresh in her mind. "I am a terrible mother," she said aloud, and bolted across the room. She laid her hands around the knife she kept for protection, and pushed the blade against her wrist.

"Shall I do it?" she asked herself. "Shall I?"

The knife fell from her hands. She buried her face in her pillow and collapsed, crying, on the bed. Weeping, she fell asleep, and a dream consumed her.

Issa, the mother of the Khazan, stood tall before her, wearing a gown of scarlet cloth. In her right hand she grasped a green staff; in her left a crescent-moon amulet, the symbol of fertility. Blue hair fell down her back, contrasting starkly with her amber skin. When she spoke, the dirt around her burst with life, and from the black earth green shoots and vines emerged: "Astarthe, my daughter, do not worry about the souls who have passed on to eternal fire, nor those who now dance in the lush fields of the Fertile Land. Take off your ashes of mourning. A task is before you, and your task is this: to wait for the conqueror god, and recognize him when he comes."

Astarthe rushed forward to fall into her embrace, but she fell away like a desert mirage, untouchable.

"Do not touch me, your mother. I am a goddess. It is not your time to touch me. Even the Fertile Land has been hidden from your sight. You have a task in the world…"

"To wait for the conqueror god, and recognize him when he comes." Her eyes were open when she spoke the words. She thought of all the books she read, all the stories she heard, all the tales that had been told to her by the fire. What Issa, her mother and goddess, meant could not be more clear… the second coming of Claudio-Valens Adamantus.

CHAPTER TWENTY-FOUR:
PRECIOUS THINGS

Numa

Against Shareeka's stern advice, Numa wore the Imperial Circlet and wielded *Imperium's Rebuke* openly when he stepped onto the dock of Carta Mega.

The heat beat unbearably on this city, hugging the edge of the desert yet somehow—according to sailors—providing water and food for a hundred thousand souls. Numa's clothes were soaked with sweat as he left the dock, with Appian and Shareeka following close behind. Leaving the artificial harbor, they found themselves in the city center. Ten domed-roof stone edifices shielded merchants from the oppressive desert sun, though they did nothing for the biting dust and the poor air. A group of men on camels were riding in from one of the side streets, their beasts of burden heavy-laden with rolls of silk.

If Numa had come to another world when he left Norriva and traveled to the southland coast, he had come to a new universe altogether when he reached Carta Mega.

"Sandstorm coming!" a voice called out in thickly-accented Imperial, and in an instant the merchants were scrambling to pack up their things.

"A sandstorm," Shareeka said from behind, "may sound like a small thing to you, Numa, but there is nothing more serious. We must find shelter."

"I think he's right, Signor Emperor," Appian said.

Numa turned around and smiled. "I think so too." His smile turned into a frown, even as the sand and dust began to whip into town, and the winds picked up. "But we didn't come here to hole up in an inn… we will go speak to the leader, and find Eudora."

"The Bel of Carta Mega would not so much as look at you," Shareeka sneered. He had not treated Numa any better since he began to wear the Imperial Circlet; in fact, it seemed Shareeka treated him worse.

"You will show me the way, Shareeka," Numa demanded.

Shareeka's whiskers twitched, and his beady pink eyes blazed fierily. "Very well," he said, and stalked off.

Beyond the city center, the flat-roofed homes had all been shuttered to protect from the coming storm. Women ran home with children in tow. Shareeka's pace was easy, despite all this, as he led them down the packed-dirt streets to the house of the bel.

The palace that stood before them rose three times the height of the highest house Numa had seen in Carta Mega. It was built not of white plaster-lined brick like the homes of the citizens, but instead of a rich red sandstone. Three of its towers ended in onion domes, carved into the shape of flower buds and painted green. The door, still a touch open, was closing, and a pair of warriors with scimitars were walking in.

Numa took off at a run.

The warriors stopped what they were doing. "The emperor?" one said.

"No, Anno, that is no emperor!" They both had the tall build and light complexion of northerners, but the accents of Khazidees.

"Signores!" Numa shouted. "I must speak with the Bel of Carta Mega."

"Who are you?" the first shouted while the second gave an uneasy eye to the whipping dust and sand.

"Numa!" he shouted.

"His Majesty Balthesar the Magnificent has no use for you—"

"Claudio-Valens Adamantus."

Shareeka groaned from behind him. Numa flushed hot, embarrassed, but the two warriors were looking at him with a mix of surprise and bafflement.

At last, the second warrior spoke. "Get inside, fool. Balthesar the Magnificent has no use for the dead."

The throne of Carta Mega was not much more than a chair, and far less impressive than the man who sat upon it.

Balthesar stood up, three-quarters the size of Numa, yet with an imposing air about him. His silk robes glistened in the torchlight, ending in dagged sleeves that fell halfway to the ground. A turban almost half his height, white like an onion, sat on his head, and a black moustache was greased and twirled, standing out starkly against his red Khazidean complexion. "Balthesar the Magnificent rises, and yet this visitor does not fall prostrate. A strange thing… very strange. But he must think much of himself… I can see it by the Imperial Circlet he wears, and a sword worth half my kingdom."

Traces of the bluish adamant were no doubt visible through the hilt. Numa had an urge to draw *Imperium's Rebuke* and display it in full, but that was too rude, even for him. "Your Majesty."

"What brings a pretender to the White Throne into the court of Balthesar the Magnificent?"

"I am looking for someone named Eudora…"

"A hundred-and-seven thousand people live in my city, Signor Pretender. A hundred-and-seven thousand profit from our fleet's overseas trade, and live from the water of our cisterns. Go door to door and house to house, and eventually—I am certain—you will find someone with the name of Eudora."

"So you do not know anyone named Eudora," Numa breathed.

"You are wasting my time, signore."

"It seems that way." Behind Numa, Shareeka groaned again.

"I wonder how much that adamant sword would fetch in the city of Melchaddad."

"By Imperium, you will not find out."

"Imperium." The bel said the word like it was curious and

foreign. A delighted smile formed over the face of Balthesar the Magnificent. "You are an Imperial, no doubt. A patriot. I thought you had all fallen away. I, the Bel of Carta Mega, do not pay taxes to your Empire… though by law, I am your friend. I wept for you, the day the lawgivers came. I had no part in it, but now, what's done is done."

"It is not done," Numa said. "It will not be done until I am dead."

"I could arrange that," Balthesar said, "but in truth, all I would want is your sword."

"You will not get it."

Balthesar's smile grew. "I wish the best for your people, Imperial; but your cause is lost. Be gone from me."

The guards tossed the three out into the howling wind and burning sand and dust. Numa tried breathing through his sleeve. Appian cursed. Shareeka signaled them to follow him, and began at a sprint.

The inn that Shareeka led them to was only a short walk away, and when they entered the below-ground dwelling, the air was thick with smoke. Divans were spread all throughout the common room, and southrons sat on them, many smoking pipes.

The innkeeper was short, handsome in a way, with the red complexion and dark hair of a Khazidee. *No doubt,* Numa thought, *he is a native of Carta Mega.* "Welcome to the Oasis," he said. "I take it you have come to wait out the storm. If you will not purchase a room, the least you could do is purchase a pipe."

Numa had never smoked before, nor did he have the inclination. "What about a glass of wine?"

"Wine is not the custom here," the innkeeper said. "The least you can do is—"

"We will purchase a room," Shareeka snapped.

The ratling's pockets ran deep.

"Very well," the Khazidee answered. "A room you will have. How long will you stay?"

"That is no one's business but our own," Shareeka answered.

"We are looking for a woman named Eudora," Numa said.

Shareeka looked back at Numa and scowled. A few of the pipe-smokers looked up at Numa, perhaps sizing him up for loot, and Appian stepped forward protectively.

"Eudora, you say, emperor," the Khazidee innkeeper went on. "Tell me your name, emperor."

"Numa," he answered, no doubt against Shareeka's wishes, but Shareeka would learn to deal with it.

"A bold one you are, Numa, to wear a replica of the Imperial Circlet. It looks very lifelike." The Khazidee's smile softened. "You ask for a woman named Eudora. Who is this Eudora you seek? I know of only one…"

Numa had no idea, in truth, why he was looking for her; only that the oracle had demanded that he find her.

"She is an Eloesian girl. Eastern women are so beautiful, don't you think?"

Numa could count the number of eastern women he had met on one hand.

"She lives outside of town, by the quarry. She won't have anything to do with us, with the men of Carta Mega. She is stuck-up. I think her father is an Imperial man… very high-up."

Numa pondered the possibility in his head. Why would the oracle send him here to Carta Mega, if only to find an Eloesian girl? And was this Eudora, who lived by the quarry, really the one he was sent to seek after? *I will find out soon.*

"Our room, please," Shareeka snapped.

The innkeeper soon acquiesced.

To Numa's surprise, Shareeka did not attack him after he shut the door. Instead, the ratling took off his cloak and went right to bed, leaving Appian and Numa alone.

Some of Appian's chubbiness had worn away on the long travel, but he was still bigger than Numa, and much better with people. *He is a good asset to have, and a good friend.*

"Some adventure we are having," Appian said as they prepared for bed.

Numa had offered to sleep on the floor. If he was going to save the Empire, he had best get used to discomfort.

"I never thought, in a thousand years, I would be in Carta Mega," Appian went on. "We are not even on Imperial soil, now, you know. And did you know who the god of Carta Mega is? Melkior, the god of precious things. There is a temple somewhere here—"

"Appian, calm down," Numa laughed. "Your excitement is a little too much to bear. I should not be surprised, though… you *were* Norriva's biggest bookworm."

Appian laughed. "A light reading of history brings out a wealth of meaning."

"Light?" Numa said, and Appian laughed again. It was good to have his friend here, and he had a feeling—a feeling he couldn't explain—that Appian would be instrumental in winning the coming war.

~

In the morning cool, Shareeka led Numa and Appian out of the inn and into the streets of Carta Mega. They narrowly missed a chariot whipping by—a pair of wealthy young men, perhaps, displaying their new purchase for all to see—and a crowd of women heading away from the city center, carrying newly-filled buckets of water.

The sun arose, and already the welcome chill was dissipating. Soon it would beat unbearably hot overhead. Numa was glad they got an early start.

Shareeka led them down the dirt streets, stopping strangers on the street to inquire for directions—and meeting a much more hospitable response than they'd gotten on the Imperial southland coast, or even Norriva for that matter. Little by little they made their way away from the flat-roofed homes and outside the city itself, until they reached the edge of the wilderness.

There, carved out of a hill in stair-like layers, was the sandstone quarry. Beyond it lay a barren country of dry, rocky soil and small pockets of scrub-brush. There, Numa guessed, a man unused to the terrain wouldn't survive a day.

"There," Shareeka said, and pointed to a house a few dozen yards away, typical of the others in Carta Mega. The constant whipping dust and earth had turned the once-white plastered walls a shade of brown.

They made their way to the door, and Numa knocked.

Minutes later, no one had answered. The sun had already begun to bake the ground, and the morning cool had vanished like a fleeting shadow. Numa dreamed of water… the endless, gushing water of the River Gad, and the nearby Coldwater Pond outside of Norriva. He realized how blessed Norriva had been, to have so much water.

"She must not be here," Appian said.

Shareeka turned around and glared. "You think?"

"Who are you?" a woman's voice called out from behind.

Numa whipped around to face her, and a lump formed in his throat.

She was young—Numa's age—with the olive skin and prominent nose that eastern beauties were said to have. Her wavy golden brown hair was tied with a length of silk, and fell the length of her back. A silk robe, dyed green, indicated her wealth. She was stunning and Numa had no business even looking at her.

He glanced away, then forced himself to meet her gaze. She looked amused.

"What are you doing at my house? You aren't from Carta

Mega, are you?"

"Carta Mega?" Numa said stupidly.

"Yes," the woman said. "That is where you are, signore. You have an accent, too… are you from Gad?"

"That is not your business."

"Oh, but it is," she went on. "And you are wearing the Imperial Circlet. I can see it is the real thing. Secondo Janus is dead and you took it. He is dead—praise the gods!"

"Indeed," Numa said. The sight of her turned his stomach to knots. All the dangers of the road, all the threats of the lawgivers and the raging war, had not done to him what this girl was doing to him now. "Are you Eudora?"

She grinned. "Indeed I am Eudora. Eudora Kyrillos. Will you all do me the honor of telling me what your names are, and why in Varda you've come to my house?"

"I am Appian, my signora."

Numa glanced over his shoulder. Appian had dropped to one knee.

"And I am Shareeka, signora." He also fell to one knee.

But Numa remained standing. He met Eudora's gaze once more. "I am Numa. And I was hoping you would tell us why we've come, Eudora Kyrillos."

Her grin widened. "I have not had the gift of such bizarre company in a long while. Not since my father left."

"Your father?"

"Yes. I have a father. Don't you?"

"My father is dead."

"That is too bad." Eudora smiled. "My father is all but dead. Surely you have heard the legend of the Lost Legions. My father has refused to serve Secondo Janus. Lysander Kyrillos, the best grand legate the Empire had ever seen. He has been in hiding and no one knows where he is."

"Except you," Numa said.

"Except me."

"Now I'll tell you why I've come," Numa said. I've come to save the Empire."

"A noble goal, for certain. Some say the Empire is beyond saving."

"Those that say that, and do not fight, deserve death."

Eudora smiled. "Very well, Claudio-Valens."

"I have been called that before."

"I believe it. You wear his crown."

"Will you tell me where your father is?" Numa asked.

Eudora's smile grew. "For Claudio-Valens Adamantus, riding forth to save the Empire and bringing news of the traitor's death… we will see."

CHAPTER TWENTY-FIVE: NEWS FROM AFAR

Pharzanes, King of Kings

On the throne of Taifun, Pharzanes sat and reigned, and for the first time in years, free from Sidathra the Traitor's poisoning words. The archmagus had been burnt alive by the magic of his brothers. *One less lawgiver,* Pharzanes thought, *is a blessing for the world.*

A messenger strode in, the train of his robe gliding across the floor. When he drew near the steps where Pharzanes' titanic stone throne began, he fell prostrate before the King of Kings.

"Rise," Pharzanes said, "and tell me the news from afar."

Gracefully the messenger stood up, and began to speak: "The lawgivers have undone the Imperial government. Some of its towns have paid the unbelieving tax which we are so very familiar with. But the provinces remain in revolt."

The news stole the breath from Pharzanes' lungs, and weighed on his soul like a bag of stones. He cursed life, and the gods, for the news. "I had thought the Empire—which has defeated us so often, and so violently—surely would never fall before the lawgivers. My heart breaks. The world has gone mad, and each day I think more of death. Death is freedom from this madness…"

"Shall we go to their aid?"

"No," Pharzanes said. "The Empire's fight is not our fight. We are not brothers or even kin. We will root out the lawgivers at home, and prepare for the final battle… our battle, not the Empire's."

The messenger nodded; a look of despair had formed on the old man's face. He turned to leave.

Pharzanes' words flashed through his mind. *The Empire's fight is not our fight… We are not brothers or even kin.*

That night he slept in his own bed, but his dreams took him far away, far not in distance but in time.

In his dream he imagined the Empire fallen, and soon thereafter, Fharas. He imagined Fharas, the Beautiful Land, hundreds of years from now. He imagined Fharas, home to the King of Kings, changed utterly from its glorious past. He imagined the Padisha Emperor replaced with a theocrat; he imagined the laws that governed Fharas and enhanced the life and beauty of the nation, replaced with the onerous Law of Mazda. He saw the fire temples of Athra replaced with black cubical *kabakhs* where preachers spewed sermons of hatred against the different, and sermons of war against those who worshiped the gods. He imagined the Beautiful Land of Fharas changed into a lawgiver republic, devoid of all its ancient beauty and culture, living forever under a gloomy and hateful sky.

Before dawn he awoke, covered in cold sweat. He determined at that moment he would call up all his troops. Every able-bodied man from Sur to Saidoon would serve under the largest army Fharas would ever seen. The stakes were far too high to do otherwise. He would go to the aid of the Empire. He would put aside old hatreds. He would go to war.

CHAPTER TWENTY-SIX:
THE WILD HORSE UNBROKEN

Cleon Adelphos, Vice Provost of the Thenoan Academy

"There is an old tale," Cleon told Priscilla as the sounds of battle in the streets echoed even into the upper-story palace window, "which I had taken as an inspiration. In the days of the Red Priestess, Lidda, the love priestess Melorra said the Imperial people were a wild horse. She said that they would resist the Red Priestess's laws. That they would fight like a wild horse, but in time, with enough pressure, they would be broken and tamed. Now, I am not so sure. Now, I have begun to wonder if they will never be broken… if they will all die to the last, before they honor Mazda's law."

"Then they all must die," Priscilla growled, "and I will watch them gladly."

Cleon turned to face her. It was so hard to take her seriously, wearing the mask of a tragic actor, with those crying eyes and the great leering frown. The lawgivers had treated her terribly, but Priscilla had continued to impress him—despite the lawgivers' harsh words and restrictions upon her, she considered it all secondary to her goal, to destroy the Empire in its current form and all the myths that propped it up. "I have such great respect for you, Priscilla." He reached out to touch her but she jerked away.

"Do not condescend to me, Cleon Adelphos. I made you what you are today. You owe the Vice Provost position to me, and to no one else."

"I know," Cleon said. "I meant every word I said."

"Spare me."

Gods, that leering frown.

"A great philosopher once said that soldiers are—by definition—criminals, for they take lives and refuse to adhere to the principles of peace," Priscilla said. "They should all be imprisoned and reeducated, he said, or executed to the last. Now, I'm not so certain."

"You think the Empire—"

"Gods, no, I am not talking about the Empire," Priscilla hissed. "I am talking about our friends, the lawgivers. I fully concur with their killing. The citizens must be brought into submission… or killed."

Cleon thought of the wild horse, unbroken. *They are likely to be killed, one by one.* "I agree, Priscilla."

"You are a fool, Cleon. I wish you would have one original thought," Priscilla barked. "Sometimes, I wonder why I put up with you. I, the Philosopher Queen, and you the useless pawn."

Sometimes Cleon thought of striking her. But to strike her was to betray all the ideals of the Academies, to betray the principles of argument and reason. And somehow, the tragic actor's mask made her appear weaker, less imposing, even less wise—more, dare he think it, pitiful.

"The people of the Empire have committed unspeakable, unforgivable crimes… and whatever comes after it cannot possible be any worse," Priscilla said. "I look forward to a land under the Law of Mazda… for it cannot possibly be anything worse than what came before."

"So you have abandoned our scheme… our grand design, our utopia?" Cleon had barely finished speaking before Priscilla laid into him, digging her fingernails hard into his shoulders.

"Shut up, you fool! I speak, but you do not listen. You hear, but do not listen." Her fingernails were almost drawing blood. "I said that whatever comes after the Empire cannot possibly be worse! You fool! You imbecile! You—"

Cleon pushed her off him. She screamed as she fell, hitting the floor hard. "You strike a woman? You answer my argument with violence? How typically Imperial!" She clambered to her feet.

A storm of voices and footsteps appeared down some narrow corridor. A group of lawgivers appeared, dressed in black as was their custom. "Cleon! A word with you," said one whose voice he recognized as the field marshal, Umar. "We need your keen mind… the conquest of Gad is within reach and some strategy is needed."

"Of course, signore." Cleon could not help but glare at Priscilla.

"I shall come too!" Priscilla said, dusting off her gown.

"No, you will not," Umar told her. "We are discussing men's affairs… war, and politics. Go to your room, Priscilla, and do not leave until I say."

"Whatever the Law of Mazda requires," Priscilla acquiesced, and snarled at Cleon through the tragic actor's mask as she left.

CHAPTER TWENTY-SEVEN: RECONQUEST

Basil, son of Basil, Prince of Harkeon, Leader of the Bluecloaks

At the shattered gate of Kersepoli, in view of the Temple of Tyros looming in many-pillared glory on the city's highest hill, Prince Basil fought for freedom, for unity, for empire, against the traitors who had sided with the Academy and by extension, the lawgivers that invaded the land. The soldier with whom he exchanged blows—a greenhorn, not a practiced warrior by any stretch of the imagination— had once been a fellow-citizen but now he was an enemy, an enemy that needed to be subdued.

The young man's spear glanced off Prince Basil's shield, throwing him off balance. Basil advanced, ducked in, then slashed with all his might. Basil's shortsword cut through the young man's shoulder, then chest, like a hot knife through butter. All around him the chaos of battle echoed, a cacophony of steel against steel and shredding flesh, the smell of blood and spilled guts in the growing heat of the morning.

The neighing of warhorses came next—a hundred mounted soldiers charging forth and driving the enemy away like leaves in the wind, the riders' flapping blue cloaks indicating their allegiance. *The battle,* Prince Basil thought as he panted, exhausted from fighting, *is won.*

Another column of riders galloped forth down the road. The way was open, and now the ten thousand Bluecloaks had free entry into Kersepoli. The city which had betrayed the Empire was once again brought, firmly and irrevocably, into its grasp. Now, Korthos and Thénai were the only great cities of Eloesus that remained disloyal.

One by one Prince Basil saw to it that the scattered resistance was picked off. Standing in the city square of Kersepoli, surrounded by the towering bronze statues of hoplites, he fought the urge to gloat at his easy victory. The warriors the Academy had hired were no doubt students, unused to war and physical exertion but trained in the minutiae of military science.

One of Basil's field marshals hurried up to him, from a side street. "My prince," he said, "the citizens are not resisting us. What shall we do with them?"

"Leave them alive," Prince Basil said. "They are not the cause of this. Arrest every lecturer and official of the Academy. We will keep them alive and in prison, until the emperor decides what to do with them." He had heard the rumor that the emperor was dead. If proven true, he would have to make some difficult decisions, but today was not that day.

Not long after the field marshal left, a messenger came running, his color ashen and his expression grim. "Your Honor, bad news… the leadership in Korthos has opened the ports, and now, hundreds of lawgiver ships arrive each day. Their numbers are already more than twenty thousand. The seas are growing unnavigable… we must thank the gods that winter has come, but we must not grow complacent."

Prince Basil nodded. The news weighed on him like a millstone tied around his neck. "We must fortify the city. We must pray… we must make an offering."

Soon Prince Basil found himself in Kersepoli's Temple of the Imperial Cult. Before the statue of Claudio-Valens Adamantus, he laid an offering in the bowl: all the silver coins Basil had. He asked that Claudio would come again.

CHAPTER TWENTY-EIGHT:
THE LOST LEGIONS

Numa

Riding on a camel, lurching from side to side as the beast made its way across the dry desert, Numa had already learned to hate the sun. He had already drunk all the water from his pouch, and though Eudora had told him the journey was less than a day, he still could think of nothing but how blessed Norriva was, with its many ponds, lakes and streams. Not for the first time, he yearned for Norriva and its simple life, but that life was gone, vanished like water into the desert sun. Now, the only life he had was this: fighting the Empire's enemy in a war that grew increasingly hopeless, in a world where it seemed inevitable the traitors would win.

Just ahead, a telltale burst of greenery appeared: a veritable forest of date palms surrounding a giant oasis. "Here we are," Eudora said. She seemed very comfortable on camel-back.

It is so good to have her with us. And soon, they had arrived.

The chirping of birds were the only sounds that greeted them as they entered the date palm forest. The further Numa rode in, the closer he grew to the life-giving waters, the more his unease grew, the sense that he, Appian, and Shareeka—even Eudora—were walking into something they did not altogether expect, something dark and grim.

When they reached the waters of the oasis, they reached two Imperial banners, still dug into the ground. Beneath it lay two skeletons, dry as the desert and beginning to crumble.

Eudora screamed a desperate scream. Appian cursed. Shareeka ran forth and stooped near the skeletons. Numa stumbled into the water, despite the desperate situation still only thinking of slaking his thirst. He fell in, totally submerging himself, and drank. A vision assailed him.

The Oracle of Hylea rose out of the water, snake twined around her body. It was night, and the moon reflected in the water; the stars gleamed, sparkling against it.

"Attend the tale of the Lost Legions, the first victims of Mazda's scourge," she bellowed. "Their armor, stolen and reforged into scimitars; their bodies wilted and dried by the foul powers of the Theomancer. Do not think you fight an enemy whose power is only of flesh and blood, Claudio-Valens Adamantus. Do not think you can succeed only by the might of the sword."

"The cause is hopeless. The Empire is lost. I should curse the lawgivers and die."

"Be gone from Claudio, devil!" the oracle barked. Her white, sightless eyes bulged with a pale fire. "Now, Claudio, listen to me and me alone. It is only a matter of weeks before Bregantium, the new seat of the government, falls. The citizens of the Empire—even the god Claudio—all believe their hope is at an end. The Empire's armies are scattered, lacking unity. And unity is what they need…"

"Why did you ask me to come here?"

"Quiet, devil!" the oracle growled like a bear. "You must take an Imperial banner, and your friend Shareeka must take the other. You must gather the Empire's armies, collect them like lost sheep. And then—when all are gathered under your banner—you must drive the lawgivers away like wild beasts, and show them not one drop of mercy."

"What of Appian?"

"Go to Haroon, the City of Issa." The oracle ignored him. "There, the last of the Imperial Navy has gathered for the winter. They are to be instrumental in the coming fight."

Perhaps she did not care about Appian. "What of Eudora?" Numa asked.

"Anthea knows what to do. Do not worry for her; she is strong." Floating an inch above the water, the oracle once again began her mad, ecstatic dance. The serpent flicked its forked tongue, drawing tighter around her flesh and then loosening suddenly. The drums he had heard on Mount Hylea pounded in the desert night. The oracle's body convulsed in the dance; she roared like a lion, then like a bear, then like a leopard.

Visions of empire filled Numa's mind.

He woke, panting, in the cold of the desert night, with Shareeka's face hovering above him. The ratling was shaking him. "Numa! Gods! Numa!" The ratling's expression hardened in an instant. "His eyes are open, now. The fool's alive."

"Thank Imperium!" Appian said. He was hovering over Numa, too, just a few inches beyond Shareeka.

"I had a dream…" Numa sat up, colder than he'd ever felt, even in the harshest Norriva winter. "Shareeka, you and I must carry the Imperial banners." He could still make out their shape in the dim moonlight. "We must go to Haroon, the City of Issa."

"I guess we must follow him now," Shareeka said. "We've followed him on this mad journey thus far. Now, we have to listen. To Haroon… thankfully I know the way."

"Where is Eudora?" The words had barely left Numa's lips before he noticed a nymphlike figure at the edge of the water, with familiar frizzy hair.

"I am here," she said, remarkably composed in the wake of discovering her father's death. "I have heard all your words. You know what you must do, Numa. I know what I must do. The Lost Legions were the Bel of Carta Mega's secret, his last resort in case of invasion. Now, I must convince him to put all his effort into supporting the Empire… to use all his wealth into fighting the lawgivers. I have a feeling I will see you again, sweet Numa."

Numa climbed to his feet. "And I have a feeling I will see you again, Eudora. But now… now, I think it is time to part ways."

"Yes." Within a few seconds' time, she had run over to him, crossing the distance and planting a kiss on his cheek. "Goodbye, sweet Numa."

Breathless, Numa watched as she mounted her camel.

From the oasis to Haroon was a journey of five days, Eudora said before she left. As her lone figure disappeared, a shadowed silhouette vanishing into the dry desert winds, Numa promised himself he would find her and meet her again.

CHAPTER TWENTY-NINE: HARD DECISIONS

Midian, Godling Priest of Atman

"Three legions, massacred." Midian repeated the words of the spy, unable or perhaps unwilling to believe it. "Three, you say, without a casualty on the enemy side…"

The spy, Haddad, had never lied to the court before. His record was spotless. "Without a casualty, no. A few hundred died—"

A few hundred was nothing.

"—but not at the legions' hands. The sorcerers in Thénai made a pact with dark forces… the power they unleashed destroyed their minds. The false king Anastasios was burned alive by hellfire. Much of the city is burned. The sorcerers have killed each other. All Thenoa is haunted, now… those with the wits to leave have already fled. Some have taken refuge in Korthos, others in Kersepoli."

Midian grabbed hold of the armrest of the Red Throne to steady himself. The news of the outer world was grim, grimmer than he had feared. But the state of Issa's beloved land, Khazidea, was even worse—the Asa nomads, converted to the faith of Mazda, burned the fields and sowed the land with salt. They piled the bodies of the peasants high as hills, and every day launched the heads of their victims over Haroon's protective wall.

The Empire did not answer Midian's pleas—the Empire itself was in peril, hanging by a thin thread. The Third Harak Legion, stationed in the southernmost portion of the province, had refused as well, stating that—despite the peril—they needed to protect the border with Fharas.

"The Empire's enemies multiply," Midian said. "Khazidea burns. Perhaps the world is at an end."

"Or a dark new world is beginning."

"I will not live to see it—I will die fighting it."

A sad smile crossed Haddad's lips.

From one narrow door, two men in blacks left—lawgiver blacks. "Stop them!" Midian screamed, heart instantly pounding out of control. Sinn ran out in their wake.

"No, brother… we were merely discussing terms."

"Terms?" Midian bit his lip, attempting to quell his rage. "I must speak with you about these terms… to see if I… agree with them."

As he left he whispered to Haddad, "Whatever you do, do *not* let those lawgivers leave."

~

Midian followed Sinn into the hallway.

"Sinn!" he snapped.

Sinn turned, the man whom Midian had considered a brother, a friend of the queen. A man he now considered his mortal enemy. "What is it, Midian?"

"You invited the lawgivers in here to discuss terms?"

"We will be allowed to live, for now. They said they do not care about our customs or practices, only the wealth of Khazidea and the wheat crop."

Midian had seen much of the Law of Mazda—that a man who wears the garb of a woman would be burned alive. A rule that would sentence all Godlings to death. "And you trust the words of a lawgiver?" A broom, sitting against the wall, would be his weapon.

"As much as I trust any man's."

Midian grabbed the broom and struck Sinn across the head. He whimpered and hit the ground; Midian leapt upon him, pinning him with his legs. Midian grabbed Sinn's neck and began to squeeze. He channeled all the rage building inside him, all the hatred that had built up in these months of constant disappointments and failure, all the anger he felt at the faint-hearted Godlings like Sinn in his midst.

Minutes later, long after Sinn had stopped struggling, long

after Sinn's limbs had fallen limp and his chest had stilled, Midian collapsed, all the strength gone from him. His arms and hands strained at the effort. He fell into tears, sobbing uncontrollably for the friend he had lost, the friend he had loved.

Asking Atman's forgiveness, he stood up and—struggling to keep his composure—headed back to the Red Throne.

Haddad disarmed the lawgivers, and now an assortment of Godling priests and handmaidens restrained them.

"What happened?" Haddad cried. "You look terrible."

"I am sure I feel much worse than I look. Nonetheless we will keep these two. They are our prisoners." Midian glared at the two lawgivers, with their square gray beards and black turbans. He had no doubts these two were high-ranking men, two lawgivers who knew much. He would extract every bit of knowledge they had, one way or another.

Over the next five days, Midian received daily reports of what the lawgivers had said under pressure—that the Theomancer's true name was Nazeer, not a particularly useful bit of information; that they had originated in a desert near the faraway eastern sea; that their religious goal was the total conquest of the world, with the Theomancer as supreme head. But then more interesting bits of information were brought before Midian as he sat near the Red Throne.

"There truly was a government-wide conspiracy to bring the Theomancer across the sea," the chief interrogator said. "But he will not name names."

"He will not name names, you say. We will see about that."

In the dark, wet room where they kept the lawgiver—his friend had already succumbed to his wounds—Midian's presence was met with a snarl, then a whimper. Perhaps he could see the anger in Midian's eyes, the anger at the Law of Mazda and his loathing for the Empire's newly weakened state.

"You will tell me. Who started the conspiracy?"

"I won't tell you, impious dog!" The interrogator at his side dunked his head under water, fully submerging it in a bowl for ten long seconds before allowing him to breathe.

"Who started the conspiracy?" Midian snapped.

"I will not—" And like that, his head was underwater.

"He has proven astonishingly resilient. He thinks his evil actions will gain him entry to paradise."

"We will see."

It was hours of dunking before they received the first name—an Imperial Councilor, Crispus Servillius, followed quickly by two more, Septimo Seánus and another, Jiacomo Lornodoris, then Decimo Kerius and Publio Martius. Midian wrote all of them down.

Once broken, the words flowed from the lawgiver like a river. "Please, stop! Oh, please!"

"Tell us what we want to know, and we will. Who else?"

"The Academies… the Academies of Eloesus…"

"The Academies?" Of all the people to aid the lawgivers, Midian would have thought the Academies would be the last—they claimed to support freedom, liberty, the rights of women and the innate value of the disadvantaged.

"Priscilla Marianus… Cleon Adelphos… and all their underlings. Cleon and Priscilla were the ones who went south and arranged it. They think they are using the lawgivers but the High Theomancer sees right through them… he endures them out of gratefulness. *Will you stop now?*"

Midian wrote the names down again. "And who let the lawgiver ships in?"

"The grand admiral Marcus Otho ordered all the ships to

stand down—he ordered them burnt. *Now will you stop?* Please, I beg of you!" The lawgiver gasped for air.

In the dark room, the sound of footsteps echoed. "Midian!" a handmaid cried.

Midian turned around, met her gaze at the door.

"Three men are trying to gain entry to the city. They claim to be friends of the Empire and of Haroon."

"Three strangers in this dark time? Shall we trust three strangers?"

"One is wearing the Imperial Circlet," she continued, "and carries an adamant sword. But he is most certainly not Secondo Janus."

The lawgiver gasped. Midian glanced over and saw his eyes widened with surprise. "Do not let him in," he said.

"Quiet, savage!" Midian hissed. "Because of your words, we will let them in…" He turned to the handmaid. "Have them escorted into the palace. I will hold an audience with them."

~

Into the Red Throne room the three men walked—two humans, both young, and a ratling carrying two Imperial eagle standards in his hands. Midian sensed something great about these men, something that gleamed of destiny. Two fell to one knee—the ratling, and the larger of the humans. The one wearing the Imperial Circlet and the adamant sword remained standing. *Perhaps he kneels for no one.*

CHAPTER THIRTY:
THE MUSTERING OF KHAZIDEA

Numa

How odd and far-removed from his life in Norriva was this—a eunuch priest who, by foreign custom, wore the garb of women. This Godling priest would have tricked him if Numa had not examined him closely and seen his faint masculine features.

"Welcome to the Red Palace," the Godling said in his high-pitched voice. "I must ask you, my domino, where you got the Imperial Circlet?"

"That is not your concern. From here on, you are to call me your emperor."

The eunuch priest fell prostrate. "Midian at your service, my domino and god."

At the word "god" Numa bristled a little bit. It was uncomfortable, perhaps, but the only way the south and east would respect him. "I understand you have ships… the last of the Imperial Navy."

"Is it the last?" Midian said, looking up from his prostrate position. "A hundred galleys locked in the harbor? That is our last hope? The sailors are here, too, but they have no fit commander. They fled disaster at the Isles of Marion."

"A flock without a shepherd," Numa observed. "The lawgivers must control the seas."

"They do… but the winter storms have begun," Midian explained.

"Numa, if I may—" Appian said from behind. "—I have read a great deal about naval strategy, about sailing and about the sea-battles that the Empire has won and lost."

Numa turned to face Appian, felt himself smile.

"I've read about the ancient Eloesian seafarers, how they

destroyed the ships of the Khazideans and the Fharese—"

"Appian, when the winter storms abate, unleash hell. I name you Admiral Appian."

Appian grinned in his familiar way, but his eyes were eager—eager to prove himself, and proud.

Just what an emperor needs. But still Numa didn't feel like an emperor at all. He was a rustic from Norriva, a flyspeck town in the middle of nowhere. Thus far, people in the Empire's interior had treated him kindly, but he dreaded interacting with the Empire's old families. Long ago on the road, Appian had told Numa, "The Adamanti were once considered rustics." But it did little to quell his doubts.

"And what shall we do, *emperor?*" Shareeka said with only a trace of sarcasm. He rose from his kneeling position, lifting the two Imperial banners high. He tossed one to Numa, who caught it.

"We command all the hosts of the Empire," Numa said. "We crush its enemies from without, but most importantly, those within."

"Idle, fancy talk," Shareeka sneered, unable to hold in his derision.

"Signor Godling, I understand that your nation is under control of another."

"In a way," Midian answered, remaining prostrate. "But to call the Asa rulers is a title they do not deserve. They are destroyers first and foremost. They would never know how to govern. They have revered the god Mazda and sworn allegiance to the Theomancer."

"Never has such a conversion been for holy reasons," Numa said.

Shareeka sighed. "We must act, Numa, not pontificate!"

Numa smiled at the ratling's impertinence. "Indeed. Are there any legions stationed in Khazidea?

"There were," Midian answered. "Two were broken up and dispersed when the Asa invaded. Their numbers are halved, at best, and they are scattered. Another traveled to Eloesus to put down the rebellion there, but met its end."

"A strange time when a legion falls to Eloesian rebels," Numa breathed.

"Not to Eloesian rebels, my domino, but to the powers of hell. And the powers of hell soon afterward destroyed the rebels themselves," Midian said. "I will sacrifice a white bull to the god Sagar, and grant you a blessing of war."

"Strange tidings," Numa said.

"Indeed, my domino. The Empire is in peril; I will pray day and night for your success, as my domina the queen has… she is a patriot as well."

"The queen?" Numa said. His complete ignorance was beginning to show… the lack of knowledge inherent in a Norriva rustic.

"The Sister-Queen of Haroon," Appian said, a hint of excitement lighting his words. "We are in her palace. The king and queen of Haroon have been brother and sister since recorded history, to the last generation."

"Not to the last," Midian said. "The queen's son now is from a different father; her brother is long-dead."

Numa recoiled at the thought of marrying his sister even though she was dead—a distant memory now.

"My domino, if I may—" Midian began.

Numa nodded.

For the first time Midian rose, standing up on his two feet. "I have a list of traitors… before you leave, I will make a copy for you. There *was* a far-ranging conspiracy to bring the lawgivers to Imperial shores… some in the government's elite, a few even in the Imperial Army and Navy. But it began in the Academies of Eloesus."

His ignorance began to show again. He knew very little about the Academies, only that they were schools. And Numa wasn't entirely confident he could point out Eloesus on a map.

Perhaps sensing his friend's distress, Appian spoke. "The Academies… the Empire's most prestigious schools, taught by the best of scholars. Who knew they would harbor traitors in our midst?"

"The Empire's problems will not be solved," Numa said, "without a restored Imperial Army, and a deluge of traitors' blood."

Midian smiled. "Stay the night… We will see to it that you are well-fed. Seven Imperial centuries stand guard here in Haroon… only seven-hundred men, perhaps a few more. I will ensure their loyalty to you, Emperor Numa."

Emperor Numa. Even now, the words rang false and hollow in his ears.

~

In Haroon, Numa bade the most difficult goodbye of his life to Appian. Then he and Shareeka traded their camels for white warhorses, and with two-hundred Imperial soldiers—all Haroon could afford—following behind them, he left through the South Gate.

In the cold morning air they rode at a slow pace south down the river. Midian had given a few pieces of advice where the remnants of the Imperial Army might be holed up—in certain forts, built in high perches near the swiftly-flowing Khazan. But he had also warned Numa's band of the imminent danger, and that was what he immediately saw.

Less than an hour's march outside Haroon, they passed in sight of a burnt village. Its homes were scorched to black husks and heaps of ash; its crops lay burned and its fields sown with salt. A mountainous pile of headless bodies stretched higher than the buildings, and even from Numa's distance the smell was nigh unbearable.

"A wonderful faith, the lawgivers have," Numa said darkly.

"Indeed." Shareeka chuckled.

That night, as they slept in the reeds of the Khazan, a horn blew—harsh and crude—but it sounded miles away. Still, Numa reactively grasped the hilt of *Imperium's Rebuke.* Only hours later did he fall asleep, and he awoke with the coming of the dawn.

Another day's journey and they reached the first fort—a stone citadel on a high hill. Four Imperial flags flapped on its towers. A few dozen Imperial soldiers waited on the wall, nocking arrows to their bows as soon as Numa's band appeared in view.

At the gate he stopped. Astride a warhorse and with the stamping of the soldier's feet echoing throughout the hills, Numa might have felt imperious but only felt like more of a fraud than ever.

"Emperor? You do not look like His Undying Glory, Secondo!" a soldier shouted.

"I do not look like him!" Numa shouted. "And I do not act like him! But nonetheless, if you ask for your emperor, I am he!"

Another soldier laughed. "What do you wish of us, *emperor*?" he sneered.

"I wish you would come out of that cowardly hole and fight for the nation you were sworn to protect!" Numa shouted. Shareeka snarled some unintelligible curse but for once he ignored his ratling friend. "I ask that you fulfill your duty and fight under the Imperial banner!"

"You are young! You cannot be a day over twenty!" a soldier shouted.

"And yet it seems… all things considered… that I am a better man than you," Numa answered.

"Get out of here, pretender!" the soldier shouted in return.

"I beg of you… the Empire is still strong. It needs unity, and it needs all its brothers-in-arms. Unless you empty out of the fort and join me, my chances of gathering all our forces together are practically nothing. The Empire needs you… it needs you to take up your sword and fight."

"Fight? For what?"

"For honor, for glory, for duty! For empire!"

"For empire!" the legionaries behind Numa repeated the words in unison.

The soldiers on the wall looked stunned. And yet, seconds

later, the gate to the fortress began to crank open. That hour, three thousand soldiers joined Numa's army.

CHAPTER THIRTY-ONE:
THE KING'S DEMAND

Councilor Augusto Vitellian

News of the world, already troubled, grew more troubled every day. And yet Augusto had never felt worse than when the messengers claimed an emissary from the northman king had come. Like a flash Augusto remembered—reparations the northmen had demanded, reparations the prior regent had agreed to pay. Not a single spare coin of gold was in the coffers… all was needed for the war.

"Gods damn it all," Augusto hissed, in the presence of the other councilors. "Our situation could not possibly grow worse."

"It could," Councilor Valerio said. "The walls of Bregantium could have failed us, and we could all be dead. Yet still we survive, and the Empire survives with us, even if we are the last patriots left."

"I doubt that," Augusto said. "There are still rebels— patriots—fighting to the bloody end." *The bloody end*—a thing he did not wish to contemplate. He turned to the pair of messengers. "Let him in. We will hold an audience with him."

The northman entered, dressed in a brocade tunic of rich forest green and a pair of tight-fitting brown trousers. A feathered cap, the same green color as his tunic, rested above his thick hair. A brown moustache fell below his chin. "His Majesty the King, Jourmande vis Bretagne, has sent me to collect the first payment of reparations… a sum totaling seven-hundred marks, paid in gold and silver."

"Signor—"

"Aloysius," the messenger answered in the thick accent of the northmen Augusto recognized.

"Our nation is in crisis," Augusto explained. "Every expense must be used to overcome an enemy that has invaded our land. When things settle down, we will pay the first installment as soon as possible… with *interest*."

The messenger smiled. "King Jourmande has demanded the first reparation now. He will not accept a delay. If you refuse, he will send an army to extract it from you personally."

Augusto frowned and took a step back, the very wind stolen from his lungs. Everything was hopeless, and many around him said the Empire was doomed—but he would not give up. A payment of seven hundred marks—more than a thousand gold libra—would wreck the already dwindling treasury. The already-imperiled government would have no purchasing power, no way of paying soldiers or hiring mercenaries. In a flash, he answered. "No. If you will not accept our generous offer of delayed payment, with interest, then go back and tell your king we refuse."

"Ah, you poor fool," the messenger Aloysius sneered.

Neither Councilor Valerio nor the others said anything—a sign of their reluctant agreement.

"You will come to regret your poor decision." Aloysius turned and left.

When he was safely out the door, Augusto spoke again. "My fellow patriots, the die is cast… we must do anything and everything in our power to regain control of Gad, and expel them from the city wall."

Valerio nodded agreement, though no doubt he—and everyone else—knew all possible strategies had been taken, to no avail.

CHAPTER THIRTY-TWO: BEFORE THE BEL

Eudora Kyrillos

The death of Father was something that pierced Eudora and wrenched her insides. Even now, wandering the sunbaked streets of Carta Mega, tears had formed in her eyes, waiting to be unleashed in unpent fury. But now was not the time for mourning; her father, if alive, would have wanted her to act, to avenge him. And now, with Numa and the ratling and that Appian fellow gone, it was clear what she needed to do. But first, she needed a blessing from Heaven, from the only god whom the Carta Megans revered.

At the seashore, where the waves washed steadily against the sand, a manmade walkway raised high above the water led unto the temple of Melkior. In its construction it differed greatly from the temples of the Imperials and those of her own people, the Eloesians; the fluted Thenoan columns with their floral capitals, flanking the doors, were a late addition. Constructed of sundried brick, it was tall rather than wide, stretching to the heavens and, by extension, the gods. Window slits at the top let in a small bit of light and air, but not much. The roof was crenellated with white stone, like a fortress.

She crossed the walkway silently and entered through the propped-open door, into the temple of Melkior the Brass God, Lord of Precious Things.

The smell of incense hit her as soon as she walked inside—it was thick, overpowering. Four brightly-burning braziers at either corner of the square room lit up the temple, with torches on sconces for good measure. Standing a titanic forty feet was the statue of Melkior, dedicated by the grand bel Haveel many hundreds of years ago. The immense brass likeness was human in form up to its neck, which branched out to six heads, each with a flaring serpentine tongue. One head had eyes of sapphire; another, ruby; another, diamond; another, emerald; another, amethyst; and the last onyx.

She stepped before the brass titan and dropped to her knees. "God of precious things, in your abode in Highest Heaven, I ask that you bless me with a silver tongue, with ears that listen and words that convince. Nothing less would be equal repayment to the precious thing that life has taken from me… my father, Lysander Kyrillos. Do not, I pray, let his death be in vain."

The great jeweled eyes did not look at her; the brass tongues did not flare or flicker. The statue was not a god, but only a representation, a sign of Haveel's great love for Melkior. Still, the immense accomplishment of metallurgy never failed to amaze her; the roof, so high the light of the braziers did not touch it, seemed to be as far-away as the night sky, bleeding into another dimension. Even on Eudora's long-ago trip to Korthos, in all her visits to its many temples, she had never seen such glorious beauty as this.

She left the Temple of Melkior with a new purpose, a new hope, and a new resolve. She prayed that not just Melkior, but all the gods in their goodness and glory, would stand with her and guide her actions from hereon. The Empire needed their rescue.

~

She had been to the House of the Bel before, on many occasions. She had viewed Balthesar the Magnificent as the uncle she never had, a friend so dear he was like a blood relative. She entered his dwelling without so much as a word from the guards, and entered his throne room without a trace of the nervousness that common Carta Megans showed.

"My sweet Eudora!" The Bel of Carta Mega rose from his humble chair-like throne. His great onion-like turban was half his height, his robes of flame-orange silk and belt of gold cloth worth the price of a mansion by themselves, but he doted on her like a niece. "I had been worried for you, my raisin. Three unsavory fellows were looking for you."

"I met them," Eudora said. "They were not as unsavory as they appeared; they went east on camels to Khazidea… they hope to save the Empire."

Balthesar smiled. "I wish the fools the best. I had told them the city of Carta Mega abounds with Eudoras, even though you are the only Eudora I know."

"My father is dead."

Balthesar's smile vanished, like water into the Carta Megan sun. "What do you mean?"

"I mean what I said. Lysander Kyrillos, my father… dead." A tear fell down Eudora's cheek.

Balthesar slumped back in his chair, his expression a storm of confusion and terror. "I had kept his presence a secret… so secret I didn't ever go there myself… too secret. Ah, curse me. Melkior curse me! When the foreigners come, we will have no choice but to surrender… to pay the tax and watch our wealth slowly trickle away, or honor Mazda."

"That is the last thing Father would have wanted," Eudora said. She wiped her eyes and struggled to remain strong, banishing the image of her dead father as much as she could. "Instead, I ask you… Balthesar, whom I have always looked up to and thought of an uncle… that we spend all the wealth of Carta Mega to fight the lawgivers, to help the Empire whose power has created peace throughout the entire Middle Sea, and allowed Carta Mega to grow prosperous and wealthy. We must aid the Imperial government—the three strangers have told me it is now centered in Bregantium."

"So I have heard," Balthesar mumbled, his eyes lost in thought.

"We must hire the best mercenaries the world can offer. We must send the Imperials silver and gold. My good Uncle Balthesar I beg of you to do not just the proper thing—what is best for the wealth of Carta Mega—but what is also the wiser thing in the long run. It is the Empire's strength and hegemony that has afforded you and me our wealth and good lives. Not many things I can say with absolute certainty, but one thing I can—the lawgivers would be far worse than the Empire."

"You speak the truth, my dear, the gods' own truth. But the Empire is lost. The lawgivers will win this fight, by anyone's estimation." Balthesar's eyes focused on Eudora. "The god Mazda has brought nothing but destruction and violence; his law is a tragedy, a 'millstone around the neck of mankind,' but I must be a realist, my dear. My first and principle duty is to Carta Mega."

Eudora frowned; the wind seemed stolen from her lungs. Her gaze dropped to the floor, and the tears she had held in fell unbidden down her cheeks. The memory of the father who had died for nothing flashed in her eyes and her strength left her. She fell to her knees.

"Eudora, my raisin…"

"A curse upon you, Balthesar, if this is truly your course of action… to live only in the moment, to not see the powers of evil growing throughout the world. To not see that the Empire's fate depends on you."

"My raisin…"

"And to have my father die in vain. That is the worst of all." She gathered her dress and turned, fleeing the House of the Bel and ignoring Balthesar's cries for her to stop.

~

It was early afternoon, when the sun scorched the land at its most hellish point, as Eudora made her way to the beach. The sea had begun to churn, and the waves crashed against Carta Mega's breakwater. The sun had dried her tears; and no longer did she feel the sadness and tragedy of defeat. Instead, the thought of her father dying in vain now filled her with anger, from her head to her toes and to her innermost sinew. His death, and the death of his legions, now filled her only with greater determination, with a focus and resolve that she could not and would not shake. She would convince Balthesar to aid the Empire or die in the effort—she promised she would live to watch the Empire's enemies, within and without, scorched and destroyed like water in the Carta Megan sun.

CHAPTER THIRTY-THREE: TO WAR!

Numa

Numa and Shareeka, bearing the Imperial war-eagle standards, had gone from fortress to fortress along the Khazan River, gathering the patriots and the soldiers that remained. With each stop the speeches came easier to Numa, the appeals to their patriotism grew more focused and refined. Thus, by the end of the first week, the small army had doubled, then quadrupled in size. To think that Numa, a rustic from Norriva, now had an army of twelve-thousand legionaries following behind him, was a thing so incomprehensible that even now he did not believe it.

Two things were clear, now, two things equal in their impossibility: that every last stronghold of Khazidea had been emptied of its soldiers, and that the Asa nomads who had destroyed the farms and the peasants' homes were completely gone, unaware of Numa's covert mission. The Asa, he had learned, had gone south, responding to the emergence of a great southron army, marching alongside the Imperial legion. The north of Khazidea, lying in smoldering ruin and strewn with carnage, was free in its deathly silence from the destroyers' grip.

When the last of the fortresses had emptied, Numa rode before them and announced their next course of action. "We will let the southrons fight the nomads, as they will. We go east, to liberate Eloesus from the traitors. We will eradicate the lawgivers, execute the traitors, and have soldiers monitor the Eloesian Academies." He would go by Midian's list. "Perhaps soldiers will stand guard in the Academies from hereon—a reminder of Imperial power that they can never shake." A few soldiers cheered at his words; speech had grown easier to Numa with each try. He knew what would rally their spirits, what would enhance their anger. "We go east, across the Imperial Road that connects Khazidea and Eloesus. I understand there are posts along the way, stocked with provisions. We will go swiftly to Eloesus, and lay upon the Academies and their lawgiver friends with all the Empire's strength. To war! No mercy!"

"No mercy!" the soldiers roared in unison, a deafening chorus. Beside Numa, Shareeka was smiling. "To war!"

"To war!" Numa cried, and yanked the reins of his horse, pivoting eastward where the Imperial Road lay in sight.

CHAPTER THIRTY-FOUR:
THE END OF JUSTICE

Twenty Days Later…

Pontio Piraeus, Chief Lecturer

Pontio no longer felt safe when he left the confines of the Academy, not even with a bodyguard of thirty lawgivers. The Theomancer had sent ten thousand soldiers to Korthos to keep the rebellion alive and make Pontio feel safe. But it wasn't enough. Thénai was a ghost town, deserted in the wake of the theurges' attack, and Kersepoli had fallen to the Bluecloaks, renewing its allegiance to the Empire. And Pontio didn't feel safe, anymore.

When Arkos, a dear friend and excellent mathematician, had attempted to confirm the rumors that a giant Imperial army was on its way to Korthos, Pontio had cursed him and lashed out, all because he didn't feel safe. "You fool! The Empire is vanquished! You are mentally unfit!" he had hissed.

The Theomancer had done the best he could—he had a war to win, after all, but Pontio could not help but grow angry at him. Ten thousand lawgivers were enough to keep the city streets relatively safe, but it wasn't enough, gods, it wasn't enough to subdue the Bluecloak counter-rebellion and ensure Pontio's safety.

Now, glancing at the city streets from a high balcony in the Academy, a deeper worry had begun to circulate in his mind, a thing that bothered him more than anything else besides his own safety. The people of Korthos were halfhearted about the rebellion; their relation to it all but soured when the lawgivers arrived. Now, they resented their liberators. They glared at Pontio when he walked by, ignoring the fact that he had dedicated his life to educating the Eloesian people. Some had even dared heckle him, though according to the Law of Mazda such an offense would result in the clipping of their tongues.

Pontio, Priscilla Marianus and Cleon Adelphos—together with the other chief lecturers—had taken a calculated risk, overthrowing the Imperial government and bringing the lawgivers in. But if Pontio had, for a single moment, thought it posed a risk to his safety, he would never have gone through with it.

Two Eloesian boys were kicking a ball around in the streets below. *How dare these common brown-bread citizens resent me? They have no right.*

Across the city, a horn-peal sounded… a horn Pontio recognized instantly. The fine-timbred horn of the Imperial Army. The war call of the oppressor. The war call of the Empire, which unjustly stood in preeminence over the world. The Empire, which stole its wealth and projected its power far and wide, which took and did not give, which refused to apologize for its many crimes and mistakes. The Empire, his sworn enemy.

Pontio had gone white and cold. The blood drained from his face. He fled from the room and down the stairs, grabbing his cloak on the way out.

At the harbor, a line of lawgivers stood guard, blocking entrance to the ships. "Gods, let me through!"

"No one leaves," a lawgiver said. "We all repel the Imperials, or die trying."

Death. Nothing was worth dying for. "Please… let me through…"

"No one leaves," he repeated. "Least of all you, the leader of the rebellion."

"*Leader?*" Pontio screamed. What if the Imperials heard that? "I am not the leader. *Let me through!*"

"Speak again," the lawgiver snarled, "and we will cut off your tongue."

A string of curses spilled from Pontio's mouth. He fled back to the Academy. He would hide there. He would cower in some forgotten room that no one would think to find. Then, if—Nature forbid it—the Imperials won, he could slip out secretly and flee to… flee to *where?* Priscilla had made it clear she wanted him to stay in Eloesus. She would not be happy if he returned to Imperial City—or, as it was now called, Melchaddad.

In a closet of the Academy, Pontio cowered, daring not to breathe. The roar of soldiers rose above the city's newfound silence. Riders—no doubt lawgivers—galloped this way and that. A shake had overtaken Pontio's body. Time seemed to slow. An hour had passed, surely, and yet the battle raged on, the insolent Imperial soldiers continued to fight. The roar of the soldiers increased in volume, and now flashed the sound of steel against steel. Open battle, he realized— they had breached the defenses somehow, gods damn it all.

The door to the closet opened. Arkos the mathematician stood there. "Signor Pontio…"

"*How did you know I was here?*" Pontio hissed.

"I could hear your whimpering… everyone could."

"*What is going on out there?*" Pontio hissed.

"Treachery. A citizen of Korthos opened the gate for the Imperials."

"When the lawgivers win, I will have all the people of Korthos *butchered!*" Pontio screamed.

"Come with me," Arkos said. "We are making a break for the harbor. We have a bit of time… the legion is overpowering our troops. We must hurry!"

Arkos, Pontio, and a few other minor scholars he did not recognize fled from the Academy as the sound of the Imperials' brutality echoed through the air. At a sprint they ran, and arrived quickly. The ships had been burnt—all of them. Now, even those desperate enough to travel in winter had no hope.

Pontio screamed. In the air, the sound of marching feet echoed. He turned and gasped. His heart pounded out of control as he beheld the sight—a hundred columns of Imperial soldiers in immediate view. Their red-gold shields bore the symbol of the war-eagle, the symbol of oppression and domination that Pontio had fought all this time to stop. He cried out, cursing Nature and Fortune, that his good and noble actions would bring him to this moment. *I do not deserve this!*

A young man rode ahead of them, astride a white horse. He had light, almost golden, brown hair and a set of piercing dark eyes. The Imperial Circlet rested on his head—the circlet once worn by Secondo Janus, and all the oppressors that came before him. In his hand was a sword of adamant. He spoke loudly: "Scholars, I see." From the folds of his cloak he drew a piece of paper. "Men and women of the Academy, your friends the lawgivers have betrayed you. A little pain, and names flow from their lips like water. Which one is Pontio Piraeus?"

At the sound of his name Pontio dashed off with a scream. The conqueror galloped after him and Pontio turned around, barreling ahead with all his might—right into the arms of an Imperial soldier. Pontio screamed and struggled, but the soldier's grip only tightened. Pontio was not strong; he was old. He was doomed.

He screamed, "Mercy! Mercy!"

"A nation has little to fear from a barbarian at the city gates!" the would-be emperor shouted. "Much more dangerous is the traitor within. A traitor corrupts the people with his honeyed words; he makes the young despise their nation. Bit by bit he destroys; little by little he weakens their resolve. The traitor is a liar, a deceiver, a devil, a worm. We have two traitors here."

"That's a lie!" Pontio screamed.

"They shall receive traitors' deaths!" the would-be emperor shouted.

"It was Arkos' fault! He made me do it!" Pontio howled. "Please, please..."

"Proud men of the Empire!" The young man pulled his horse toward the troops. "Patriots who put your lives at risk for Imperial glory… you are the shining paragons of our nation, the representative of all that is still good about the Empire. You are the mirror opposite of these five we have, here, today. The mirror opposite of Pontio Piraeus, and Arkos Theonos, who began the Eloesian rebellion in order to further the lawgivers and realize the Academies' perverse goals."

Perverse! Pontio couldn't believe the words. He spoke like a Getan, and he was as ignorant as one. He struggled again but the soldier's hands were too tight, his grip too strong.

"Bring me two crosses!"

Pontio screamed. *"No! No! No!"* At worst he had imagined a beheading, but this was simply too much. "Have mercy! Mercy, *please!*"

"No mercy for traitors!" the young man shouted, and when his dark eyes met Pontio's, Pontio gasped and staggered back—there was power in that conqueror's eyes.

"Please! I beg of you!" Pontio screamed.

"Your cries for mercy—as with all traitors, from hereon—fall on deaf, nay, hostile ears."

Pontio screamed, unable to think of anything but escape, as pieces of wood were hauled out toward the harbor. *This is the end of peace and knowledge… the end of justice!*

CHAPTER THIRTY-FIVE:
GLORY

Numa

The speeches came easier and easier to him—most of all because he felt and believed every word. He left the screaming, bloodied traitors, nailed in agony to crosses, to confer with his inferiors. The traitors were less than garbage, but like garbage he would leave them, food for vultures.

Shareeka caught up with Numa as he headed down the avenue—toward the House of the Magistrate, where he had set up headquarters. "A bit extreme—they were citizens," the ratling mumbled.

"A traitor who yearns for the nation's destruction is not a citizen—nor, in my mind, a human being," Numa answered. "All the traitors will die that way, I will ensure it."

"You have changed," Shareeka said. "You are not the simple boy from Norriva, anymore. I think you've let the Imperial Circlet and all this power go to your head."

"Enough lectures, Shareeka." Numa smiled. "Though I do appreciate your commentary, as always."

In the House of the Magistrate's feasting hall, Numa took a seat at the head table. Almost instantly, messengers and informants began arriving, telling tales of the trouble brewing throughout the world.

"The southron army has turned back, accepting defeat," one told him. "The Asa are impossible to catch—they are too swift."

"Excellent destroyers, but terrible conquerors," Numa muttered. An empire built by the Asa would vanish within a generation.

"Haroon holds fast."

An hour later, another informant arrived. "Bregantium is under siege," he said. "The last bits of the Imperial government are there. Seventy thousand lawgivers surround it. Their commander is Crispus Servillius, newly converted to the faith of Mazda."

Seventy thousand. Even with the reinforcements he had received at Imperiopoli, Numa's army only had fifteen thousand fighting men. The news was a stark warning, a grim reminder that his work was not done—as things stood now, the Empire would fail, if he cast the die and met them in open combat

"The lawgivers are unopposed in Anthania—the rebellion still remains, but our citizens have resorted to sudden attacks and stabbings. Most of the lawgiver force has left Anthania for Gad. The islands of Imperial District have fought them off, thus far, successfully. That means only Gad and the Isles remain nominally in the Empire's control."

"Gad, the Isles, and Eloesus," Numa said.

"Well, there is Kersepoli…"

"Yes, Kersepoli." The mysterious Bluecloak Revolt held control of the last of the Eloesian cities, while Thénai lay ravaged, a ghost town. By all accounts the Bluecloaks despised the lawgivers, but would Eloesian freedom fighters truly honor the Empire? Once freed from the Imperial yoke, would it take some strategic victory—a thing Numa could not count on—before they would submit again to the Empire's rule? "We will wait," he replied. "That is the best we can do."

~

Days later, on a cool, rainy morning, a loud trumpet pealed, sounding loudly across the otherwise quiet city. Numa knew who had come, but not why, or what intentions they brought. The message he had sent to the Bluecloak Revolt had finally borne fruit, but whether good or bad fruit he did not know.

In Heaven's Square, in sight of Korthos' myriad pillared temples, Numa waited. The sound of many thousands of stamping feet echoed. At the fore marched a man with olive Eloesian skin, a head of short dark hair, and a face marred by a battle-scar. He lifted his hand, and all at once the marching stopped; the soldiers behind him, blue cloaks flapping in the wind, stood as still as statues.

"Greetings!" Numa shouted. *I am not the simple boy from Norriva anymore.*

"I am Basil, son of Basil, prince of Harkeon, its keep and all its holdings. I am the leader of the Bluecloak Rebellion… but in truth it was not a rebellion, but an act of patriotism and valor. I serve the Empire, as my father and grandfather have, from the days of Claudio-Valens Adamantus until now. I pledge myself, and all the ten thousand who serve under me, unto your name, Emperor Numa."

Emperor. Still it sounded false—it couldn't possibly be. *I am a rustic from Norriva.*

"Eloesus has been liberated from the traitors," Prince Basil said. "Imperial rule has been restored. And I know the people rejoice. We shall seize the traitors and do unto them what you have done by example."

No doubt he referred to Pontio Piraeus and Arkos Theonos, their bodies still rotting on crosses.

"Agony is what traitors deserve!" Prince Basil thundered. "We march with you, Numa! To war! To glory! To Empire!"

CHAPTER THIRTY-SIX:
TIME, RUNNING SHORT

Astarthe, Queen of Haroon

From the least knowledgeable of citizens to the upper echelons of the fractured Imperial government, the future was clear, grim and bleak. It rested on Astarthe to reverse the inevitable, with the only measure of power she had.

The ceaseless battering of the city gate had gone on, day and night, with few signs of remission. The seventy-thousand lawgivers outside the city walls of Bregantium had doubled, then tripled in size. Worst of all and most disheartening, the leader of the rapacious horde was none other than Councilor Crispus Servillius. The deathly-old bureaucrat now called himself Amal the Pious.

Ignoring the concerned shouts of the soldiers she began her climb up the city walls, onto the battlements. The sight below her stole her breath.

A sea of lawgivers stretched before her, endless as the ocean, the black cloth of their hoods and robes reflecting grimly against the steel-gray sky. Just below, a few yards distant from the bruised and battered city gate, Crispus Servillius sat raised aloft on a litter, dressed in lawgiver blacks but without a hood. His egg-white head stood out starkly in the dark-garbed crowd.

"*Crispus!*" she shouted above the sounds of the innumerable mass.

"You will use my true name, witch!" Crispus hissed.

"*Amal the Pious!*" Astarthe screamed. "*On behalf of the Imperial government I wish to negotiate our terms… of surrender!*"

A few soldiers on the wall gasped and looked at her, wild-eyed, furious, angry beyond words. But there was no informing them of her ruse; Astarthe's last resort was too important, too desperate, to fail.

Crispus laughed deeply. "Very well! I see not even the mighty Empire can stand up to the forces of Mazda!"

A ladder clacked against the wall. Astarthe loathed Crispus Servillius more than any human being she ever had, even the Theomancer, even the death-god Mazda himself.

"Don't you *dare* go down there!" a soldier snapped but she hurried past him; this was too important, too critical, to fail.

~

In the tent she finally met Crispus Servillius face to face. Crispus was not just old—he was ancient. He could not be a day younger than ninety, and was likely older than that. His wrinkled, egg-white head was marred with blemishes and warts; his face, small and plain. Had the daughters of Empire ever before birthed such an ugly creature?

"Crispus…"

His face flashed red in an instant; his eyes burned with anger. "Amal the Pious…"

His snarl lessened only incrementally. He had brought no lawgiver guards; what did Crispus Servillius think he had to fear from a short, unarmed girl?

Astarthe launched her mental attack, throwing her hands forward. The mind of Crispus Servillius was weak and short of will, even for a senile old man: she gained control of him in that instant, and impressed her command—"*You must return to the Theomancer with all your armies… only he has the proper siege equipment to effectively breach Bregantium. You will let no one question your demand.*"

In his mind Astarthe lingered for only a brief second, but all of his character and beliefs revealed themselves to her—the wealthy yet unexceptional man of the August Class, born into purple and fed by a silver spoon. He had debated with his peers, in their villas in

Paradise Gardens, of the great evil the Empire had foisted upon the world; at a young age, he had made it his life goal to destroy it. He had bided his time while he served under Claudian Adamantus the "ignorant patriot," gathering his strength and planting the seeds of the insurrection to come. The lawgivers had not been nearly as receptive to Servillius' notions of liberty and freedom, but in the end one goal trumped all others, even the dramatically opposite views of the lawgivers: Crispus Servillius' undying mission to destroy the Empire.

She drew back with a gasp, feeling like she had bathed in a cesspool. She felt dirty, having inhabited the mind of such a slug. It would take days, perhaps weeks, to fully recover and feel clean again.

"You have stated your case," Crispus Servillius said to her. "We have come to an impasse. When I return with the proper equipment, your city will burn; your people, taken slave; and none shall stand against the forces of Mazda, against reason and progress."

Astarthe turned and left the tent. She made her way up the ladder to the wall's battlements. The Imperial soldiers were staring daggers at her. "Wait," she said, though she understood their anger.

She waited on the battlements as a commotion overtook the camp, as heated argument spread through the camp and lawgivers shouted at Crispus Servillius. But he was the field marshal, the leader personally appointed by the Theomancer—the very Hand of Mazda—so who could argue?

Before night fell, the lawgivers were gone.

CHAPTER THIRTY-SEVEN: TO SAND

Four Weeks Later…

Priscilla Marianus, Provost of the Thenoan Academy

"Bregantium is surely fallen by now…"

Priscilla watched the lawgivers discuss their plans in the way that they demanded of her—from a distance, in silence.

"The cities of Eloesus, as far as we know, are practically under our control," the lawgiver continued his report to Field Marshal Umar. "Imperiopoli has probably fallen."

What was the Law of Mazda but another societal construct? Priscilla had been oppressed by Imperial men her whole life; why in Varda would she question her course of action now? The Theomancer had put to death all her friends—all the scholars who had come with her, who had tried to engage him on the finer points of debate—except for Cleon Adelphos, who knew better than to question Mazda's law. She had poured her whole life into destroying the Empire. She had intended to rebuild it from the ground up, but now that rebuilding it was out of the question, having lost all her power over the insurrection, why shouldn't she rejoice that her most pressing concern had been accomplished?

"The question is not whether we succeed," the lawgiver continued. "The question is what we shall do when the Empire is totally destroyed."

Priscilla smiled behind her mask.

"We shall levy a nationwide tax," Umar answered. "A tax on unbelievers… that has been, by far, our most successful method of conversion. Then we will look further… south to Fharas, and north. We will not stop until the Theomancer rules all of Varda."

"And then what?" The lawgiver's question was more

profound than many she had heard.

When they control the world, then what?

"Then Mazda shall rule in physical form," Umar said.

Superstition, Priscilla knew, but she dared not say it. Instead she left, down the winding halls of the Imperial Palace.

In the past weeks the rebels had continued to fight, but the lawgivers by now had slain them, culling their numbers to near extinction. When Priscilla left the Imperial Palace with a cohort of lawgivers, she had witnessed the sniveling commoners' hatred for her. Only surrounded by the Theomancer's soldiers was she safe from those wild, hungry dogs, who had the gall to judge her. They were part of the problem she had solved—leftovers of Imperial power, who clung unswervingly to the doctrine of blind patriotism and notions of glory and honor. It was they who conquered the people of Eloesus, much superior in intellect to themselves. It was they who conquered Khazidea and subjugated her people.

Priscilla dared not even contemplate the fact that the Queen of Haroon fought for the Empire—a brainwashed, simple fool of a girl. She was a willing pawn of Imperial men, a doe-eyed lover of the world's rude, violent conquerors. No wonder, the lawgivers wanted her head. The forces of power and oppression Priscilla had spurned, Astarthe had relished and embraced. No doubt, when Astarthe met her death-day, her eyes would glare with the same condemnation and judgment Priscilla had encountered on the streets of Imperial City. But then Astarthe would die—beheaded, or burnt alive.

Priscilla found herself in a balcony overlooking the silent city of Melchaddad. The city's advertisements had been removed from the apartment blocks—all images were blasphemy in Mazda's eyes. No more did the sound of music play in the streets. The aqueducts still brought in endless supplies of fresh water; the stores of food showed no signs of running out; and yet, the former Imperial City had become a ghost town, a fraction of what it once had been. The blind patriots and supporters of the military had all fled north and west, joining the rebellion or taking refuge in fortresses.

Silence reigned in Melchaddad, that was, until the sound of marching feet began to echo. A dark shape on the horizon had turned into a near-infinite column of lawgiver soldiers.

"Look at that." She jumped at Cleon's voice, despite herself. "That is Crispus Servillius's army."

"What?" Priscilla snapped. "Impossible! Don't be stupid, Cleon… any more than you have to be."

"He must have failed to take Bregantium."

The words sent Priscilla into a hot rage. She turned around and grabbed his shoulders, digging her nails in hard. "Don't even joke about failure! We will *never* fail!"

Cleon shook her off him, so hard she stumbled and would have fallen, had she not grabbed the balcony railing. "And you use physical violence against me!" Priscilla howled. "How dare you?"

"Your nails are sharp, Priscilla… and I did not do anything that the lawgivers have not already done."

"How dare you? You have a small mind, much smaller than mine!"

"I concede that. I agree."

"Do not presume to act like I have a double standard about Imperials and lawgivers—that is *just* what an Imperial would do."

"I am sorry," Cleon said.

"Too little, too late," Priscilla shouted back, and fled past him, through the door.

In Imperial Square, the army stopped its marching. Indeed, Crispus Servillius rode at the front of the ranks—but why? Why in Varda would he come all the way back here, to Imperial City? He should be in Bregantium, winning the Empire's battles.

Seconds later, the Theomancer came running out, howling incomprehensible curses. "What is the meaning of this? Why are you not in Gad?"

"Simple, Your Holiness," Crispus answered. "I require excellent siege equipment to finish the attack—the gate is nearly broken."

Priscilla gasped. *He has gone mad.*

The Theomancer howled more curses. "Tell me, Crispus, what you remember right before deciding on this course of action."

"I met with the Queen of Haroon," he answered.

The curses the Theomancer howled were louder, angrier, this time. "She has bewitched you!" he at last said. "I want to kill you for your foolishness but it is not your fault, Crispus Servillius—you have served Mazda in the best way you know how. I want your lesser leaders—every last one of them! The chief men of every battalion.

Some were dragged; others were pushed to the front of the line. Their hands were bound tight with rope. Priscilla had never before witnessed the supernatural power the Theomancer was said to have but she had a feeling she would see it now.

A sickly white light enveloped the Theomancer's hand; the air grew dryer, and all vapor from the previous night's rain quickly vanished. He thrust the desiccation forward; and little by little all fifty of the men whitened—their skin turned to scales, then to dust. Before long, clothing and all, they had become sand. Winds blew their wispy remains away across the street, toward the sea.

"March back to Bregantium at once, Servillius," the Theomancer snarled. "Bring me the Sister-Queen's head on a pole!"

CHAPTER THIRTY-EIGHT:
THE MUSTERING OF PALADIUM

Numa

As winter showed its first signs of fading, Numa began the march northwest. His army had swelled to thirty thousand—all the Imperial garrisons in Thenoa and the Vale of Isteros had emptied from their holds and fastnesses, hoping for glory and retribution under the banner of Numa.

What would Mother think? Numa wondered. His mother was gone—a fact that sobered him in his best moments. The memory of her lived on, the memory of a woman he had never fully appreciated and loved—the woman who had brought him into this world.

On a sunny day Numa and his army reached the River Sulis and the walled town of Pallister. The gate towered before them, closed—for good reason, perhaps, but closed.

A warrior in full steel plate eyed them warily from the battlements. "State your business!" he shouted.

"I am Numa!" he shouted. "I am your emperor. We wish to cross the River Sulis, nothing more!"

"Dorimer, the most holy Exarch of Pallister, has no wish for trouble—from the Empire, or from the lawgivers!"

"You are part of the Empire!" Numa answered.

"Indeed, so it appears! And yet, no army shall pass! The Exarch of Pallister has maintained a strict policy of neutrality, and to let you pass would indicate to the lawgivers that we have chosen sides!"

"Words from Dorimer—who claims to be a man of god!" Numa shouted. There was no other way to transport thirty-thousand men except this bridge. "Your ruler is a coward."

"And yet he is alive! More than the Exarch of Paladris can say."

"He will not be alive when I am done with him! Let us by.

This is your last chance—for *your* life, and for the exarch's."

The spokesman had no answer—Numa had no doubts he was nervous, a man under the strict control of his superior. Yet Numa would punish the exarch and all who fought for him alike.

That night, the siege of Pallister began.

Crossbowmen shot from the high perch of the wall and Imperial bowmen answered, yet the battering ram continued to pound against Pallister's city gate. It was not until late in the night, when the wood had splintered, that Numa ordered his men to relent. In the morning they would continue—and, he swore, by the day's end, the exarch would suffer a coward's death.

In the rain the legion continued heaving the battering ram. Bit by bit the gate began to splinter, even as the crossbows unleashed bolts like hail and Imperial bowmen returned with volleys. Ladders fell against Pallister's city walls, yet the Imperials failed to gain control of the battlements. The day ended with Numa's vow unfulfilled.

Early in the morning a new figure appeared in the battlements—a lion of a man with a giant hammer strapped to his back, wearing a suit of plate armor lined with gold filigree. "Numa… *that*, I gather, is your name! I am Dorimer! This has gone on far too long. We will let your army pass; but do not think it is a sign of our allegiance to the Empire! We remain completely neutral!"

"If you will not pledge allegiance to the Empire's cause," Numa answered, "then the siege goes on, until your unconditional surrender!"

Dorimer's curses were soon drowned out as Numa's soldiers cheered deafeningly. Dorimer turned and left, snarling.

The battle raged on that day; and in late afternoon, the gate at last burst open.

Astride his horse, Numa drew *Imperium's Rebuke* and led the charge into Pallister. A hundred Templars and a thousand lesser warriors met them head-on. Blinded by battle he fought as his soldiers filtered into the city and gradually overwhelmed it, surrounding the soldiers who fought in the city square.

Numa and Shareeka found Dorimer in the entry hall of his palace. The man regarded them with two baleful blue eyes. A long golden moustache fell below his chin in the Paladian style. He wore no armor. He greeted them with a snarl. "The followers of Mazda are devout—more devout than god-fearers in the Empire."

"Devout, you say." Numa laughed lightly. "Devoted to destruction and darkness. There is one way you can avoid crucifixion, Dorimer."

The exarch's eyes narrowed.

"You may fly the Imperial flags on every city turret. I will leave five centuries here with you to ensure you do."

"That can be arranged…"

"And there is something else… an irrevocable sign of your allegiance."

"What do you have in mind?" the exarch said.

"You will see soon enough."

~

A day later, Numa's soldiers led Dorimer into Pallister's city square, where white marble temples towered high above. Dorimer had stripped down to his underclothes, leaving his chest and legs bare. Numa watched as one of his soldiers brought out the red-hot brand he had customized. Dorimer cried out in pain as it made its mark—on his arms, his chest, and at last his forehead—the words "I LOVE THE

EMPIRE" burned forever into his flesh.

That afternoon, Numa and his thousands of soldiers left Pallister, heading northwest along the Imperial Road.

~

The Imperial Road ran straight and unyielding through the wetland of Paladium, raised high above the water, broad enough for thirty walking side-by-side. Numa rode at the front with Shareeka by his side, marveling at the Imperial ingenuity. These roads had allowed swift travel, not just for armies but for traders, travelers, and pilgrims.

"There is an Imperial fort outside Sanctum," Shareeka told him.

Numa didn't think the ratling approved of his methods—for one, the crucifixion in Korthos, and for another the branding of Dorimer the Exarch.

"Fort Luminor. Five thousand soldiers were stationed there when I visited."

"Then we will go," Numa answered.

A milestone lay on the edge of the road: TO SANCTUM—132 MILES.

~

It was six cold, miserable days before a road branched off, veering west toward the sea. A small town had cropped up in the crossroads—a stone-walled inn with a thatch roof, a few shops, and a small cluster of homes, all raised high above the marsh like the Imperial Road.

The army's food supplies had already worn thin, and the stop in Sanctum—far from unnecessary—was vital. Numa merely hoped to the gods they wouldn't resist him. A siege of Pallister was one thing, but Sanctum was well-fortified, well-stocked with provisions, and filled with holy warriors of all kinds.

The citizens of the small crossroads town hailed the soldiers as they turned west.

Fort Luminor lay on a high perch, a manmade hill a hundred feet high, within sight of the white walls of Sanctum. On its thick stone walls were statues of the god Lunas, lord of the moon, depicted not in his human form but instead as the King Moth. Numa had seen a temple to Lunas before in Gad, in the town of Arreba—it had amazed him, though its statues were nothing compared to these. They looked like giant moths, turned to stone by the gaze of a gorgon. At the gate he waited, and within moments the doors had opened, without even a word.

Within Fort Luminor's spacious confines, the legate met with Numa.

A giant of a man, he wore steel-plated Imperial armor ornamented with jewels and gold filigree patterns, and on his head a bright steel helmet with a red horsehair crest. "Tidus Varro, legate, at your service."

No doubt a mere greeting, Numa thought.

"Where did you get the Imperial Circlet?" Varro asked.

"It does not matter. I am your emperor, and I ask that you and all your soldiers join me."

"The garrison at Fort Luminor is commanded to protect the city of Sanctum… and ensure its loyalty," Varro said.

"And is Sanctum disloyal? Has the Pontifex become fast friends with the lawgivers?"

"His fiery denunciations are something to behold," Varro said, and smiled. "He has all the monks and vestals worked up into united opposition. I do not fear any sympathies with the lawgivers from the Pontifex or the establishment in Sanctum, signore."

"Then come with me. We are thirty-thousand strong. We need your numbers to restore the Empire."

"I was sworn to protect the Empire… but Emperor Secondo Janus has demanded that I keep watch on Sanctum."

"Emperor Secondo Janus is gone. Your emperor Numa demands you join him."

"Numa… a name I have not heard before. Yet he wears the Imperial Circlet."

"If you love your nation," Numa said, and drew *Imperium's Rebuke*, "and wish to crush its enemies—from without and within— then join me, Tidus Varro, for the sake of honor, and glory, and empire!"

Varro smiled. "A Getan you are—but I will follow an emperor from Gad, if he is as much a patriot as you. Tonight Fort Luminor empties… for you, for honor, for glory, for empire."

"For empire!" Numa shouted.

"For empire!" a chorus of voices—on the walls and within them, a countless group of soldiers—shouted deafeningly in unison.

~

The gates of Sanctum opened for the thirty-five thousand soldiers—to Numa's surprise, after he had seen the treachery and weakness of Dorimer the Exarch. That night the Imperial soldiers had their rest, ate well and drank wine as they were able to pay. They cheered for music, for wine, for singing and dancing, for joy—all the things the lawgivers hated. They left in the morning, well-rested and well-fed, energized and ready for the journey ahead.

CHAPTER THIRTY-NINE:
PREPARATIONS

Appian

He had studied every book on naval warfare in Haroon's massive library, read them over and over again until he could recite all the concepts from memory, though even Appian—Norriva's biggest bookworm—knew he could not truly understand them until he put them into practice. He may not have the brilliant talent that led admirals to victory, but he would try—try as best he could, with the remains of the Imperial Navy, to recapture control of the seas.

The Godlings—the only adult males allowed in the Red Palace—checked on Appian frequently while he studied in the Imperial garrison. The cross-dressing eunuchs had once frightened him, but now had become all but a normal part of life. If he had to fear anyone it was the men of war, and the Asa outside the city walls, not the Godlings.

One morning in late winter he left the confines of the garrison. The air had already grown warm. A cloudless sky hung above, and the onion domes of Haroon's temples stretched high above along the skyline, their red sandstone painted in bright greens and blues. He wondered just how to put himself to use today, and began to turn toward the library when a man shouted, "Hail, Appian!" in a Fharese accent.

The man before him wore a colorful tunic—dyed an off-purple, with a gold four-pointed star—and woolen pants. In one hand he held a rolled-up letter; in the other, the reins of his horse. He had a full beard in the manner of the southrons. "I asked who the leader of Haroon was, and they told me you."

Me? The leader of Haroon?

"Words from His Glorious Majesty, Beloved-of-His-Father, Helper of the Empire, the padisha Pharzanes. I bid you good fortune.

Fharas stands with you. Goodbye."

Appian supposed, with the Sister-Queen gone, and his closeness to the current "emperor," he was the highest ranking man in Haroon. What would his mother, father, and sisters back in Norriva think? He had brought honor to the Appia family again!

He retreated back into the garrison, toward his quarters—small and plain, for the leading man of Haroon, he thought.

On his desk he spread out the letter, written in the fine handwriting of a scribe. At once he began to read:

To the Leader of the Empire in Haroon,

Words from the glorious Pharzanes, King of Kings, His Inimitable Majesty, the well-born sovereign of the Beautiful Land, Fharas...

What has Mazda brought besides destruction and death? Whether the faith of Mazda is a creation of dark spirits or a tragic and mournful mistake of man, it is nonetheless a heavy millstone around the neck of humankind. I have seen visions, and dreamed dreams, of Fharas changed from what it was, into a realm ruled by a theocrat. I have done all I can to stop it, and yet I have not achieved success.

I have fought with the horsemen nomads who plague your land, and lost six thousand of my men. Their horses are too swift;

their bows and arrows, too true. And yet I have slain their leader... while they slept a knife was plunged into his heart. A poor trade, but I have at least done some damage. Let this be a token of our friendship, and—should the Empire rise again— let us always live in respect and in peace, from here to eternity.

When Numa sat on the throne—he could see it even now—Appian would make sure he respected the King of Kings, that he saw him as a rival but never as an enemy. He wondered where Numa was now, whether he had succeeded in gathering all the Empire's legions, or if he'd met a horrid fate at the end of the nomads' arrows. The thought was too terrible for Appian to contemplate.

CHAPTER FORTY:
A TIME FOR WAR

Far North, in Zarubain…

Honey Crumbles, Court Jester

Honey Crumbles had eaten woodchips and fallen to the floor six times after telling every joke he could remember, and still the wrinkled gray face of King Jourmande had remained solemn and unamused. Honey Crumbles had heard horror stories of what Jourmande had done to his old jester, Twinkle-Bells, after she'd failed to amuse him. Now, as Honey Crumbles began—out of desperation—striking himself with a stick in view of the Lion Throne, a loud knocking echoed on the door.

"Enough, buffoon! To the shadows with you!"

Honey Crumbles breathed a sigh of relief and drew back into the darkness. *I like shadows best.*

The door opened and in walked a man Honey Crumbles recognized only vaguely—Aloysius, he remembered. Honey Crumbles welcomed the distraction from his ever-worsening performance.

"Have you brought the money, Aloysius? The kingdom is in good need of seven-hundred marks."

"The government has refused, Your Majesty," Aloysius said. "The Empire is in a shambles."

"*What?*" The old man rose from his throne, eyes burning with the un-pent rage Honey Crumbles had always feared.

At least it is not directed at me.

"They have refused," Aloysius repeated.

"The Empire has refused their first payment. We will demand all of it, then. We will have all seven-thousand marks at once. An army shall be gathered—knights and soldiers, from every able lord!" King Jourmande was beside himself. "We shall demand the Wizards Council join us."

From the shadows, the wizard Uriel emerged in his bright green robes—a man Honey Crumbles had always known was there, yet whose sudden appearances always frightened him. "The Archwizard Odo will want nothing to do with this war. It does not align with our interests. The Council of the Twelve shall remain neutral in this affair."

King Jourmande knew better than to lash out in anger at Uriel—a man of such power he could level the palace and slay everyone in it. Instead, the king ground his teeth together and said, "Very well. If the Empire is in shambles, as you say, we will overcome them quite quickly—or, if they know what is best for them, they will pay the sum immediately. In a few months, the army shall be assembled… to war, my subjects… to war!"

"To war!" everyone—including Honey Crumbles—shouted. Uriel disappeared again into the shadows of the throne.

As Aloysius left, a gnawing nervousness overtook Honey Crumbles. The distraction had been far too short. He shuddered as he walked back into view of the now-unsettled King Jourmande. He had a grand performance ahead of him, and its results meant life or death.

CHAPTER FORTY-ONE:
DOOM, DELAYED

Astarthe, Queen of Haroon

The seas had grown calmer, and the sailing season drew near. The air hinted at spring—though it was autumn for the Empire, nearing the winter of desolation and utter destruction. Once, the people of Bregantium would have greeted the warmer weather with celebration. They would have dove into the waters of the Imperial Sea, basked in the sunshine among the palmettos. But now, when Astarthe walked the ancient stone streets, the atmosphere was anything but joy—she sensed trepidation from all corners. The Rite of Spring approached, but precious little had been prepared for the celebration. The celebration likely would not happen at all.

In her bedroom she brushed her long black hair by herself. She had left her handmaids and Godlings behind in Haroon. It was good—she would not want any of them to experience the doom she felt, but neither would she abandon the Empire's cause. Astarthe would live with the city, or die with the city, for in this city—Bregantium—rested the last best hope of the Empire.

There was a knock at the door.

"Signora?" Astarthe said, then remembered it was not one of her handmaids, likely a man.

"We are meeting," said the voice of Augusto Vitellian.

"I will be there in just a moment," she answered him.

In the spacious room of the Governor's Mansion that now served as Imperial headquarters, Astarthe met the last vestige of the Empire's government—Vitellian, Alba, Geta, Longus and Anderis—and waited for the last bout of dire news. Had Haroon finally fallen? That news would only come with sailing ships.

Yet the dark pessimism that haunted Vitellian's face for months seemed to have lessened. He almost looked hopeful. "Thanks to your spell, my queen," Vitellian said, "Bregantium may yet hold for another year. An army—eighty thousand strong—has driven the lawgivers from Paladris and crossed the River Hyber."

"The Hyber? Paladris?" Paladris had been lost many months ago. The exarch Thormer had capitulated after the siege, yet the treacherous lawgivers executed him despite their promises of mercy.

"Every last lawgiver within the walls has been executed. The Pontifex has sent another Templar to replace Thormer," Vitellian explained.

"That is great news!" Astarthe exclaimed.

"The leader of the army calls himself Numa," Vitellian went on. "The informant tells me he wears the Imperial Circlet—somehow stolen from Secondo Janus—and has a sword of adamant."

To wait for the conqueror god, and recognize him when he comes—the task that Issa had set upon Astarthe's heart reverberated in her mind. Was this him? "Numa… a strange name."

Councilor Geta answered. "In the dialect of northern Gad, it means 'eagle.' I think we have ourselves an emperor from Gad… or a pretender."

"An emperor from Gad who loves the nation is better than Secondo Janus—" Vitellian murmured. "—and he cannot possibly be worse than what we have now."

"Gods, to see that adamant sword through Crispus Servillius' neck!" Councilor Longus cried—and Astarthe did not blame him, for the thirst for blood had also seeped into her. "I will do all I can to make it happen."

"Four thousand soldiers remain to protect Bregantium." Astarthe could not help but feel her optimism crumble. "Eighty-four thousand soldiers—even Imperial soldiers, the best in the world— against hundreds of thousands of lawgivers."

"Do not abandon hope," Vitellian said. "If we—the Imperial government—abandon hope, then all hope fades with us. We must stay strong and optimistic—for the people of the Empire."

"Yes… for the people of the Empire," Astarthe said.

They repeated the words in unison—"For the people of the Empire!"—as a gust of sweet spring wind blew into the room.

PART THREE

A deep darkness overcomes me and a heavy shadow haunts me. The Empire will fall, I think with a shudder. The barbarians are too strong… The forces of destruction are too great… The people of the Empire do not love their country… In every heart there is sedition, in none, strength…

The dark and tragic law will surely overshadow us and weigh us down for all our days.

CHAPTER FORTY-TWO: HOPE, QUICKLY FADING

The eagle soared high above the green grass, searching for prey. The flowers were in full bloom, the beasts of the field bountiful, but the eagle had not yet found its quarry. High above the eagle flew, far from its home near the River Hyber. On the road echoed a chorus of stamping feet… a group of humans thousands strong, glittering with steel and carrying red and gold banners, like the men the eagle used to see, not the ones in black whom it despised.

Numa

The army would reach Bregantium in a day. Spring had begun, and the chill in the air had left; the sun shone bright in a sky with precious few clouds. Along the road, myrtles bloomed, and in the air the scent of pollen and springtime hung thickly. Back in Norriva, farmers no doubt busied themselves planting their fields—but that life was gone from him, a thing forever relegated to memory. He had shaken off his old identity; now, he was Numa, the aspirant emperor, with eighty-thousand men at his command.

A village appeared, un-walled like much of the Imperial interior—a cluster of houses and shops with red tile roofs—and a temple that, on closer inspection, had been defaced. The statues of Bregeto, god of wealth and plenty, stood at the temple gates headless.

As soon as Numa drew near, a group of citizens came rushing out—both men and women—crying out frantically with joy. "Ah! Our salvation!" a man cried. "I had to sell my clothing and my house to pay the unbelieving tax… I refused to worship Mazda, and was punished."

"Signor Tyrenas worships Mazda!" a woman in a roughspun woolen gown shouted. "The old magistrate of our town gets paid from our tax… he gets rewarded for his treachery!"

"I will see to it that he is punished," Numa said. "Never again will treachery be rewarded in the Empire."

From the words of the locals he discerned the location of the magistrate's house—a giant stone mansion with an iron-rimmed gate, guarded, as Numa expected, by lawgivers. There were thirteen, dressed in flowing blacks, with hoods covering their heads and bandanas over their mouths. At once they drew scimitars; but it was only seconds before Imperial century engaged.

The lawgivers fought with grace and skill, twirling and blocking with their sabers, but the battle did not last long; before a minute had passed, all lay dead, slashed open by Imperial swords and bleeding on the road.

"What is the meaning of this?" a voice cried from within. The gates opened, revealing a man in purple silk, but just as soon began to shut.

A soldier dashed into the courtyard, grabbed the man—no doubt, Signor Tyrenas—by the throat, forcing him inside.

"What is the meaning of this?" he repeated his plaintive cry.

"Signor Tyrenas," Numa said.

"Fabian Tyrenas!" he corrected with a snarl. "And who do you think you are, signore, wearing the Imperial Circlet of an empire that is dead?"

"I am your emperor," Numa answered.

"You're a rustic from the North Country—I can tell it by your accent. The gall, of you claiming to be emperor!" Fabian howled.

"I am your emperor," Numa repeated. "And you will refer to me as Your Undying Glory."

"I will not," Fabian insisted.

"Cut out his tongue!" The soldier that held Fabian looked at Numa questioningly, but Numa nodded in approval.

Fabian's cries of protest turned to screams as the soldier obeyed.

"You swore to protect the people of the Empire. As

magistrate, your people depended on you," Numa said. "You profited from your people's misery. You strove to protect your life. But now, you will receive the worst of all possible deaths, and all your wealth will be donated to the ones you betrayed."

Naked and bloodied they affixed Fabian to his cross; his wounds were mortal but his death would be slow. Some citizens looked aghast at their former leader, disliking his punishment; others openly cheered, threw stones, and spat on him. Once every last gold libra was removed from the house, Numa set the bags of money out in the city square.

"Hail Numa! Hail Numa!" the townspeople cried as he left.

~

Through wide-open gates, Numa and the eighty thousand entered the city of Bregantium. Amid the cobbled streets, people peeked through windows at the aspirant emperor. Others gathered by the road and threw flowers in their wake. Despite their joy they looked thin and gaunt, unhealthy and heavy-hearted after the months-long siege. Yet Numa provided a flicker of hope—a hope, he knew, that would quickly be extinguished.

CHAPTER FORTY-THREE:
IMPOSSIBLE NEWS

Priscilla Marianus, Provost of the Thenoan Academy

"What do you mean?" Priscilla howled in the Imperial Palace library, beside herself at Cleon's words. "You cannot possibly be serious!"

"The cities of Eloesus have rejoined the Empire. The warriors we sent to Korthos… slaughtered."

Priscilla grabbed him. "You have your facts wrong."

"The Theomancer does not seem to think so."

Priscilla screamed. "Pontio Piraeus… I had left him in charge. He was so capable, I thought. So shrewd and wise. To convince that common street-rat he was a king, and foment a rebellion."

"Pontio Piraeus was crucified," Cleon told her.

Her shock was too great to elicit a scream; instead, she fell back, limp and cold, drained of blood. "I think I will be sick."

"The Theomancer has no choice but to send an army to Eloesus," Cleon said. "We will take the cities by force rather than rebellion. The Empire has emptied its garrison there—an army has marched north."

Priscilla groaned.

"An army small enough to crush with focused effort. It is the least of our concerns," Cleon told her. "There is another bit of bad news."

"What could be worse?" she replied, and steadied herself with a bookshelf.

"Khazidea is a desolation but Haroon has remained firm… they have several years' supply of food—Astarthe was a better ruler than we thought."

"And that is the bad news?" Priscilla asked.

"The blockade of Haroon was broken… smashed by a sudden

maneuver of the Imperial Navy. A hundred war galleys are now in the open water."

Priscilla glared at Cleon, though he surely could not see her through his mask. She could not help—despite the irrationality of the thought—that this was all Cleon's fault. "The Empire… the great bully of the world. They do not realize their time on the world stage is up. Priscilla Marianus has brought about a new and better world… the world of Mazda."

She had never spoken so boldly before—she and the conspirators had ferried the lawgivers here as tools, but they refused to obey orders. Now, any insular concerns about the Law of Mazda did not matter—her goal was to destroy the Empire, and any method toward that end was good.

"Your optimism encourages me, Priscilla," Cleon said with a smile.

She could not bear to look at him.

"A young man claims to be the emperor. He is wearing the Imperial Circlet… the Circlet he somehow stole from Secondo Janus."

She snarled some curse. "And what is the fool's name?"

"Numa. He ordered Pontio's crucifixion."

"Then he will be crucified in turn," Priscilla said. "Anyone who supports the Empire, the great bully, will suffer. Anyone who proclaims its virtues will suffer. We will drive its supporters to the ground, and then, to the grave."

"Mazda be with us!" Cleon said.

"Mazda be with us, indeed," Priscilla answered.

CHAPTER FORTY-FOUR: THE GOD ARRIVES

Astarthe, Queen of Haroon

So this is the conqueror god, Astarthe thought to herself as she ran her eyes over the one who called himself Numa. His salvation of the city was undeniable; the value of his eighty thousand soldiers, incalculable; but she could not help but think she had expected something different—a hawk-eyed, black-haired commander of the Empire. Not a young man with light, almost golden brown hair, whose speech and mannerisms indicated a country peasant visiting the interior for the first time. Not a young man with a strange name— Numa—with no family line to speak of. He was the definition of a "new man"; but this was the one whom the gods sent, and Astarthe would accept their gift.

"Four hundred thousand *warriors?*" Numa repeated Councilor Vitellian's words, apparently incredulous.

"The traitors have brought an entire nation over the sea—in concert, they burned most all the ships of the Imperial Navy, allowing the way for the lawgivers," Vitellian explained.

"Not all," Numa said. "A hundred war galleys remain in Haroon."

"Truly?" Vitellian gasped.

Numa nodded; his features were light, yet hard and stern. Beside him stood a ratling who called himself Shareeka, wearing a hooded cloak. Astarthe had never liked ratlings—the sight of him, even know, made her skin crawl.

"I have a list of traitors," Numa went on. Out of the folds of his worn, dirty cloak, he pulled a rolled-up piece of paper. "They came from a Godling in Haroon."

Councilor Vitellian allowed the paper to unravel, began to run his eyes over the entries. "Some I recognize—Crispus Servillius, of course. But these others… Septimo Seánus? Even the Seáni family—the best in the Empire—have betrayed us? I thought Septimo died with the rest of the Imperial Council." The further he read down the list, the whiter his expression grew. "Priscilla Marianus is the architect? And Cleon Adelphos? Cleon taught Septimo's son mathematics for years… Priscilla Marianus was a great scholar, a prolific author. Her work was a bit critical of the Empire, but I never once thought she would betray us all."

"Marcus Otho, too. The Grand Admiral." Numa's words sent another shock through Vitellian.

"Our own military," Vitellian breathed. "The Otho family… a great knightly family, wealthy beyond compare. I thought they were unswerving patriots, all."

"And yet they are not… a sickness has infected the elite," Numa said.

"A sickness," Vitellian repeated. "Yes, a sickness endemic to the Augusts and the Knightly classes. A sickness present in the days of Claudio-Valens Adamantus. A fatal sickness we cannot repair."

"We can repair," Numa asserted, "and we will."

His confidence refreshed Astarthe's heart, but she could not help but feel it was misplaced. For all intents and purposes, the great army lay trapped in the city of Bregantium, and to go outside meant slaughter.

CHAPTER FORTY-FIVE: THE DIE IS CAST

Thirteen Days Later…

Numa

In his room in the Governor's Mansion, Numa read and re-read the reports swirling about—that some citizens of Bregantium were growing restless and desperate; that an army of lawgivers was destined for Eloesus to utterly destroy the undermanned, under-protected cities, to "destroy their temples and melt their works of art into gold"; and the only ray of good news, that rebel activity had once again surged in Imperial City; but still, all he could think of, now, was of Appian and the girl he'd left behind in Carta Mega—but most importantly, of Appian.

Where is he? With the last remaining navy he had surely left Haroon, but where did he have a mind to go? He missed his best friend, the one he'd grown up with in Norriva. Where Shareeka was harsh and critical, Appian was easily-humored and warm.

A knock on the door startled him from his thoughts.

"Come in!"

The door opened, revealing Councilor Vitellian. "Good news and bad news, Signor Numa, but mostly bad."

"Tell me the good news first," Numa said.

"Crispus Servillius has only brought three-hundred thousand lawgivers around the city walls."

Numa laughed grimly. "And the bad?"

"The same—and that a hundred thousand have been sent to Eloesus, to utterly destroy everything that remains of Imperial culture," Vitellian explained. "Signore, if we wait, and hole up here, then it is only a matter of time—eventually the city of Bregantium will fall, and the lawgivers will slaughter us all."

"Then what do you propose we do?"

"Wait," Vitellian sighed. "What else is there? No other options remain."

"We will wait," Numa agreed. "But we will have hope. We owe the people nothing less. We will win this war, somehow."

"Hope," Vitellian sighed. "I will do my best, Signor Emperor."

Numa nodded. "That is all you can do."

Around the city walls the mass of black surrounded them, an army dressed uniformly in dark clothing, bearing sharp scimitars of steel. Their banners, too, were black, and raised high on a litter was Crispus Servillius—an ancient man, Numa thought as he surveyed him from the battlements. He was dressed not with the purple sash of an Imperial Councilor, but in the black cloth of a lawgiver. A shield of alchemical glass protected him from arrows.

"I wish to speak with the pretender… the rustic from Gad who calls himself an emperor!" he cried.

"I am he!" Numa answered with a shout. "If your eyesight were just a little better, Signor Crispus, you would see the Imperial Circlet that I wear!"

"If you surrender unconditionally, ensure the death of all remaining councilors, honor the god Mazda, and sell the Bregantines into slavery, I have word from the Theomancer… *that he would still have you burnt alive.*"

"A noble death is better than what you describe!" Numa answered. "A noble death is better than how you have lived… a life of safety, gained by treachery."

"Soon the cities of Eloesus will all be burnt down," Crispus hissed. "All its libraries, its temples and its works of art, all the remains of its glory will be a smoking ruin. And on the ashes of each city will instead be a great black *kabakh.*"

Numa felt his hackles rising, but anger was what Crispus wanted; he craved hatred and desperation, and Numa would make sure he didn't get anything he wanted. "It is strange to hear that from you, Crispus Servillius. The entire coup was planned by the Eloesian Academies… the Academies that stand for free thought, for arts and science, and liberty."

"Liberty!" Crispus laughed. He spoke the word like a filthy curse. "You bore me, Getan rustic. I cannot wait to bring you back to my associate, the Theomancer."

"Your associate, you say. You mean your domino…"

Crispus snarled. "Surrender and receive the death that is due you."

"Goodbye, Crispus Servillius," Numa said. He turned and left, ignoring the shouts.

The sounds of the siege echoed through the night. Volley answered volley, and Numa remained ever-close to the army, though his skill was not in strategy—his presence added to their morale, nothing more, a well-fortuned young man wearing the Imperial Circlet on his head, and a sword of adamant in his hand.

From the battlements he called out, "Forward! For empire!"

And his men shouted back, "For empire!" as they unleashed volleys of arrows on the lawgivers trying to break through the gate. Servants brought pots of boiling water up onto the wall, and with each charge of the battering ram another lawgiver cried out at the burning liquid. In time, the lawgiver forces retreated, swearing to renew the fight tomorrow.

Bregantium will hold, Numa told himself. *I will make sure it will hold.* The walls of the city had held it fast. Yet this strategy was a losing one—sooner or later the city would starve, or the gates burst asunder; then, the flood of lawgivers would overpower them by sheer numbers. Something riskier, something daring, had to be tried—but what could he possibly do?

~

For two days and two nights, the siege continued. The Imperial forces continued their losing fight; then, the light of the third day dawned, and Councilor Vitellian came rushing to the city gate where Numa had already arisen. "Ships! Ships, my friend! Ships in the harbor!" Yet his voice burst with joy, not sorrow.

"Imperial ships?" Numa said, aghast. Could it be? Could Appian truly have prevailed? Could he truly have won the naval battles, and somehow crossed a thousand miles of sea?

Indeed, the galleys in the harbor bore Imperial sails: the gold war eagle against a red field; and already they had begun to dock. Imperial sailors and Khazidees, working in concert, unloaded bags full of flour and barley, and kegs filled with Khazidean beer. On one of the ships—the flagship with an eagle prow—Appian stood on the foredeck, looking different from the simple Norriva boy Numa had remembered.

He rushed over to him, sprinting toward his friend—the friend who had prevailed against these impossible odds, and filled Numa with a tiny sliver of hope. He met Appian in an embrace, and for a moment refused to let him go.

"Numa," Appian breathed. "It is good to see you, friend."

"Appian," he managed to say, yet staring into the harbors he knew, in an instant, what he had to do. Something far-fetched, something risky, a command no one would obey if Numa weren't emperor.

"Wait here. Thank Imperium for you," Numa said, and turned, hopping off the war galley and sprinting down the road, out of the harbor.

In the Governor's Mansion, before the elated members of the Imperial government—Queen Astarthe included—Numa shamelessly announced his mad plan. "We will take forty thousand of my men in war galleys… we will strike Imperial City and drive the lawgivers out."

"Madness!" Councilor Anderis shouted.

"Madness, indeed," Vitellian said. "But now is the time for madness; a desperate chance, a terrible risk, and totally unexpected."

"I will not have the last bits of our military strength wasted on this fruitless exercise!" Anderis thundered. "I will not see our last chance squandered."

The other councilors nodded in agreement.

"Your presence is welcome, Numa," Anderis began, "but your command is—"

"My command is final!" Numa shouted, his words quaking with a power he had never felt before. "*I am your emperor!*"

A hush fell over the room; Anderis looked down, not daring to meet Numa's gaze. Astarthe's eyes beamed with wonderment, and admiration.

"And I will go with you," the Sister-Queen said. "I will follow you to the ends of the earth, conqueror god. I will see the lawgivers defeated and humiliated at your hands."

Numa risked a smile. "Very well. She will go with me. In the end, your words, councilors, are only an afterthought—my commands are final. I will leave a force here to defend your city. I will do my best to protect your lives."

Four legions, thirty thousand men in all, he left under the command of grand legate Salvatore Jiovanucci. Vitellian he left in command of the city itself, and the newly-refreshed food supply. Numa had high hopes the city would stand firm for months, perhaps a year.

Forty thousand legionaries filtered into the hundred war galleys, packed tight in their spacious hulls. On the deck of *The Will of Imperium,* Numa stood with Appian and Astarthe, knowing full well he had taken a remote and incalculable risk. "The die is cast," Numa said.

"To victory or death. To empire."

"To empire!" Appian shouted.

"To empire!" Astarthe repeated, and the ship's crew followed, then thousands of the legion.

"To victory or death! To empire! Onward!"

CHAPTER FORTY-SIX:
DESPAIR

Eudora Kyrillos

The summer sun beat, heavy and oppressive, on the dry, baking-hot roads of Carta Mega. Business had slowed to its summer standstill; few had the madness to go outside, like Eudora did. The heat had grown unbearable, yet the worst had not yet come; still on the edge of summer, Carta Mega would soon go from unbearable to a living hell on earth.

But nonetheless Eudora stood outside on this oppressive day, walking across the sun-scorched dirt road in nothing more than her sandals. Eventually she made her way to the House of the Bel. The two guards let her by without a word.

~

Sitting on the throne in his great onion-white turban, Balthesar the Magnificent greeted Eudora with a frown. "Eudora, my dear."

"Uncle Balthesar," Eudora answered. "The seas are good for sailing. Have you thought any more of my proposition? The Empire needs your help. A thousand gold pieces would only scratch the surface of our wealth, and help them greatly—"

"Eudora." Balthesar's voice had gone from polite to openly annoyed. His eyes hardened into a glare. "I have word from the cities of the east. Two hundred thousand lawgivers have landed in Eloesus. And in Khazidea, Haroon stands alone amid a great desolation. The war is lost, Eudora. I will not grant aid to the losing side, and risk the wrath of the Theomancer."

"You are not a man," she snapped.

"Excuse me?" Balthesar rose, his face gone red, his irritation replaced with rage. "You will apologize to me now, or I will have my guards escort you out. Your father was a great man, a dear friend, Eudora; but you should know better than to insult the bel of Carta Mega, the greatest city in the world."

"The greatest city in the world, soon to be under the Law of Mazda. My words stand. You are not a man, Balthesar Bel. You are a coward, a weakling, a worm."

"*Guards!*"

Two blond-haired, blue-eyed soldiers in scale-mail armor came rushing out from some alcove—warriors of Gad, both with crescent-moon axes strapped across their backs.

"Show this *lupa* out," Balthesar said, "and make sure she never enters the House of the Bel again."

They threw her out in the hot sun, as visions of failure swirled in her head, of a world under the rule of Mazda, of the Empire utterly destroyed. She cried out at the thought, and in desperation decided on her course of action—if the Bel of Carta Mega would not help her, she would need to find help elsewhere. She would ride her camel across the desert. *To Haroon,* she thought. *No, to Zoar.*

To Zoar, the City of Stone, where the Great King ruled. It was a long shot, a desperate action, but she would not give up, not now. Eudora would fight for the Empire, with all she had in her. She would never abandon hope, not until she breathed her last breath. The Great King in Zoar had an army. He had warriors. He had wealth—some wealth, at least. Perhaps if the scales would not fall of Uncle Balthesar's eyes, the Great King would listen.

She left the precincts of Cartha Mega as soon as the midday sun began to fade, eyes welling with tears, her thoughts filled with grand notions of hope and victory but her body and soul overcome with despair and fear of defeat.

CHAPTER FORTY-SEVEN:
A TIME FOR VIOLENCE

Ten Days Later…

Cleon Adelphos, Vice Provost of the Thenoan Academy

"'There is a time for violence, in its season,' says Nestor," Priscilla read from a book in the Imperial Palace library. "The Empire has committed so many crimes, Nestor would agree with me, don't you think?"

All Cleon could think about was the mask of the tragic actor that covered his old friend's face. He could scarcely even acknowledge Nestor, the favored disciple of Theiarkos and proponent of Thenoan Philosophy. "Of course, Priscilla," he said—all he could manage at that moment. Visions returned to him of lawgivers putting young women to death for "impurity," burning cross-dressed priests of Atman alive, setting the Imperial City Library to the torch. "Who are you trying to convince? I am on your side," he said.

Maybe, Cleon thought, *Priscilla is only trying to convince herself.*

"I know you are," Priscilla said. "And yet you do not comfort me… you do not soothe me. Your presence does not reassure me. I believe you are halfhearted about our mission—I believe deep down, you despise the lawgivers… I believe you despise me. I believe you blame *me* for this nightmare we are in."

"Nightmare?" Cleon said.

"I spoke without thinking," Priscilla said. "I meant, of course, the nightmare that the people resist us… even dare to hate us."

"I do not despise the lawgivers," Cleon answered truthfully. "I think whatever comes after the Empire cannot be worse than what happened before. I think, Priscilla, that you destroyed the Empire singlehandedly—and that is an accomplishment worthy of the highest praise, no matter which side you are on."

Cleon could sense Priscilla's smile behind the black mask.

Gods, that mask. That leering frown, those sad eyes.

A bell rang—the lawgivers were summoning Cleon to a meeting. They did not allow Priscilla into such meetings, preferring her to keep to the shadows.

~

The Theomancer stood in the White Chamber in view of the throne, dressed in his black turban and black robes. A handful of the highest-ranking priests stood there with him. Umar, the highest-ranking field marshal, had long since left with Crispus Servillius, to make sure the Khazidean witch did not cast a spell over him again.

"I have some news which is not particularly good," the Theomancer said. "The Imperial Navy escaped from Haroon and brought food to Bregantium—enough, some say, for a year or more. The blockade has since returned over Haroon and Bregantium, but another of our fleets was utterly destroyed off the coast of the chaparral barrens."

Off the coast of the barrens, in Anthania, Cleon thought. That was uncomfortably close.

"I thought we had destroyed the entire Imperial Navy," a senior priest said.

"Marcus Otho ensured me it was so," the Theomancer answered. "There will be hell to pay when I see him next."

"Where is he?" the priest asked.

"In Nichaeus. But he is the least of our concerns right now. We must destroy those ships, as soon as possible," the Theomancer continued. "All our soldiers are in Bregantium and Eloesus."

A coldness infused Cleon. Over the room, dread spread its long black wings. The threat was probably empty; the danger, probably insignificant. But the possibility—the mere possibility—of the hundred Imperial galleys filled with soldiers, sent a shudder through him. *The Imperial Army is destroyed,* he remembered. It had taken the entire population of the lawgivers to overcome them, but it was done.

The Empire was in shambles. Imperium, the Spirit of Empire, had abandoned its nation; the gods were shown as empty ideas, devoid of power. Yet still… Priscilla had to be warned.

~

"What do you mean?" Priscilla hissed. "You cannot possibly be serious. Off the coast of the barrens? But what if there are soldiers on those ships?"

"My thoughts exactly," Cleon told her. "Do not be worried?"

"Do not be worried? Do not be worried about my safety? Typical Imperial man!" Priscilla hissed. "My life is precious. I am leaving in the night. I am going to Nichaeus and taking a small ship to Bregantium. There I will help Crispus Servillius with his siege. There, I will be safe."

"The Theomancer will kill you if you leave without his permission," Cleon said bluntly.

"The Theomancer will not know—unless you tell him," Priscilla sneered.

"Shall I put your mask back in the library?"

"If Mazda's holy law demands my face be covered, then so be it," Priscilla hissed. "Though you would not know, heathen—the law is only a tool for you."

And so it was with you, once. Cleon did not bother to say goodbye; her mistake was grave, the Theomancer's wrath unquenchable. She had as good as sentenced herself to death, all for some notion of safety; yet Cleon would not stop her.

That night, dark dreams plagued him, of fires and floods, of battles and bloodshed, of a great beast rising from the ashes of ruin, and the horned visage of Imperium in the wilderness, calling out for Cleon's blood.

CHAPTER FORTY-EIGHT: MORNING AT THE WELL

Lexis Avidicci

At the fountain in Imperial Square, in the dark hours of early morning, Lexis met a rare sight—the women of the lawgivers in their full-bodied robes, their faces covered by veils. She dipped her bucket into the water, and one of them shouted some indistinguishable curse. She looked around, saw the black shapes before her but no eyes to gaze at. She did not much care about what the women thought of her; they had no power among the lawgivers, no rights or ability to speak.

"What gives you the idea," one croaked, "that you can dip your hands in the same water we do?"

Lexis did not care what they thought. Their presence here, in Imperial City, was an abomination—though one which showed no signs of abating.

"The Imperial whore," another said, "the heathen lawbreaker, thinks she can drink the same water as us. Wait until I tell my husband Malihl… he will have her head."

At their words, Lexis laughed, her bucket filled with water for the day's necessities. She turned and left toward her upper-story apartment.

How strange, she thought, *that these women who have no rights and no respect still consider themselves superior to me.*

CHAPTER FORTY-NINE: BLOOD ON THE STONES

Cleon Adelphos

Still shaken from his nightmares, Cleon took an afternoon walk through the streets of Imperial City. The bright blue skies overhead reassured him; the warming spring air had all the promise of summer. His fears had been so foolish—the Empire lay dead from a mortal wound he and Priscilla had inflicted.

In the Walk of Triumph he gazed at the still-standing giant statues. As of yet, the lawgivers did not have the technology or the knowledge to destroy these, which—as images—they considered idolatrous. Still, the titanic statues of King Anthans loomed above Cleon, of Empress Irena—worst of all, to the lawgivers—a circlet of command on her head, and of Horatio the Citizen Soldier, bearing the eagle banner. They were all symbols of unjust power, of oppression and inequality, of dominance and aggression. Yet that, at heart, *was* the Empire—this represented everything it stood on. Its foundations were violence. Its spirit was inequality. Its heart was domination.

A horn blew, echoing across the empty streets. *An Imperial horn.* Two more blew, then four, then ten.

"No," Cleon began to say. "No, no, no, no. No. No! *No!*"

He should not have worn his lawgiver blacks. He began to run. He would hide in the Imperial Palace, yes. He turned, feeling the colossal statue of Claudio-Valens Adamantus was staring at him, scorning him with its oppressing, bullying eyes. *The world bully is here. The world's self-proclaimed ruler.*

"Where is justice?" Cleon screamed. "Where is justice, for me?"

The horn pealed, deathly close. Cleon tossed a look over his shoulder. Soldiers had appeared behind him, in steel breastplates, carrying red-gold eagle banners. Warhorses came thundering ahead.

Cleon ran with all his strength, his heart threatening to explode. The joyful cheering of citizens rose above even the war cries of the Imperial Army. *Gods be damned.*

"Where is justice?" Cleon screamed. "Where is justice? O Lady Justice, deliver to me what I deserve!" A long life is what he deserved—a long life, on the ruins of the Empire he had utterly destroyed. *"Where is justice? Gods! Gods be damned!"*

Though he ran as fast as he could, the thundering of the horses' hooves was growing closer by the second. The war horns blew again. The oppressor, the world bully, had returned to the center-point of unjust power.

"Gods help me!" he screamed, though he knew even then that his cry was empty. He screamed for the Empire's victims. He screamed for the Academies. He screamed for learning and enlightenment, for the liberty and intellectual excellence he had always strived to bring. He screamed for Priscilla, but most of all he screamed for himself.

A sword took him in the back of the head.

CHAPTER FIFTY: DEATH TO TRAITORS

Numa

In the midst of Imperial Square, a group of augurs restrained the Theomancer's powers of desiccation and sand as legionaries led him toward the chopping block. It had been a struggle to carry him here, a concerted effort to locate him in the Imperial Palace and then force him from his hiding place. But now the Theomancer feebly walked before him, not a demon of the pits but an old man with a square gray beard, his old eyes showing a hint of fear.

Around the perimeter of Imperial Square, a vast crowd of citizens had gathered, cheering his death. Yet the Theomancer's death was not the one he craved.

"Where is Priscilla Marianus?" he asked for the third time. "Where is Jiacomo Lornodoris? Publio Martius? Septimo S——"

"For the last time," the Theomancer howled, "I do not know. Priscilla escaped in the night. I have not seen Jiacomo in months… not Septimo Seánus, either."

"I will let you sail home with all your men if you tell me right now," Numa informed him.

The Theomancer's eyes lighted with hope. "Priscilla Marianus… she has gone into hiding in… in Carta Mega! And Septimo Seánus—yes, Septimo and Jiacomo and Publio, they've all gone to Eloesus to besiege Imperiopoli. Yes, that is what they are."

"A pity you are such a bad liar." Numa glared into the man's already-enfeebled eyes. "I have heard the lawgivers are allowed to lie, if it advances their cause. No dishonor is inadmissible if it furthers the Theomancer."

The Theomancer bared his teeth. "Not true. Not true at all."

"More deceits. What else should I expect from a lawgiver?" Numa motioned to the soldiers who restrained him. "Off with his head!"

The crowd roared at the words, as the soldiers hauled the Theomancer to the chopping block. One kicked him into position. The executioner pitched back his sword. The crowd wanted a crucifixion, but that was a punishment fit only for the lowest of worms—traitors—and not foreign enemies such as this.

"Impious! Idolater! Arrogant boy!" the Theomancer shouted. "Mazda strike him dead!"

The sword fell. The clean cut split his neck clean in two. The head rolled off and the blood began to collect. The crowd erupted with a deafening cheer. Numa drew *Imperium's Rebuke* and thrust it twice, then three times, into the air.

When the noise of the crowd began to die down, Numa seized the opportunity and shouted: "Such is the punishment for the invaders! Yet the punishment for treason will be far worse! A man who follows the Law of Mazda will not be punished for his barbarism—only viewed with disgust and shame! Yet anyone who has extorted from Imperials, who has collected money from the unbelievers' tax—who has stolen from the brave and profited from his cowardice—a crucifixion shall be his death! So, too, shall anyone who took up arms against the Empire!"

The crowd roared again, louder than before.

Yet Numa's work was not done; his death would only anger the lawgivers, who still outnumbered him by hundreds of thousands.

~

The lawgivers had depleted the treasury; they had cut the heads off statues, painted over advertisements on the wall; they had desecrated Imperial City with their black stone *kabakh*; they had smashed the stores of Korthian wine; and attempted to destroy their way of life.

At the smoldering ruin that remained of the Imperial City Library, Numa viewed the collapsed pillars, the shattered roof, and the burnt husks of books, and cursed. "Not even Fharas was this barbaric... not even the northern kingdoms. All that knowledge, destroyed... to think of a world that values ignorance."

Appian, beside him, was too enraged to speak.

A woman came rushing up to them, a slave judging by her unornamented brown dress. "Your Undying Glory, there is a story behind this outrage. That *lupa*, Priscilla Marianus, was trying to convince the Theomancer not to burn it. But the Theomancer said 'Any book that contradicts the Law of Mazda is worthless; any book that agrees with it is superfluous.' And he set the whole thing aflame."

"Gods damn it all!" Appian at last snapped. "I had dreamed of visiting this place long ago. I had dreamed of learning. I had dreamed—*Gods damn it, barbarians!* An execution was too kind, Numa. You've really done us all a disservice. Gods damn you." He stormed off.

Numa shook his head. Perhaps Appian was right, but still, Numa believed Crispus, Priscilla, Septimo and the others on the list deserved worse fates. And the success of his mission was still in the air; things could come crashing down so easily.

Most of the temples had survived, bereft though they were of statues and ornaments. Only the Temple of Imperium lay in ruin—the Theomancer's idea, no doubt, of destroying Imperial pride. Yet Numa swore he would rebuild the city—and most of the all, the Temple of Imperium—grander than before. Beautiful statues would stand high on every street; wine sellers would have a reduced tax; music would play without cease; and on the ruins of the library a much bigger and more awe-inspiring one would take its place. Rebuilding would take time and great resources, but Numa swore—if he succeeded—he would leave Imperial City a city of marble, of brightly-painted statues, of grand temples, of joy and music and wine. From ruin it would rise grander than ever before.

"*Emperor!*" The sarcasm in the voice meant Shareeka was behind him—no one but the ratling dared to treat him with such disrespect. "Mighty bit of work these lawgivers did. So many wanted to see the Theomancer burned alive… they might be a bit angry at you, with only a beheading."

Numa turned to face the ratling. He was carrying a scroll in his hand.

"I stole this from the *kabakh* as the lawgivers fled. It has the snake symbol on its seal."

Numa took it and broke the seal—a crime punishable by death, if it were an Imperial one, but the snake insignia made it clear it belonged to the lawgivers.

He opened it, expecting foreign lawgiver writing, but found its instructions in Imperial lettering. *This,* Numa thought, *is meant for a traitor.*

"To Amal the Pious in Bregantium," he read aloud. *The false name of Crispus Servillius.* "It is with great regret that I announce the rebellion in Anthania remains strong. Focus all your effort on destroying Bregantium. When you are done, burn down its libraries as I have done, and then level all of it to the ground. Build a great *kabakh* so that you and your fellow-soldiers may worship."

Astarthe was approaching him, radiant in her blue silk garments.

"Marcus Otho has told me," Numa continued reading, "from Nichaeus, all the forts where the Imperial Army may be hiding. Capture those forts, and the rebellion shall be crushed. I have them listed below."

Some he vaguely recognized, like Fort Lorenus in the halfling kingdom—others he didn't, yet the directions were specific and exact.

"A gold mine?" Astarthe said.

"No," Numa answered her question. "I cannot leave Imperial City undefended. If I do, the lawgivers will demolish it in full."

Astarthe's eyes were sad, though thoughtful. "Whatever you command," she said. "You, after all, are the conqueror god… you are the Undying Glory, the Unconquered Son."

God. Glory. Unconquered Son. Numa bristled at the words. Those were all the things a boy from Norriva was not.

Shareeka snatched the letter away. "It *is* a gold mine, Numa. And if you don't have the manhood to follow up on it, then I do."

"I will leave a cohort to you—"

"Nonsense," Shareeka snapped. "You humans have no idea how to sneak, and skulk. I am going into enemy territory. Say a prayer to Imperium for me, Numa. I am going to need all the luck I can get."

"Farewell, friend," Numa said. The gaze of Shareeka softened—in all this time the ratling had never once called him friend.

Numa reached out his hand… and Shareeka grabbed it, then met him in an embrace. "Farewell, Emperor Numa… and good luck."

CHAPTER FIFTY-ONE: SALVATORE'S LAST CHARGE

Salvatore Jiovanucci, Grand Legate

The north gate of Bregantium at last buckled and cracked under the force of the battering ram. Flaming arrows from the lawgivers rained down on the city; there was only a century left. A century, and Salvatore.

Eyeing the hundred men who survived, who had endured hell for the past weeks and fought this losing battle, Salvatore raised his sword. For these men, many wounded, all thoroughly exhausted, he did his best to rally their spirits. "We will die as free Imperials! It does not matter whether history will record our fight. It does not matter whether the gods in heaven reward us. All that matters, my friends—"

The gate burst open.

"—is that we fight to our last breath, for our nation, for our people, for our way of life. Onward! For wine, for music! For empire!"

"Empire!" the men roared.

Salvatore led the charge into the black mass, dropping his shield halfway. He stabbed a lawgiver, then severed another's head. He slashed and cut wildly, even as an arrow pierced his shoulder. In front of him, a dozen yards away, Crispus Servillius the traitor viewed the battle from his litter. A dagger pierced Salvatore's side, but the sight of Crispus filled him with new rage. He slashed and hacked wildly with his sword.

He was within inches of cutting Crispus down when an axe took him in the chest. Bleeding, in the spasms of death, he knew that Imperium, on high, smiled at him; that he had given the battle his all; that he had died for the sake of the Empire, and that his death, somehow, would not be in vain.

CHAPTER FIFTY-TWO:
THE FALL OF BREGANTIUM

Crispus Servillius, August

In Bregantium, rocks flew at him from windows. Some emptied their chamber pots on the lawgivers. It did not matter; in time, Crispus knew full-well they would submit or die. Justice, and Mazda, demanded it. First, of course, they needed to root out the source of the problem—the government, which refused to yield.

At the Governor's Mansion, they were already waiting—the five councilors, that was, not the southron witch Astarthe. He recognized them all: Augusto Vitellian, Lucius Alba, Marco Geta, Niko Longus and Valerio Anderis. They were the lowest of the Augusts, representatives of the most minor of the noble families. They were scum, unable to understand true intellect. Crispus had been wise not to trust them.

"You have made your deaths very easy," Crispus said, and laughed at their stupidity.

"We accept our fate with honor," Vitellian said. "Honor and dignity… more than you ever exhibited. You are the betrayer of the Empire."

Crispus laughed again. "Not the only. There were many. I was merely the leader. Your armies are crushed. The Empire is gone. Everything you fought so hard to save has vanished into the wind. Soon all the Imperial books will burn, too, and there will be nothing left to remember what came before—"

"Burning books," Niko Longus sneered. "You once claimed to be a man of intellect and learning."

"There is no good or evil. There is nothing," Crispus repeated the tenets of Thenoan Philosophy. "There is nothing worth fighting for. Nothing worth dying for. Not even books… and certainly not the Empire."

"Know this, Crispus, when you put me to death," Vitellian said. "The Imperial Army remains strong. Most of it, we sent over the sea to Imperial City."

"You lie." Crispus felt himself go white. "The Imperial Navy is destroyed. That is impossible."

"I am not a worm like you. I do not lie," Vitellian said. "You will know, soon enough."

"*Kill them*!" Crispus howled, and the lawgivers fell upon them with scimitars.

A bloody, slashed mess he left them. He would not bury them as the Law of Maza demanded.

In the week that followed, many citizens slipped away from Bregantium. Others rebelled openly and met sudden deaths. The air of anger and resentment was palpable: resentment toward the lawgivers, yes, but also to Crispus.

He had taken up quarters in the Governor's Mansion after demolishing its statues and burning its once-fine paintings. Resting his old bones, he thirsted badly for a glass of wine. That was one thing he disliked about the Law of Mazda; but in the end it remained a small price to pay for the destruction of the Empire.

One morning on the balcony, his thoughts turned as they frequently had to the councilors' lie about the army, to Imperial City, to Priscilla. Trumpets blared. The mansion gates had opened, and in walked a woman dressed in a fine purple cloak, her face hidden by a hood. Crispus had a feeling it was Priscilla Marianus, the co-architect of the rebellion.

~

He met her in the entrance hall.

When she lowered her hood, a masked face greeted him—a tragic actor's mask, the one they wore in stage plays. Those had long been banned. Yet the voice which spoke belonged to Priscilla. "Signor Crispus."

"Amal the Pious," he answered her. "That is what they call me now." He paused, running his eyes along the fine black contours of the mask. "I cannot take you seriously, Priscilla, when you wear that."

"It is the Law of Mazda. A woman must be hidden," Priscilla said. "I made a commitment to the Theomancer. I made a commitment to him… and now he is dead."

Crispus thought his heart might rupture. "You are joking. The Theomancer—dead?"

"The oppressors have named a new emperor," Priscilla said. "While the lawgiver armies focused on Eloesus and… *here*… a great army arrived, took back the city, and now rules in the Imperial Palace. The common brown-bread citizens are *so* happy that their leader is a coward."

"A coward?" Crispus said. The news had weakened him, infused him with a deathly chill. "It seems daring. It seems brave… and maybe, just maybe, a little bit wise."

Priscilla's hand caught him off guard; her slap burned his cheek. "You compliment the oppressor?"

"You strike an old man?" Crispus answered. "I have killed for less."

"As have I," Priscilla snapped, and walked inside.

~

The bright summer sun filled Crispus' private room with light.

"Marcus is on his way, with Septimo and Jiacomo and the others," Priscilla told him. "It seems our friends in Nichaeus saw the omens long before the Theomancer."

"As did you," Crispus said.

"No flattery—that is what poisoned me against Cleon Adelphos."

"Where is Cleon?"

"I assume, dead. He did not reach Nichaeus, at least, before the Imperial Army swept in." Priscilla glanced out the window. "It is probably for the best. I had truly grown to loathe that man."

Just as Crispus had loathed using Marcus Otho in the coup. Yes, he had proven a useful asset, but Marcus Otho was, at heart, a military man; he had patrolled the seas, and sworn an oath to defend the Empire. His actions had poisoned Crispus Servillius against him, and no doubt, Priscilla, too, but she seemed less hateful toward him.

There was a knock at the door. "Come in!" Crispus shouted.

A group of lawgivers arrived, dressed in black and bearing gem-encrusted scimitars. These were the highest ranked lawgivers, the field marshals. They would not interrupt him without reason.

"Amal the Pious. The spirit of the Theomancer has left his body," one said. "His ghost has departed for the realm of fire, where he will judge the lawbreakers; but first, it told me this. You are the Theomancer, now. We, the community of the faithful, imbue you with his wisdom, with his power, with his desiccating hand."

"I… I don't know what to say…"

"Then say nothing." A ghost appeared around the field marshal, a white swirling spirit with only vaguely human features. A low moan echoed through the air, a strained and mournful sob. The air grew cold and quiet. Crispus backed away, suddenly unwilling to endure this. He hit the wall, trying to avoid the ghost, but it dove for him anyway, burrowed into his heart until it pounded out of control, until his breaths grew cold and shallow. Another person lived inside of him, a person that immediately began to whisper: *"Kill Nagal."*

Crispus lifted his hands, and one of the field marshals screamed. His skin and clothing began to dry out; all water vanished; he shrank, and then bit by bit, turned to sand. The field marshals clapped at the sight. Priscilla backed away and gasped, perhaps in horror.

Yet Crispus smiled. Now—regardless of the natural explanation of his newfound power—he was more equipped than ever to finish what he began, to utterly destroy and demolish the Empire he was born into.

CHAPTER FIFTY-THREE:
IN THE CITY OF STONE

Eudora Kyrillos

From the scorching desert around Carta Mega to the wheat and barley fields of Kheroe, she had traveled only a few days on her camel. Small villages appeared every mile, and the land was rich with life—plant, animal, and human. It seemed these country peasants had escaped the travail that plagued the Empire. Big towns appeared—some nearly as large as Carta Mega—but the Great King of Kheroe did not live anywhere nearby. No city was fit for the Great King except for Zoar, the City of Stone.

A week of easy traveling passed by along the dirt roads of Kheroe. The air had already grown oppressively hot; gnats gnawed at her constantly, sweat and grime soiled her once-fine gown, and she spoke the Kheroese tongue in a thick Carta Megan accent, but she had arrived, and for now, her hopes for success remained.

The City of Zoar overlooked the choppy western seas from a high precipice. To reach it, a traveler had to undertake an exhausting climb. From the low lands of the harbor to the top she struggled up stone steps for what seemed like an hour, always in view of the city's crowning achievement—a lighthouse that stretched four-hundred feet into the sky.

When at last she reached the city proper, she gasped at the sight, though she had been here before, and met the Great King, Magon. The buildings, carved from stone into a beehive-like shape, stretched thirty, sometimes forty feet in the air. All around it, the scent of spices wafted up from the harbor far below. The people looked so different from those in Carta Mega, though in history they were kin. These were pure Kheroans, unmixed like those of Carta Mega and the wider empire. They were short with beautiful coppery complexions, with raven hair dark as the night. Even the poor wore finery—if not silk, then linen dyed sky blues and ruby reds.

Twenty thousand souls called these great works of stone their homes. At the far end, against the rock mountain from which Zoar was carved, lay the palace of the Great King. She had been younger when she visited Magon's court, though the Great King had called her the apple of his eye. An endless stream of noblemen flocked to his court—from Zoar's Council of Elders and the Kheroe's wealthy bels to visiting dignitaries of the Empire, which had ruled it in all but name—yet Magon had delighted in Eudora's father most of all. They shared a loathing for the soft Secondo Janus, a hatred for the arrogant Augusts of the Imperial Council, and an equal desire for change. Magon wanted less interference from the Empire, while Lysander Kyrillos wanted strong Imperial leadership; yet a shared dislike for the status quo brought them together.

How terrible it would be when Eudora told Magon he was dead.

Eudora stuck out in the streets of Zoar, a lone Imperial in a sea of Kheroans. Some looked at her askance, but most only went about their business. In time she reached the palace of the Great King.

~

The guards—recognizing her from those early days—let her beyond the humble mountain door and into the opulence of the Great King's court.

On a throne King Magon sat, dressed in a rainbow robe of silk. Each layer of color gleamed with a different gem: sky-blue sapphires, flaming rubies, and forest-green emeralds. Gold thread interwove the raiment in vine-like patterns, and a golden sunray crown glistened on his head; yet when Eudora entered the room, his austere expression melted away. He stood up and shouted, "Eudora!"

"Uncle Magon," she called out to him, as she had long before, many years ago.

The Great King removed his sunray crown, revealing a head of bright gray hair. With eyes as warm as a grandfather's, he said, "It has been too long." He descended the steps of his throne and met her in an embrace. "You have grown… in height, and in beauty."

"And yet I come to you in desperate need," Eudora said.

"You may stay here forever, if you wish," Magon said. "You are like a daughter to me."

"My father is dead."

"Dead?" Magon gasped. "Lysander Kyrillos? I thought that man would never die."

"The lawgivers slew him, I know it. The lawgivers destroyed the legions, as they destroy everything—whatever came before, they demolish. Everything that is beautiful, everything that is joyous." She had begun to cry.

"Enough!" Magon snapped with a terseness that, in a hundred years, she did not expect. "Words such as those may cost you your life."

"And they already have!" A man's voice spoke Kheroan through an accent she did not recognize. A man had stepped from the shadows, dressed in black, with a scimitar clipped to his belt.

"Surely not!" Eudora backed away, head spinning. "Not here… not in the City of Stone." She turned around toward the exit. A dozen more lawgivers had appeared.

"I have done what I must to preserve our way of life," Magon said.

The world has gone mad. Eudora screamed some curse, indistinguishable even to her.

"She has blasphemed," the lawgiver said. "She must be burnt alive."

"*No!*" the Great King howled. "Under no circumstances will you take my Eudora's life. I view her as a daughter."

Yet in an instant he had become dead to her, a mortal enemy.

"She will be kept alive. She will be kept alive, or…" Magon

sounded spent. "Or I will revolt. You would win the war, but it would be unnecessary for you to struggle, all for the sake of one life. By the gods, she will be kept alive!"

"I want to go," Eudora muttered. "There is nothing for me here."

"You will not go," the lawgiver said. "And yet, our Great King has been too great an asset to follow Mazda's Law to the letter. She will be kept alive, in chains… in the dungeon."

"Gods preserve me," Eudora said. She did not know which was worse: a long death in the dark dungeon, or a blazing death by fire. One thing she knew above all else: all warm feelings toward Magon had vanished. Uncle Magon was, now and forevermore, her enemy.

The coward's eyes watered as she was led away.

CHAPTER FIFTY-FOUR:
BEST-LAID PLANS

Priscilla Marianus, Provost of the Thenoan Academy

"News," the messenger announced boldly in the presence of Priscilla, Crispus, and Marcus Otho. "Korthos has fallen; the Bluecloaks there have been slaughtered. The field marshal had held off on its destruction, awaiting further instruction from the Most High Theomancer. Do you, truly, want them to burn the libraries? You have a chance to stop this madness."

"Madness!" Crispus howled in rage. "I would turn you to sand now if I had half a mind. But you must relay this message. All the libraries must be burned. All books must be set to the torch. All remnants of the Empire must be destroyed; any evidence it existed, any so-called learning its people have uncovered. Anything that might shed doubt on the truth of Mazda must be eliminated."

He has changed, Priscilla thought. Yet she understood him. She supported him.

Across the room, Marcus Otho stood, looking less excited about the prospect of burning the library, maybe even a bit regretful. The stern Marcus Otho had the solemn features of a military man; gray peppered his brown hair, and he had the aquiline nose of an Imperial. Priscilla understood his use—the destruction of the Navy would have been impossible without him—yet she had a harder time than Crispus Servillius with accepting him. He was a military man, a man who killed, who had sworn an oath to defend the Empire. How could such a thing be forgiven?

The messenger left with a look of disgust on his face. *How dare he.*

And yet a shadow had already overcome the room—the shadow of the other bit of news they had received, which seemed to outweigh the destruction of the East.

"Southern Anthania," Crispus said, "lost. A young man from *Gad*, proclaiming the Empire's virtues in front of the brown-bread populace. Stirring them up against the forces of intellect, reason, and culture."

Servillius' words seemed at odds with his command to burn the Korthos libraries. It was a thing difficult even for Priscilla to reconcile—a symptom of her Imperial-centric upbringing, her Empire-tainted worldview.

"It is now summer," Servillius said. "We can sail briskly, with a bit of fortune from Mazda. A hundred thousand soldiers will put this minor rebellion at an end."

"I think that is too low," Marcus Otho offered. "Our strength is in our numbers. Man for man, the legions are better. The boy commands eighty-thousand—"

"*Imperial scum!*" Servillius howled like a shrieking ghost, his face a bright cherry red. He had become something other than human, something more frightening than a beast. His eyes burned with a hatred Priscilla had never seen in anyone.

Was it possible he hated the Empire more than she?

Impossible, she corrected herself.

Servillius reached out with his desiccating hand; Marcus dried up, then disintegrated. Priscilla stood alone with Servillius. She looked at the pile of sand, then at Crispus Servillius gloating at his victory. Chills ran up her spine at the sight of him; gooseflesh tore across her skin. Crispus had become someone altogether different, something more hateful than she had ever imagined.

But I hate the Empire as much as he.

Crispus fixed his eyes on her. "We will send one hundred thousand troops, no questions asked."

CHAPTER FIFTY-FIVE:
A NATION ARMED

Numa

Imperial City was, to a large extent, ruined. Yet a great darkness had left, and Numa could see it in the hordes of men and women returning. Each day, crowds of thousands filtered in along the Imperial Roads. These once proud Imperials now unswervingly accepted Numa as their emperor—*Numa*, a rustic from Norriva, the son of an invalid.

In Imperial Square he gave the order to his legates: "They will all be armed."

His legate Marcusio nodded. "Under Secondo Janus, the Empire began to confiscate the citizens' weapons."

Numa nodded. What a dark thought, that the Imperial Council had orchestrated the nation's fall. "Everyone shall have a sword and shield—man, woman, slave and free. We will all be warriors."

"And shall we build a wall around Imperial City?" asked his legate Valentus.

"No." Numa's answer drew some surprised looks from the legates. "We will not go backwards. We will not let the lawgivers turn us into a nation of fear. Imperial City will remain a city of peace and prosperity. When we fight, we will fight them on the open field or in the city streets—with an entire nation of soldiers."

Valentus smiled. "Indeed."

Imperial City was vast, but Numa always knew where to find Appian. He had taken to the water—as the new admiral of the Empire, he had learned to love the sea.

As Numa expected, Appian was there on the docks—with

Astarthe. He had not expected the southron queen. But there she was, sitting next to Numa with her feet in the water. She was laughing.

Appian and Astarthe? The thought of them together, a couple, elicited a chuckle from Numa—a chuckle that drew their attention.

"Where have you been, Numa?" Appian heaved his legs onto the dock and stood up, suddenly self-conscious. "Don't you have some grand scheme to plan? Don't you have an Empire to save?"

"We both do," Numa answered, and grinned.

Astarthe rose as well. "This Appian fellow knows more about Khazidea than the queen herself."

"Appian was always a bookworm," Numa said. "The biggest bookworm in Norriva."

Appian looked down, bashful.

"I have a mission for you." It had long been on Numa's mind. He did not want to put his friend in danger, but he could not see the Empire falter. "I want you to wreak hell on the lawgiver navy. I want you to make sure they never command the seas again. No doubt they have already blockaded Haroon again. Break the blockade of Haroon, and Eloesus, too. Work your magic again, Admiral Appian."

Appian laughed. "There is no magic, my signore. Just luck."

"Not luck," Numa answered.

"I will go with him," Astarthe said. "I have grown rather fond of this fat Getan boy."

Numa smiled. "May Imperium guide you."

He turned to leave. By the morning, Appian had departed with Astarthe and his sailors. Good for the Empire, Numa thought—but now he was alone to fight the nation's battles, without any close friends left.

~

Two weeks later—two weeks of constant forging, two weeks

of new arrivals to Imperial City—word arrived that an impossibly vast lawgiver army had landed on the shore.

CHAPTER FIFTY-SIX:
A GIFT FOR CLAUDIO

Days Later...

Tertio Araceli, Legate

Tertio was not a demigod, nor was he made of steel, as some of his soldiers thought. The news that Korthos had fallen had gutted him—he knew what the lawgivers had done to all previous cities. Libraries would burn; statues would be dashed to bits; all traces of culture would be exterminated. At least Pontio Piraeus had put up a pretense of culture and sophistication; at least he had left the libraries, academies, and temples alone. *Perhaps crucifying him was a mistake.*

Kersepoli lay within days of the same fate. Even here, in Imperiopoli, lawgivers massed around the city walls. Tertio stood in the city square, in view of a great limestone temple, its towering pillars stretching to the sky, its triangular roof gleaming with red tiles, its pediment bearing the words GRAND TEMPLE OF THE IMPERIAL CULT. Tertio had never believed emperors were truly gods; he thought it pure superstition. Yet what did he have to lose, seeking wisdom before its giant statues, reflecting in the quiet solitude?

Ten braziers lit the way before the giant statue of Claudio-Valens Adamantus. The stone effigy depicted a very young man, twenty perhaps, with short-cut hair and a proud masculine nose; his eyes, even here in this statue, seemed to pierce the soul, to see through all lies and all falsehoods. His stone breastplate bore the Imperial war eagle.

Breathless, Tertio approached the statue. An offering plate was piled high with gold coins, jeweled rings, and silver necklaces. At the base of the statue lay a stone tablet with words etched into it:

CLAUDIO-VALENS, THE UNCONQUERED SON
THE GOD OF PATRIOTISM, OF IRON WILL, AND OF REFUSAL TO SURRENDER, WHO GUIDES OUR NATION TO THIS DAY.

"Do you guide our nation to this day?" Tertio spoke aloud. A few dark-garbed worshipers turned to look at him in the shadows. He continued to speak nonetheless. "Our nation is on the brink of annihilation. What kind of god are you, Claudio-Valens? Perhaps the Thenoan Philosophers are right."

There is no good, no evil; there is nothing. The words tasted bitter in his mouth, sent him closer to despair.

"Claudio-Valens will guide us." A female worshipper stood there, her face darkened by a hood. "The purposes of the god Claudio are inscrutable to the mortal eye. Yet they wind their way to new hope, to prosperity."

Her words sounded desperate to Tertio, the last cries of a doomed animal before it is slaughtered. If there had ever been gods in heaven, they were dead.

"Make an offering," the worshipper continued. "Make an offering, and perhaps he will save us."

"Like hell he will." The words seethed with anger, anger this woman did not deserve. Yet nonetheless he crossed the distance to the offering plate and emptied his pockets—all his silver denara and copper aesa, down to the last coin. They were useless—the effort was mere showmanship, a desperate plea to a pile of ashes in a limestone urn, to a long-dead mortal man, to a god who did not exist.

He turned and walked away from the statue, leaving the worshipers behind, out of the Grand Temple of the Imperial Cult, overcome with despair.

~

In the bright-skied day, one of his soldiers came rushing up to him. Basil met his joyful smile with a snarl—anger that anyone could possibly be happy on a day such as this.

"Signor Prince, the blockade is broken."

The words did not lift his dark mood in the slightest.

"Anthania has been retaken. Emperor Numa now sits enthroned in Imperial City. And yet… Bregantium has fallen."

Even the good news had failed to soothe his soul; the bad news he had expected.

"The ships have docked in the harbor. The sailors have brought some food. The admiral calls himself Appian—and the southron queen is with him, Astarthe."

Tertio Araceli had never liked the fact that Claudian Adamantus gave Astarthe back her throne. Yet perhaps now, seeing her love for the Empire, perhaps his edict had been wise; perhaps he had installed a woman devoted to the cause of the nation.

Nonetheless, Tertio cursed his fate, marooned here with ten thousand, fighting a force twice his number. *The gods are dead,* he thought, *and Claudio-Valens is a pile of ashes in a limestone urn, nothing more.*

CHAPTER FIFTY-SEVEN:
THE NOBLE AND THE GOOD

Janno Kerius, August

Thousands of lawgivers walked in front of Kerius. He rode, as he preferred, behind the screaming mob of warriors. Their cries, and the commotion that—he had heard—followed a battle, would injure his old ears.

"I hear the common folk say Numa is Claudio-Valens Adamantus, reborn," said his protégé, the young Alexus Caro. "A typical brown-bread thought. They are so simple minded, so naïve."

"Claudio-Valens was an oppressor, a destroyer," Kerius said. This long ride from the ships to the edge of Imperial City had made him sweat; no doubt his gray hair had grown untidy and tousled. "Imperials have never known how to deal properly with other nations; they have always been rude warriors, uncivilized, unwilling to consider any other opinions beside their own."

Kerius wished they could take a rest. His legs had grown saddle-sore after these many hours of riding. He needed a mirror and a comb. He had spent many hours on the ship attempting to touch up his hair, but now all that effort had gone to waste.

"Do you know what else the brown-bread say?" Alexus said.

"What?" Kerius could also use a touch of powder. They helped hide his wrinkles. A government man simply had to look good, even in the midst of a war—it had been rule number one of politics, back when he lived in Imperial City.

"They say the Law of Mazda is barbaric."

"The Empire has never been able to seat itself in the grand table of nations." He had put little thought into those words. What he wouldn't give for a pair of tweezers. He recalled earlier in the morning, when they'd hopped off the ship, he had seen an untidy hair sticking out of his eyebrow. He hadn't thought about it too much at the time—

he'd been too occupied with disembarking from the ship. It was so typical, to realize it now, when his cosmetics kit was packed somewhere deep in his luggage.

They had entered the suburbs—the tight-packed towns, the grim concrete apartment blocks. They'd grown empty, now. On the side of one of the apartment blocks, some imbecile had painted offensive words: "*Mazda is a cross-dressing pig!*"

A few cries of anger arose from those who could read Imperial writing. "Stay the course!" Kerius hollered. "The community of nations will have its vengeance soon enough!"

Eventually the angry cries died down. They continued down the road in the baking hot sun, drawing near Imperial City proper.

"Why would anyone write that?" Alexus Caro asked. "Why would anyone ever be intentionally hurtful? Why would anyone purposefully offend? The Imperials are such bullies."

"Stop!" Kerius shouted at the top of his lungs. The field marshals gave the orders. Kerius dismounted and dug through the saddlebag. At last his prying fingers found the cosmetics kit. He propped it against the saddle, opened it and grabbed the mirror. "Gods!" he said. His hair had grown wild. He straightened it with a comb. He dashed a bit of powder on his face, watched the wrinkles quickly dissipate. He grabbed the tweezers and plucked the hairs that stuck out so stubbornly against his wishes. He softened his lips with a damp towel, and then colored them just a touch with some balm. At last he looked presentable. He packed the items back into the kit, shut it, and dropped it in the saddlebags. At last, he could continue and focus.

Yet when he mounted his horse again, a commotion had overtaken the front lines. Curious, he rode all the way to the front, leaving poor Alexus behind, and found a field marshal at the front, talking with a pair of a hundred lawgivers.

"Your Highness!" one of them shouted—perhaps to Kerius.

"I have just spoken with your underling Umaz. There are still lawgivers in Anthania—quite a huge number of us native converts. There are fifty thousand of us. We have inside information. We want to help you."

"It is good to see native Imperials joining the community of nations. Yes, we can use your help," Kerius answered.

Umaz looked up at him, eyes unsure. "Very well," he said. "Lead us there… try anything, and we will burn you alive."

"We would never commit a deed so egregious." The native lawgivers turned down a different road than they were expecting. Kerius kept still on his horse, allowing the entire army to pass him by. He rode in the very back with Alexus Caro. War was not suitable for an August; since the Empire's founding the ignoble, the uneducated, and the underprivileged had served in battle. Besides, in the heat of battle the effort he had poured into perfecting his appearance might prove fruitless. He had never seen a battle or read much about them, but he imagined they were nasty things.

For hours Kerius followed in the train of the army. The day grew hotter and hotter; the sun beat down hard and reflected on the road. Kerius imagined throwing himself into the sea to cool off. No matter how much he drank from his canteen, he only grew hotter and hotter, more and more miserable. He wondered why in Varda he had agreed to this, why he had told Crispus Servillius he would do this. *It will be easy,* he had promised Kerius. *The Imperials are worthless dogs.*

It was late afternoon when the soldiers stopped their marching. "What is going on?" A lawgiver hollered. "Why are we stopped?"

Kerius looked up toward the glaring sun. Huge rows of concrete apartment blocks towered above-head. It dawned on him, they were just outside the city precincts, in a two-mile stretch of road dominated by the housing of the urban poor. The Imperial government had housed the refuse in these towering buildings, these folk who worked menial jobs or fed off the city's free Khazidean bread like parasites.

The uproar grew. Kerius looked around, then looked behind—and caught the glittering war-eagle banners of the Imperial Army. Thousands marched toward them. Kerius uttered a wild scream. *"Look out, Alexus!"*

Alexus turned back, screamed, then galloped ahead in a panic. As a column of Imperial horse charged the lawgivers, Kerius followed Alexus' lead, galloping ahead. Archers appeared on top of the apartment blocks and arrows fell like rain. One arrow took his horse in the side, then another whizzed an inch away, nearly taking off Kerius' thigh. He tried to dismount but only fell hard onto the ground, bruising some bone he did not know. "We've been betrayed!" Kerius screamed, though he did not know to whom. A maelstrom of death had consumed them; the Imperial horsemen were dashing the lawgivers down like lambs to the slaughter. Every second, another dozen lawgivers fell to Imperial arrows. Unable to walk, Kerius dragged himself across the road, toward the relative safety of an apartment block. Blood began to flow, a red river carrying bodies with it. Where rain was meant to trickle down, blood instead fell into the sewers. Desperate screams rang through the hot summer air, but the cries of Imperial triumphalism overwhelmed it, the rabid cheers of the victorious oppressors, the jubilant roar of a people who—despite the best efforts of the noble and the good—had, at least in this skirmish, won. The slaughter of the horsemen continued, and death swept Kerius by as he hauled himself into the cool of the apartment block. The red river sloshed bodies across the way. The arrows continued, raining hard as ever.

Death had consumed them. *Death.*

CHAPTER FIFTY-EIGHT:
HELD CAPTIVE

Numa

The death of a hundred thousand lawgivers with only ten Imperial casualties was a grand accomplishment even Shareeka couldn't deny, if he had been there. Yet Numa's heart weighed heavy for those lives lost, for those ten lives that mattered. A red river now flowed through the streets of Imperial City, and the battlefield—once a residential area for the urban poor—lay thick with bodies.

The disposal of these countless corpses would prove a confounding logical task. Yet the victory, Numa thought as he rode beside the flooded street, was undeniable.

"Signor Emperor!" A tribune had come, girt in a standard-issue breastplate and a horsehair-crested helmet. In his steel gauntlets he gripped the hand of an old man, dressed in lawgiver blacks but clearly Imperial. His skin had the wrinkles of an old man; his eyes, the aloof stare of a nobleman, an August.

Numa did not know the man's name, nor did he care. He was merely an enemy. "Who is this?"

"Councilor Janno Kerius, Your Undying Glory," he answered.

He was the first traitor to refer to Numa that way. Yet nonetheless he remembered the name on the list of traitors. "Why were you with the lawgivers, Signor Kerius?"

"I was held captive, Your Undying Glory," Kerius said. He was a good liar. "Now I am free—and I thank you."

"Deceit is second nature to the Augusts; no word from their mouths can be trusted." Numa glared at Kerius, yet the former councilor put on a brave face. "The way of the Council House, I hear, was lies, but no more. You will no longer lie to the people. You are a traitor, Kerius, and I have ample evidence. I hold you captive. A punishment awaits you, Kerius—a punishment you cannot even begin to imagine."

The austerity vanished from Kerius' face for a moment, yet he regained it quickly. The blood had drained from his face. His gray hair was intricately combed; his face was softened with powder. "Signor Numa, I do not know the customs of Gad, but in the Empire, no punishment may be delivered to a citizen without trial. I am certain, before a justice, I will be proven innocent."

"No man that fights against his own nation can be considered a citizen." Numa's blood burned within him. "I strip you of citizenship, Kerius."

"Impossible!" he squawked.

"From here-on, you will be considered a slave; no, worse. A captive of war. You will stay in prison until the time of your punishment… you will be fed the poorest of fare… you will sleep in the roughest of beds."

"Not without trial!"

"Be gone, worm." The tribune led him away despite his wild protests.

A quick death might be more sensible, but a grand display was needed… a grand display Numa had yet to devise.

~

In the end they burned the bodies, clothing and all, in a field outside the city. The process took days, but when a column of smoke rose high above Numa, toward the sky, he knew that Imperium in highest heaven smelled the pleasing burnt offering, the gift of traitors' blood.

From the sheaths of the dead lawgivers, a hundred thousand citizens were armed with scimitars, men and women both. For once Numa had a bare flicker of hope.

~

The next night they fell upon the city of Nichaeus in the dark hours. The garrison of lawgivers was far too small to resist, and quickly fell to Imperial swords. The home port of the Imperial Navy, the Empire's ancient military town, now lay in Imperial hands. Soldiers seized the registry, the archives, and the docks in one rapid operation; yet with the dawn a new surprise awaited him.

Numa had thought the lawgivers did not bring their families with them—either that, or they sprang up, spawned from holes in the ground—yet in the light of day the women and children appeared, begging for mercy.

The mob of newly-armed citizens were thirsty for blood. "We will make them suffer as we suffered!" a woman screamed.

"I want to see them bleed!" a man howled.

"No!" Numa shouted, surprising even himself. Yet he was certain of what to do; he was an Imperial, not a barbarian. "The women and children will be kept alive."

"Thank you! Thank you!" A fat lawgiver woman, her body completely covered in cloth, fell to her knees and knit her hands together. "Thank you, merciful emperor! *Thank you!*"

Numa turned from her, still unwilling to befriend a lawgiver. No doubt many hundreds of thousands of women hid within apartment blocks in Nichaeus and the greater area surrounding it. He understood full-well the mob's desire to put them all to the sword, but an Imperial mob was still Imperial, still better than barbarians.

From the archives, a few days' search did not unveil much—except reports on the steady removal of all weaponry in the years preceding the coup, the steady reduction of the Imperial Army, the steady destruction of seaworthy ships. The entire calamity had been elaborately planned and perfectly executed, so well and so completely that even now the Empire hung by a thread.

Still, I might fail Imperium. Still, the traitors may win.

CHAPTER FIFTY-NINE: HAUNTED MEMORIES

Priscilla Marianus, Provost of the Thenoan Academies

It did not matter whether Priscilla was waking or sleeping, whether she hid within the confines of the palace or walked the streets in the still-seething, still-resentful Bregantium; the image of Bregantium's library, burning, had seared an image forever in her mind, an image she wished to forget. She thought of the histories that might shed light on the Empire's evil behavior, forever lost; she thought of the books of geometry, mathematics, and natural science now burned to husks; she thought of her own books, widely circulated throughout the Empire's libraries and booksellers, discussed by intellectuals in every city, gone forever. She thought of the burning library, and felt a heavy burden of regret.

Regret that the library burned, yes. Regret that all that knowledge was permanently lost. Yet there were other regrets—memories of the life she had forever left behind, as a writer of philosophical texts, a traveling speaker. Yet that world—the Empire—was forever gone, and only its memory lived on. It was her hand that had stricken the death blow.

Looking out from the balcony onto the steep roofs of Bregantium, seeing its cobblestone streets and its brick buildings mostly silent and empty, she reminded herself that she had done the world a service. She should not—and would not—feel regret. Yet spending all this time with Crispus Servillius—a man she thought she knew, but did not—put all her exuberance to the test.

Yes, he represented what blind patriots called the "sickness" that "infected" the Imperial Council—a concern for its unfair power over the world, a desire to see its strength removed, a determination to give other nations concessions—but of late, his faith in Mazda had begun to seem genuine. His derision for Priscilla grew more and more severe; his demeanor exuded woman-hatred worse than even the old Theomancer, and his right-hand man Umar. It baffled her that Crispus Servillius—a man educated at the Thenoan Academy, who up until now had shown every inclination of scholarship and wisdom—now truly believed in Mazda and his supposed law.

Now, observing the silent streets of Bregantium, Priscilla had an itch to remove the mask that hid her face. Yet if she did, Crispus would fly into a wild rage. His anger had grown legendary among the lawgivers; he used his powers of desiccation and drying impulsively. Priscilla could not risk his rage. No one could.

She looked over Bregantium, the same Bregantium that had stood over a thousand years—the same Bregantium, yet not the same. She thought of the life, the Imperial world that had been lost. She had, at last, accomplished her goal; but what was there for her, now? The Academies of Eloesus were in all likelihood burning; the books, scrolls, and tomes of learning were no doubt engulfed in flames. The old world had passed away, and in its wake a new one had arrived.

"Whatever comes after the Empire," she muttered to herself, "it cannot be worse than what came before."

The door behind her opened. She hoped to gods it wasn't Crispus. She turned, and met the eyes of Umar.

The lawgiver captain could have been handsome, if his black beard and wild hair were cut off. But as of now, he looked like a wild-man of the woods, unfit for love, unfit for anything except war and survival. "I have left just in time, my sweet Priscilla," he said. "The news has just reached Crispus. He turned the messenger to dust."

"What news?" Priscilla asked, feeling herself go cold.

"A massacre. An ambush. A hundred thousand of our men, gone in an instant." Umar looked strangely jubilant.

Priscilla's gut clenched.

"He did not send enough soldiers to fight," Umar said. "Our strength is in numbers, not in skill."

"Marcus Otho said that." But Marcus Otho was dust, forever gone from the Empire. Crispus Servillius had ensured it.

Umar does not like Crispus. Priscilla could see it in his eyes. "No doubt he will send me to right this wrong. He will sit in a cushioned room and let me fight his battles."

"Do not speak of the Most High Theomancer so," Priscilla snapped, though she believed it herself.

"I am going for a walk. The streets need patrolling." Umar smiled at her. She shirked at his glance, turned around and looked away.

CHAPTER SIXTY:
SECRET MEETING

Massimo Tivernas, Imperial Agent

The Poison Arrow Inn had an unfortunate name, and a more unfortunate reputation. Now, with the sale of alcohol banned, not even its few regulars bothered coming. No one was there, not even the innkeeper—no one except Massimo, sitting alone in the Poison Arrow's Red Room.

At last his scheduled guest arrived, dressed in lawgiver blacks. A scimitar hung from his side in a sheath. Massimo was in great danger, yes, but the Empire was in far worse, and far more meaningful danger. "Signor Snake's-Eye." As part of the agreement Massimo promised to never use his name. "I am so glad to see you."

"Enough with the small talk," he said. "What is your offer?"

"One-hundred gold libra."

"Gold means nothing to a lawgiver," Snake's-Eye answered. "The only metal with value is iron."

"Would you like iron, Snake's-Eye?"

"Don't be foolish, Massimo."

"I can offer you a villa in Paradise Gardens, with ample space for a farm, and slaves to staff it."

"What else?"

"The Servillius family townhome in Peregoth. The Servillius family mansion in Kings Terrace."

"An Imperial wife," Snake's-Eye said. "Ten Imperial wives."

"Polygamy is not allowed in the Empire, nor will it ever be." On that issue, Massimo was firm. He could lie, certainly, but he had every intention of holding his end of the deal, if Snake's-Eye held up his.

"Very well," Snake's-Eye said. "An Imperial wife. One wife. And I want a seat on the Imperial Council."

"If you are elected, Snake's-Eye, you can have one. But I can elevate you to the August class, and that is all."

"Then we have a deal," Snake's-Eye said. "Tell no one about this, not even your friends."

"Of course not, Snake's-Eye. I have better sense than that."

CHAPTER SIXTY-ONE:
AN END FOR THE EMPIRE

Crispus Servillius, August

In the dark of night they set out. With the lawgivers having lost control of the seas, the grand field marshal Umar decided a land journey was best; and so, they marched the road. Three-hundred thousand lawgivers in and around the city fell into rank. Crispus went with them, carried aloft on a litter, to finish the task he had begun long ago—to destroy the Empire his teachers had taught him to hate, that his friends had sworn a pact to eradicate one summer night long ago, in Paradise Gardens.

He still remembered that summer, sitting in the solarium with a then-young Septimo Seánus. They sat there, glasses of sweetwine in hand—a drink he had, of late, foregone—and spoke of the Empire, its dark and violence-laden history, its unjust practices. All in one summer night, they had realized everything the August class was supposed to uphold, everything the Knightly class was supposed to defend, truly wasn't worth fighting for. Crispus' father, Primo, had only a tangential sense of patriotism. Primo had loathed the Adamanti family and all they represented; he had spoken nothing but ill of the emperor Claudian.

"That fool halfwit," Primo Servillius had said. "His only virtue… he's the son of a rustic from Gad, from a family without any prior distinction." And Primo had loathed Claudio-Valens Adamantus above all.

Claudio's predecessor, Emperor Julio Seánus, had made plenty of terrible mistakes… fighting for the Empire's interests in Zoar, for one, and supporting the military. But Julio had been infinitely better, Father said, than Claudio, who rebelled against the wishes of the Imperial Council, even executed them.

When I have full control over the Empire, Servillius thought as the litter swayed to and fro, *I will hunt down every last Adamantus, every last blood relative of Claudio.* The only one who had any rights to the White Throne was the son of the southron witch, Astarthe, but Servillius would go further. He would research the genealogies of the Adamanti, discover who married whom, and would hunt down and kill every last one. He would not spare anyone related by marriage; to love an Adamantus was to love the Empire.

Down the road the army marched, down the great road toward Anthania, toward Imperial City, toward the heart of empire.

~

Days later—or was it weeks?—in the hot dry weather of the Central Valley, where the sun baked the bright gold grass, an eagle soared above the army. *An eagle,* a parched Crispus Servillius thought, *the symbol of the Empire.* The symbol of the nation he had sworn to destroy on that hot summer night, years and decades and life ages ago.

Servillius lifted up his left hand, which had grown rigid and stone-gray with his newfound power. He dried the eagle to its most infinitesimal part; it fell to the ground as dust, as sand.

"Crispus!" The army had stopped its marching, and Umar had drawn close; Crispus had been so distracted by the eagle to notice. "We must change our route. If we continue this path we will walk into an ambush. One of our men betrayed us."

"The Path of Tidus is open and free from ambush." The treason did not surprise Crispus—pay a man enough money, and he will do anything—though an ambush on this road seemed highly unlikely.

"I will not risk it," Umar said. "The Imperials are crafty. They cannot be trusted. They do not act like normal men."

"Indeed," Crispus growled. Yet still, it seemed unlikely to him. Regardless, he trusted Umar's judgment. "Who is the traitor?"

"He is gone, Crispus." Umar's tone was harsh, final. "He confessed and then ran off."

Crispus did not have time to deal with the threat. The damage, after all, had been done—and corrected. "Lead on, field marshal. Lead on, to victory."

CHAPTER SIXTY-TWO: LAST CHANCE

Numa

The lawgivers outnumbered them more than three to one. On equal footing they would be slaughtered, and a new empire would take the nation's place, a nation under the Law of Mazda. All hope hinged on this ambush, this last desperate maneuver, Numa thought as he surveyed the eighty thousand soldiers bunched around him. *All hope on a lawgiver's word… all hope on a turncoat's promise.*

A week would come before they took this last chance, this last hope, this last cast of the die.

CHAPTER SIXTY-THREE:
A MEMORY OF LIFE

Priscilla Marianus, Provost of the Thenoan Academies

The riots had broken out just hours after the lawgivers left Bregantium. Complete disorder had consumed the streets. Lawgiver women and children—those that had journeyed here, to the far north—had met terrible fates at the hands of the Imperial mob. If an Imperial ruler knew one thing, it was to fear the mob. In a world such as this, loud and violent rabble held unthinkable power. In a world such as this, the windows of the Governor's Mansion she hid in had been boarded up after the mob shattered them. The city was in chaos, and the rule of law was exchanged for carnage, violence, and brutality. The anger of the Imperial mob was something Priscilla could feel even here, in this fortified mansion. It was overwhelming.

"Priscilla!" a lawgiver met her in the upper room. "An Imperial wishes to speak with you. He is unarmed. I've checked him for blades. He says he has information."

"Send him up here," Priscilla said, not knowing why, but only wanting to see the face of an Imperial after all these long, dark days, after Crispus Servillius, after Jiacomo and Septimo and the others.

It was shameful to admit her desire. Still, Priscilla wanted nothing more than to see the Empire crushed. But still, she had grown tired of the entire situation. Her emotions threatened to overwhelm her, to cloud her judgment.

Minutes later he arrived, an Imperial with dark brown hair, wearing plain, un-dyed clothes of wool. "Signora Priscilla… why are you wearing a mask?"

"Enough!" she cried.

He turned, shut the door.

If I die now, so be it.

"Signora, I bring some news."

"Speak, then. Do not waste my time," Priscilla snapped.

"I want restitution in the world to come... the world of Mazda. If I spill a secret, you must reward me, no?"

Priscilla sighed. "Another traitor."

The Imperial smiled. "Just like you." The glowing expression evaporated. "Signora, your cause has been betrayed. There is a traitor, even among traitors."

"Traitors seem to spring up wherever I go."

"Umar, the one you call field marshal, is leading you into an ambush. My friend Massimo told me in confidence, but he has misplaced his faith in me."

She had grown to loathe this man, this man who was helping her. This man who was telling him a life-changing truth. "Umar? Surely not."

"Umar, indeed. The one you count on even now. You must ride to Crispus and tell him before it is too late... tell him, and reward me."

Priscilla shut her eyes and did not open them for a few long seconds. In the silent darkness she saw a terrible vision, a vision of knowledge lost, of a culture destroyed, of libraries in flame, of theaters demolished, of academies converted into religious schools. Then, in the vision, she looked at her hand and saw that it was covered in blood; the blood of the nation she had murdered. *It is all my doing.*

"Signora?"

"Who else knows? Have you told anyone else?"

"None but you, signora. None but you."

In her mind's eye, the Library of Thénai was burning... so many books set aflame that a great fireball rose up. The black smoke wafted up and coalesced into words, words that sent a shudder through her very being: *All this, by Priscilla's hand.*

"I would ride away at once," the traitor said. "He may have gotten far already."

Priscilla remembered her life as a little girl, vowing to make something of herself, vowing to become a scholar against all the pressures of her sex. She had achieved it… she had become leader of the Academies. And now look… look what she had done. She had used her power to destroy everything she had known. She had brought the Empire to its destruction. A thought—a tiny whispering thought—entered her mind that perhaps she was wrong, that there were worse things than the Empire, that what came after may not be as good as what came before. "Signore," she told the traitor. "Shut the door. We must discuss this."

As he obeyed the command, she walked to the window, grabbed the curtain and yanked it free.

Deep down she knew what she intended to do, yet still her conscious mind failed to grasp it. With his back still turned, she wrapped the cloth around his neck. His scream was softened by her tightening pull. She harnessed all her rage, all her frustration, all her anger and disappointment in herself, all the thoughts of libraries burning, and focused on this task with all her might. The struggle to snuff out this man's life took her across the room and back again, breaking priceless porcelain dishes, upturning tables and sending a trail of silverware everywhere; the struggle lasted many minutes, but eventually the traitor gave up his spirit.

Exhausted, she stumbled backward and screamed. She had failed in so many ways. Yet she had not failed in this. She screamed again, then removed the tragic actor's mask and threw it to the floor.

CHAPTER SIXTY-FOUR:
THE EMPIRE'S END

Tertio Araceli, Legate

A day, perhaps, from its inevitable destruction, Tertio nonetheless stood guard faithfully over Imperiopoli. The gods had failed him. The gods had failed everybody. The gods were nothing, and Claudio-Valens Adamantus was just a pile of ashes in a limestone urn. All the people's prayers to gods human and divine had been rejected. There was nothing, only death.

A face appeared in the crowd, a face Tertio thought he had seen before. It was an Imperial face, not southron. It was an old face, wrinkled, with eyes that indicated an old spirit, a spirit that should be wiser than to join the lawgivers.

Perhaps I am the fool. And yet this man wore a purple sash around his lawgiver attire. This man had once been a noble, even a councilor. Perhaps a nation that produced a man such as this had little hope; but Tertio would do all he could to see this man fail, to see him suffer. When the lawgivers finally broke through the gate, Tertio would seek this one out and cut his throat.

But all hope was gone. There was nothing left. The Empire would die. But Tertio would not live to see that day; he would fight to his last breath. To die was better than to see failure.

CHAPTER SIXTY-FIVE:
AMBUSH

Numa

At night they fell upon the lawgivers, and Numa led the charge. In the span of a minute a hundred died, before any had woken up. Yet they readied themselves quickly, drew the swords they slept with. In an instant the eighty-thousand legionaries began to see resistance. In the heat of the battle a lawgiver swung a mace and crushed the head of Numa's horse, and the beast fell. Numa rolled to the ground, felt grass already thick with blood. He stood up to a scene of frenzy, of wild fighting and a bit of panic. A cudgel hit him in the head; he fell to the floor, to a bed of blood. He had failed. The Empire itself had failed. The Empire was dead.

~

The bones of his brothers-in-arms formed wings, and Numa flew on them, from the sight of the disaster to the starry heights above.

On a cloud, dancing to the rhythm of drums, was the very one he had expected. Io the Oracle danced, her naked body entwined with a snake, her hips pounding to the drums, her skin lathed in sweat.

"Am I dead?" Numa asked. "Have I gone to heaven?"

"Quiet, Claudio. You are a fool. You have not earned heaven… yet. The Empire is not saved."

"The Empire is lost!"

Her eyes blazed with an anger that undid Numa, that sent him tumbling toward the ground. "I would have expected better from you, Claudio-Valens Adamantus. I have never known you to give up."

"I won't give up. But what can I do? What can I possibly do?"

"Go to Imperial City," Io answered. "Then, you will know."

"I won't see defeat—I will not bear it."

"Then go to Imperial City," Io snapped. "Go to Imperial City and behold your handiwork."

"My handiwork?" The words baffled him, tasted empty in his mouth. Failure was palpable, even here on the roof of the world. He had done his best to save the Empire, but the cause was lost.

"Go, Claudio-Valens Adamantus. Do not wash the blood that drenches your clothing, the red gold that drips from your sword and armor."

"Io…" His failure was a heavy burden, the weight of a mountain.

"To kill is to be a man; to shed blood is to be a patriot. Ride all night and all day… do not stop for water or food. In Imperial City, ride through the Walk of Triumph. Then you will see the end result of your handiwork… a new empire."

"An empire of lawgivers."

Her eyes blazed with inconsolable, insane rage. Her body transformed into that of a leopard—a leopard with the feet of a bear and the mouth of a lion, and iron claws. She dashed toward him, tore him to pieces, removed every bit of cowardice, every bit of bad faith, every bit of him that questioned his love for the Empire.

~

The day had grown late, the air hot and thick with the stench of blood and death. Numa rose above the field of slaughter. The twitching bodies of lawgivers and Imperial soldiers lay before him. The blood reached to his ankles. The pines that surrounded him—in the thicket of the Iron Mountains where the lawgiver armies had been led—dripped, too, with blood and flesh. Yet over the bodies— rammed into the body of a lawgiver—was a war-eagle banner of the Empire.

The Imperials had not lost the battle, it seemed—they had merely left, thinking Numa was dead. He removed the iron helmet from his head. A horse approached, a roan charger whose rider had died. Without a second's thought, Numa hopped on and urged it forward, riding down the mountain toward Imperial City, which lay only a day's journey away.

~

The hours bled into each other, endless as Numa galloped, then trotted down the Path of Tidus. He had grown mad with thirst, yet still he did not stop to drink as the sun dawned in red colors over the eastern sky. It was not until evening when he arrived at the Path of Tidus, and found himself in a city gone wild.

CHAPTER SIXTY-SIX:
THE BEGINNING OF THE END

Numa

The citizens of Imperial City—all armed—had set upon the lawgivers with an irate fury. Blood sprayed even the lofty statues of the Walk of Triumph, and the corpses of the Empire's enemies lay around the street, discarded like trash.

Numa, still in the Imperial Circlet, still with *Imperium's Rebuke* in his hand, rode quickly with increasing worry, unwilling to believe what he saw, still denying that the Empire had won.

"Hail Numa!" a woman cried.

"Hail Numa! Hail our emperor!" a man screamed, gripping a head by the hair.

"Hail Numa!" someone cried at regular intervals, as he guided the horse through the streets, indirectly yet inevitably toward Imperial Square.

~

There, those lawgivers who surrendered lay entrapped by the furious mob, protected only by Imperial soldiers intending to keep order. Numa rode past his brothers-in-arms, where the surviving lawgivers—no more than a thousand remaining—stood rigid, eyes shallow with fear. Yet these were not southrons; these were Imperials all, the ones who had abandoned their nation for security and safety yet would—Numa swore—lose everything. Perched high on the fountain, his foul magic held at bay by a group of nearby augurs, stood the architect of the treason.

Crispus Servillius was an ancient man, his face wrinkled like a prune, his black eyes terrified, yet nonetheless holding a hatred for Numa and everything Numa represented.

"The game is up. The die is cast, and the day is won," Numa said. "Not by you. The true lawgivers fought to the end, and fell to the slaughter. They are not the true enemy. The true enemy is you, all of you… the ones who dare to hate the Empire, who switched sides when it became convenient for you. Of all creatures that slither about the earth, you are the lowest of the low. And you will receive traitors' deaths. Each one of you will suffer unimaginably."

"Please!" one screamed. "I have a family!"

"And so did your victims. You will all perish in unimaginable pain." Numa's anger was only building, his blood heating to a boiling point.

"Hail Numa!" the crowd surrounding the square had begun to chant in unison. "Hail Numa!"

"You have lost, Crispus. You have lost, Julio Seánus. You have lost, Septimo, and all the August classes… all the so-called noblemen who sought to destroy the nation that gave them their comfort, their privilege."

Two men, nearly as old as Crispus, yet wearing the same lawgiver blacks, snarled at his words. "You are a rustic from Norriva!" one hissed. "You should be tending to swine, stomping grapes in a vineyard."

"I would react in anger," Numa answered the worm, "but you will learn to regret your words… your words, and actions. All of you will. You will all be driven mad by the time I am done with you… yet your desperate pleas for mercy will fall on deaf, nay, hostile ears." He struggled to quiet his anger, his desire to see them slain. But he would not just slay these men; he would make an example of them for the ages. "This," he shouted, "is the beginning of the end for all your plans… the beginning of the end for traitors, and a great and glorious beginning for the Empire.

~

From that day onward, the ceaseless barrage of bad news

became an endless stream of good.

"Bregantium has revolted against the lawgivers… a mighty slaughter in the streets!" a sailor told him the next day.

"The lawgivers have retreated from Eloesus!" another said the next day. "They are heading south, toward Khazidea and Fharas!"

Khazidea, Numa thought. That alone remained the troubled point—the breadbasket of the Empire, ravaged by raiders. He would kill every last raider; he would obliterate them from the face of the earth.

CHAPTER SIXTY-SEVEN: THE LITTLE GIRL IN THE WHITE DRESS

Priscilla Marianus

Long before Bregantium fell, Priscilla had ridden away, south through the little-traveled land of southern Gad. She had left the tragic actor's mask behind—a symbol, she had come to realize, of oppression far beyond what the Empire had ever forced upon her. She knew she had reversed all the things she worked for her entire life. She had come at last just outside a small seaside inn. She watched the whitecaps roll in, heard the seagulls sing a new song. The water was cool and refreshing against her bare feet. She had journeyed here to bathe and wash her dark past away in the Imperial—not the Middle—Sea.

It seemed just yesterday that she had been a little girl, in a small fishing village of western Anthania. Her father never had much money, but one birthday he had bought her a white dress of fine-spun wool, told Priscilla she could do anything, be anybody she wanted.

In the Academies of Eloesus, the lecturers had filled her mind with tales of Imperial injustice; they had called the Empire the worst nation which had ever existed. As a young woman, she had believed them. Now, as an old woman, she no longer did.

Hot tears streaked her cheeks. She did not know what would come after this. She did not know if the Empire would forgive her. But she did know the plans of Crispus, of Septimo Seánus, of the Augusts with their loathing for the Empire, and of the Academies with their grand utopian vision, had failed, evaporated before the might of the great Imperial beast. Her father would loathe her, at this point, for her failure. He had never hated the Empire as Priscilla and her friends at the Academies did, but he had hated failure, had never accepted it in the Marianus home.

She wept, not for the first time, certainly not for the last. She gave a moment's thought to drowning herself in the sea.

"Hail, woman!"

Priscilla turned around. A fat man stood there at the doorway, perhaps the innkeeper.

"Do you need some lodging?" His eyes alighted with shock. "Hey, that's the traitor woman! That woman that brought the lawgivers over the sea. That woman from the Academies, that author!"

At the words an angry crowd poured out of the inn, their eyes blazing with fury.

Priscilla walked up to them, accepting their captivity. She had dug this hole for herself, and she would live with the consequences of her actions. At the least, Father would be accepting of that. No longer was she the little girl in the dress, but a woman full-grown, regretful and brought to ruin by her own hand.

CHAPTER SIXTY-EIGHT:
LONG-AWAITED VENGEANCE

Weeks Later…

Tidus Tivernas, Marshal of the Imperial Guard

The last of the Asa nomads stood before Emperor Numa the God. The pursuit of these useless destroyers, these savage killers, had cost thousands of denars the Empire could ill afford to lose and many more thousands of Imperial lives, but His Undying Glory had never yielded from his goal. The last hundred lay at his mercy, their horses wounded or driven away.

Here, in the rocky desert, the chieftain of the Asa had fallen to his knees, hands knit together, eyes teary, mouth trembling. "Please," he sobbed. "Please… mercy."

Yet an anger filled Numa's eyes, an anger such as Tidus had never seen, in Numa or anyone else. Not even Crispus Servillius had displayed such a terrifying visage.

"You kill thousands… pile up the bodies of men and women and children and babes, then leave them to rot… and ask for *mercy?*"

Numa's voice did not sound his own.

"You and I have never seen eye-to-eye, Nued."

How in Varda does Numa know his name?

"My name is Ahram!" the chieftain screamed. "You are mistaken. I beg of you. *Mercy!*"

"No mercy. No quarter. No peace. Only death." His eyes blazed with empire. A command thundered from his lips: "Kill them all!"

Across the wasteland of Khazidea, Tidus followed Emperor Numa the God, amazed that this boy from the hinterlands had saved the Empire. In the streets of Haroon a crowd roared, chanting his name: "Numa! Numa, the god! Numa! Numa the god!"

His original reluctance and humility had evaporated; he now acknowledged that he was a god, the divine ruler of the greatest nation in the world.

Khazidean girls threw flower petals before his feet. Behind them, outside the city gates, the recovery from the Asa's ravaging had only just begun. It would take years, likely decades, to recover. But under Emperor Numa the God, Tidus had no doubts they would.

CHAPTER SIXTY-NINE:
ASTARTHE APPENINA

Astarthe, Queen of Haroon

Astarthe had never been happier in her life, looking into her betrothed's eyes and reveling the thought of a new beginning for the Empire, and a new beginning for herself, as a member of the Line of Appia. Appian—a rustic from Gad—did not have the muscle of a warrior, but he had a mind far beyond any of the so-called scholars that hated the Empire. His brown eyes were so rich, his dark hair so imperious. They stood in the open air, in the ruins of the Temple of Imperium, with common citizens gathered to watch.

A priest of Imperium in red and gold robes peered into her eyes. "Do you, Astarthe, take Appian of Norriva as your husband?"

"I do." Joy was rising up within her, the uncontainable expectation of a future life.

Numa the emperor stood by, the Empire's sovereign ruler whom Astarthe had grown to look upon like a brother.

"And do you, Appian, take Astarthe as your wife?"

"I do."

"Then," the priest of Imperium said, "by the power of the Empire, the greatest nation in Varda, and its heavenly spirit, Imperium, I pronounce you man and wife."

Astarthe Appenina. She met Appian in an embrace, then a kiss. The women of the Line of Appia might take the name Appenina alone, but Astarthe would only add it to her own. The name Astarthe was a sign of her roots—she was a daughter of the River Khazan, forever— and it was a sign of the priceless thing she had forever lost, Adamantion. She knew her son, now dancing in bliss in the Fertile Land, would want her to be happy.

And in Appian's embrace, she was.

CHAPTER SEVENTY: THE BEAST UNCHAINED

Emperor Numa the God

Thirty thousand traitors, even out of a population of many millions, was a number high enough to aggrieve Numa, to fill his soul—at the thought—with a deep darkness. Yet these traitors—the dozen Imperial Councilors, the thousands of their August conspirators, and the many more Knights and common folk who swore allegiance to Mazda to preserve their lives, then fought against the Empire—would all get the punishment that was due.

A cross had been prepared every hundred or so feet along the Path of Tidus, throughout the length of Anthania. These people—these worms—whom Numa punished were the shackles that held back the Empire's strength, the dread disease that weakened it and could well have been fatal. Now the chains were broken, and the Empire would never falter again.

~

Naked, beaten, and scourged, Crispus Servillius was fixed to his cross. The hatred and derision with which he had treated Numa had evaporated, given way to panic. "Please!" he begged. "Please! I do not deserve this! I did not commit any crimes! I did not fight the Empire! It was someone else! It was all Septimo Seánus!"

Septimo screamed, "Lies! It was all Crispus!" as he, too, was led beaten and bloody to his own execution place.

"Rub salt into Crispus's wounds," Numa growled. The legionaries at his side quickly obeyed.

A wild screech of pain echoed through the air. The bloodied

body of Priscilla Marianus was next. Yet she did not utter any screams or groans; her eyes reflected a strange sense of peace.

"Do you regret your actions, traitor?" Numa asked her.

"Yes," she answered, her eyes streaming with tears. "Yes, I do."

Why, Numa wondered, *of all people, is she most calm?*

Weeks later, the task was complete. By the time Numa returned the way he had come, the bodies of Crispus, Priscilla, Septimo and the others had given way to rot and foul smells. Yet Numa would never take their bodies down; they were a symbol of what happened to traitors, a symbol of what happened to those who betrayed their nation, who acted with fear and perversion rather than duty and honor.

The beast had broken free of its chains. The nation's strength was unchecked. The Empire's most glorious days were yet to come.

A NEW EMPIRE

In Bregantium, in the depths of my despair, I have all but abandoned the Imperial Chronicles. Yet then the news arrives: the traitor armies decimated, the Empire recaptured, a new day dawning, brighter and more glorious than any before...

CHAPTER SEVENTY-ONE:
BECAUSE WE CAN

Emperor Numa the God

In the Imperial Council chambers, Numa stood before the thirty newly-elected Augusts. He did not particularly like these people—the same political class which had betrayed the Empire and sought to destroy it—but the ancient law of the Empire could never be rewritten.

"Councilors, Augusts all," Numa said. "I have a proposition for you, one which I demand you accept. I demand we seize Zoar and Kheroe, and end the nonsense about a 'client kingdom.' I demand we rule as their master, once and for all."

A bitter expression appeared on the face of Juno Seánus. "Signor *Emperor…*"

Numa despised that a Seánus was on the council, but the Augusts were so few, and so many had died in the war.

"Kheroe is a client kingdom but it is sovereign. No nation can or should dictate its affairs." Seánus chuckled darkly. "Perhaps in *Gad*, might makes right, but in the larger world we must not interfere except without reason. So tell me, my dear little Getan emperor, why we should invade Kheroe?"

"Because we can."

At Numa's answer, the Imperial Council burst into laughter. An anger welled up within Numa—an anger that felt ancient, as if from a former life—and then, he saw clearly just who he was dealing with. These Augusts would betray him an instant, assassinate him without a moment's thought. Great change was needed.

He left the room, and the laughter vanished from his ears.

"Kill them all," Numa told the Marshal of the Guard, Tidus.

"But—"

"Your emperor's word is final."

Tidus nodded reluctantly.

~

At noon that day, Numa walked to the High Podium before an innumerable crowd in Imperial Square. With the Imperial Guard standing behind him, he began his reform of the Empire: "I, Numa the God, effect the following laws. Any citizen possessing land, with wealth of one-hundred thousand libra or more, may join the August class. Any citizen possessing land, with wealth enough to purchase a horse, sword, and armor, may join the Knightly class."

The crowd roared with cheers at the words, a deafening sound that shook the High Podium.

"Every emperor from hereon will take the family name Adamantus; and under no circumstance shall the title pass from father to son."

When the crowd's roar died down, he finished the last—and most difficult—bit.

"The Imperial Council has been slain by the hands of patriots. New elections must, therefore, take place! Anyone matching the prior requirements may submit a bid for office! From now on, the August Class will be based on merit, not birth!"

The roars of the crowd grew from loud to deafening. The wealthy merchants, the successful traders and actors and musicians, were now on par with their unworthy predecessors. A new August class would rule the Empire, a class which Numa had a feeling he would join.

CHAPTER SEVENTY-TWO: NORTH AND SOUTH

One Week Earlier…

Shareeka, Ratling Skulk

The battle lines were drawn, but not the ones Shareeka expected. The enemy stood before him, but not the ones Shareeka had set out to fight. The northerners had come, a column of knights in the front with feather-plumed iron greathelms and richly-colored surcoats bearing lions, swans, and bears—the symbols of great noble houses. Behind them, thousands of peasant archers stood at the ready, and thousands more common men-at-arms. Yet it was the knights that the Imperial legate, Marco Falcono, feared most of all.

Yes—despite the fact that Shareeka had drawn the soldiers out of their hiding places in cities, frontier outposts, and hill forts—a ratling would never lead the legion. Nor did Shareeka want to. It was his duty, as a ratling skulk, to move about unseen and unnoticed, to strike devastating damage upon the enemy while they turned a blind eye.

~

Marco Falcono walked ahead of the front line into the open, trusting the northmen's honor. Resplendent in a great black Imperial helm with a red horsehair crest, he beat his sword against his shield and shouted, "What grievance do you have against the Empire?"

Out of the lines of knights a white stallion sallied forth, revealing the king—a man of honor as well, it appeared.

The northman king had no use for the Imperial inhibitions over splendor and majesty. Both sides of his purple, fur-lined robe fell halfway down his horse; a crown of gold, inset with fiery rubies, verdant emeralds, and blue sapphires rested on his head of white hair. A sword hung from his side in an eelskin sheath, and his beard was white like cotton. "Your sovereign," the king began in his thick northern accent, "the honorable King Secondo Janus, agreed to a yearly indemnity of seven hundred marks, paid in gold. You have the obligation to obey the rule of law. It does not matter if your Empire is in decline. It does not matter if you are weakened and ready to collapse. Laws govern the nations, codes of honor that must be upheld."

I have found my target, Shareeka thought as he fixed his eyes on the king.

"The Empire is not in decline!" Marco Falcono thundered back. "The Empire is rising! We are not weak; we are strong! And no world laws apply to the Empire! Only one law rules in the Empire… Imperial law!"

"Neither of us wants war—" the king began, but his words were drowned out by the deafening sound of legionaries.

"Empire!" they shouted, and Shareeka joined them. "Empire! Empire! Empire! *Empire!*"

The king turned and fled back into the innumerable host. The peasant archers let loose a volley. The Imperial front lines moved forward with the ordered precision they always had, and the soldiers in the back—Shareeka included—held their shields up like turtle-shells as the rain of steel fell uselessly upon them.

~

As the Empire and the northerners fought a bloody battle on the north plain of Gad, Shareeka darted this way and that, tumbling through the blood-drenched grass as he made his way deep into the enemy ranks, taking advantage of the confusion to remain unseen.

It was long, late in the day, before he at last fixed his eyes on the prize: the northern king in his priceless robes and ostentatious crown, guarded by a column of dismounted knights. The swords they wielded were large enough to chop an Imperial man in two—to cleave open a skull, helmet and all—yet they were clumsy.

Still, Shareeka faced the real possibility of death. He shuddered at the thought of Numa running the Empire without him—that fool boy would ruin everything, if left alone. He hesitated, pondering his next course of action.

He turned, unnoticed. The northern lines were faltering, driven back by an Imperial force much smaller than themselves. The renewed morale of a rising empire had infused the Imperial Army with strength; their confidence would take them to the finish. Shareeka had no doubts the victory was theirs.

"Enough blood has been spilled," Shareeka muttered to himself, and decided to spare the king's life—the king's life, and his own.

~

The Imperials had, one by one, slain or driven back most of the knights, and the men-at-arms were dwindling by the moment. At dark, the northmen began to shout: "Surrender! We surrender!"

But nothing less than total victory would satisfy Marco Falcono. Shareeka watched as he pressed onward, as the northmen's spirits were broken and one-by-one, they fled or fell to Imperial swords.

~

In the dawn hours, while the Imperial Army slept, Shareeka realized two things—there was no sign of the king amid the sea of bodies, and they had left their coffers behind. A bit of fiddling with the locks, and a stream of glittering silver sparkled in the sun—coins marked with the face of a woman, with the name "FEANARA THE LADY," and on the back the bearded visage of the king.

Perhaps at a younger age, before these times of trouble, before the Empire had stood on the threshold of death, before he had seen citizens die and seen grave, unspeakable injustices committed, he would have pocketed the money himself. But instead he dragged the two wooden crates all the way to Marco Falcono's tent. Endless wealth would have been irresistible to the Shareeka of a year ago, but now, the good of the Empire was the best reward of all.

Woken from his sleep, gray-haired Marco Falcono said, "You will keep one of these, Shareeka. You are a hero, after all."

CHAPTER SEVENTY-THREE: THE PATRIOTS

Emperor Numa Adamantus the God

Along the Walk of Triumph, the Imperial Army marched, declaring victory over the northmen and the confiscation of great treasure. Reports had already reached their emperor, Numa Adamantus; the good news swirling about the four winds had invigorated the soldiers, their morale had brought them to a victorious finish, and they had made a resounding victory against the northmen.

At the High Podium, Numa Adamantus, their emperor, met them, these brave men who risked their lives for the betterment of the nation. "Soldiers! You, I will always honor. There is no higher profession; no better way to spend your days. You represent everything good that remains in our nation; you represent everything that the traitors are not. There is a good reason why they rot, crucified along the Path of Tidus, and you are here, in honor and glory and prosperity!" A spirit guided Numa, a spirit around and inside of him, the spirit of Claudio-Valens Adamantus. "The lawgivers are not the ultimate enemy. The southrons are not the ultimate enemy. The northmen are not the ultimate enemy. The true enemy of the Empire is treason… the ones I hate most are not the lawgivers but our ruling class, the men of ancient blood and little wisdom, the Augusts who— idle, yet having everything—dedicate their lives to grand schemes, yet bring the Empire to ruin!" A god guided Numa, the god of his people and his nation, the all-conquering god Imperium. "Never more will we judge a man for anything but his merit! Elect good councilors, my fellow soldiers and my fellow citizens!"

"Numa! Numa!" the crowd roared, and the soldiers joined them, beating their swords against their shields. "Numa! Numa!"

From the great red and gold throng of legionaries, a ratling appeared, dressed in a gray hooded cloak. Only one ratling would dare approach him. The Imperial Guard rushed to cut him down as he sprang up the podium and heaved himself upon it, but Numa stopped them. "Shareeka!"

"Great bit of work you did," the ratling snapped. "The Path of Tidus smells like death, but the visuals… what artistry!"

"They only got what they deserved." Even now, watched by many tens of thousands of people, Numa could not help but feel the grin forming on his face at the sight of his ratling friend. He would never have made it to the oracle without him; he would never have gotten this far, or saved the Empire, without his ratling friend.

"I want to submit my bid for the Ricci. I bought an apartment block with my spoils. I am a landowner. I am an August."

The Ricci. Numa smiled at the words. The ratling enclave had been represented by a human councilor for all its history—a human or something less, an August. "Very well." He took the ratling by the hand, and lifted it up before the crowd. "We have a new bid, my citizens… a ratling for the Ricci!"

~

The same day the elections began, the foundations for the new Temple of Imperium were laid. The building would be taller, grander, and with more images than the first. Wine would be served within, in commemoration for their victory, and music and dancing would fill its halls.

It was the same day they sent the lawgiver women and children away by the sea, back to their homeland. It was the same day that thirty new Imperial Councilors stood before him.

None had illustrious names, or old blood. These were successful merchants, great traders and artisans, even the owner of the Imperial Arena—and Shareeka. Of course, there was Shareeka. The first ratling councilor ever looked very pleased with himself in his purple-sashed white robe, standing amongst his peers in the Council House.

"My fellow councilors, 'Augusts' all. I have a proposition for you that would anger the elite," Emperor Numa announced. "Like all things that anger the elite, it would benefit the Empire. I propose we launch an invasion of Kheroe and end the nonsense about a 'client state.' Then we will go to Carta Mega… announce our sovereignty there."

All thirty councilors raised their hands in agreement: the last and final affront to the old ruling class of the Empire.

~

In bed, in the rich Imperial chamber, Numa's thoughts turned toward Carta Mega, toward the beautiful and queenly woman he had left behind. What better wife could there be, what better empress? The daughter of a patriot, of Eloesian origin with not a trace of August blood within her? She was perfect for him… but before Carta Mega fell, the invasion of Kheroe and Zoar had to be complete.

CHAPTER SEVENTY-FOUR: AN END FOR THE SUN KING

Emperor Numa Adamantus the God

Thousands of Imperial soldiers emptied from the ships along the sun-browned grass of Kheroe. Panic soon overtook the harbor, and a rider came galloping out to meet Numa: "Signor Emperor… what in Varda is going on? No Imperial soldier may lay a foot in the royal city, by world law."

"There is no world law," Numa answered. "There is only Imperial law."

The rider galloped away as the army grew, emptying from the great war-galleys. Above, the stone city of the Great King stretched to the sky, and a great lighthouse towered high as a mountain. The sight stole his breath, yet his commitment was firm. No more pretense of self-rule would be afforded.

Eudora Kyrillos

"What news?" Eudora spat and struggled in her chains. They had fed her meager bread today but already she was shaking with hunger.

The prison warden eyed her over. "Signora… the Imperial Army has arrived on the shore. King Magon has asked the Fingers of Barukh for help."

Eudora cursed. With her luck, the legendary arcane archers would decimate them.

"But the Fingers of Barukh hate the Great King. He sold the nation to the lawgivers for his own safety… they will not come to his aid."

Still Eudora cursed, sure somehow this would all end in her disfavor.

Emperor Numa Adamantus the God

In the hot late summer sun, sweating through his tunic, Numa led the army up the steep stone ramp. Some generals had dissuaded him from finalizing the conquest of Kheroe, saying the risks and involved were too great, warning him of the devastating barrages of the arcane archers. But still he climbed, leading the eighty-thousand soldiers up the exhausting black-stone switchbacks to the Great King's city.

When Numa reached the beehive-shaped buildings, he stopped his horse and gasped at the sight. The city was carved completely from stone, lying in the shadow of the colossal lighthouse. The air had a refreshing coolness this high up.

No archers with crystal arrows or white bows greeted them, only confused and frightened citizens. The Imperial Army marched down the stone streets, to the hole in the mountainside where the Great King's palace lay.

~

The soldiers found the Sun King hid in one of the palace's many rooms. By the time Numa reached him, his wrists were slashed. A knife wet with blood lay in his trembling hand. "My people have abandoned me… even the lawgivers have left me… my god, Atman, lord of the sun, has left me too. Curse him! And curse you, too, Numa the conqueror. Curse you, Empire!"

In his splendid robe of purple silk, the Sun King bled all over the floor. From his lifeless corpse they took his sunray crown.

"We will leave a great garrison here. We have won ourselves another province," Numa said.

A soldier cheered, "Hail Numa!"

"Hail Numa!" shouted another.

Numa smiled. "Take everything of value in the palace. A grand triumph is in store when we get back home."

He made his way out of the palace. He had just reached the doorway when he fainted, lost in a vision.

~

The oracle's sightless white eyes greeted him. The cosmic serpent lay wrapped around her nude body, itself set against a starry black canvas. She had become all-powerful, all-wise, all-triumphant. She had become Wisdom herself; she had become madness and supreme intelligence, bound into one.

"The god Claudio-Valens Adamantus must have his Anthea."

Anthea, he had gathered, was his wife.

"My Anthea is not here," Claudio answered, but then he thought to himself quietly. She had to be—Anthea was here, somewhere. Anthea was in the Sun King's palace. He sensed her. She was below him, in a deep dark place.

"Go find her!" Wisdom shouted, and the vision vanished from Claudio's eyes.

~

Numa Adamantus immediately rose, ignoring the soldier's concerned exclamations. He pored through every winding corridor, every ill-lit hall. He searched for an hour, then another. Then, at last, he found a trapdoor, leading downward, into darkness.

The further Numa Adamantus scaled the ladder, the heavier the scent of blood, salt, and human waste grew. In the dim light of torches he found himself in a subterranean tunnel. The lash of a whip cracked in the air, the sound of rending flesh echoed, and a desperate howling scream pierced the loneliness of the tunnel.

But Numa was not afraid; an Adamantus was never afraid. Instead, he followed the scream down the lonely tunnel, until it opened up into a grand chamber.

Thirteen copper-skinned Kheroans lay bound in manacles, their skin shredded and torn by whips. They sat in piles of their own filth—urine, scat, and vomit—and though some were muttering in pain, the majority had eyes devoid of consciousness. These were men and women who had given up.

The black-garbed torturer lowered his hood. This was a Kheroan, also. In his hand was a whip, its thong covered in broken glass. His eyes seethed with rage at the sight of Numa Adamantus.

"An Imperial dares show his face here? He dares think to rescue the traitors? I will kill them all before he touches them." He drew a knife from the folds of his black robe. He darted at the victim on the far end, but Numa charged him, drew *Imperium's Rebuke* as he ran, pitched back the sword and lopped off the torturer's head.

But the tortured only responded with groans. Numa did not think even the best physicians could save them. The tears in their skin had exposed raw red flesh, and many of the wounds oozed yellow with infection. On one's hand he spotted black flesh, the telltale sign of necrosis. His heart broke for these men and women, these innocents. What crime could possibly deserve this?

Treason, he thought, but somehow he doubted it. What would this torturer consider treason? What would the Sun King consider treason, besides?

"*Help!*" a woman's voice shouted from elsewhere. Numa took off through another corridor and found a spacious room with only one torch. In the dim light were many more captives, most in little better shape. Some of these were Imperials—a dark-haired Anthanian among them, and a light-haired Getan like Numa.

Then there was the woman whose voice he had heard. There, in chains, was Eudora.

He had not recognized her voice; it seemed to have lost all spirit, all hope. It was a voice that had given up. The sharp wit he remembered in Eudora had vanished, replaced with a woman defeated.

And in the body, she did not fare much better. Her rich Eloesian complexion had turned wan; her dark brown hair was a tangled mess. She, too, lay in filth, and her prisoner clothes of undyed wool did not become the daughter of a legate. Yet her flesh was not torn by whips, and not a single bruise marred her skin. Numa Adamantus wondered why the Sun King had spared her. But it seemed that she alone would survive her ordeal. As for the others, Numa Adamantus would do his very best, try as hard as he could to save them.

He returned to the chamber, grabbed the key from the torturer's corpse. One by one, he unlocked the manacles. Some victims screamed in pain when the pressure of the chains lifted.

He saved Eudora for last.

He grabbed her bare shoulders, looked into her chestnut eyes, feared that someday, somewhere, she would break his heart. Then, weakly, she fell upon him, met him in a kiss. "My hero," she said. "My emperor."

"My wife," he answered.

~

Though the City of Stone had lain long under the control of its weak king, the one who capitulated to the lawgivers to save his life, there was much to be done. For an hour, Numa wandered the streets alone. The air had a refreshing coolness and a smell of spice wafting up from the harbor. Above, the impossibly tall Lighthouse of Zoar stood out against a cloudless blue canvas. At the base of the lighthouse, Numa found what he was looking for. A poor man in flea-bitten gray rags, taking shelter in the shade.

"Signore!" Numa called out, and the man looked up. Numa could not trust a man of noble birth, an elite who spent his life in study.

"What is your name?"

"Marukh," he answered.

"Marukh," Numa repeated.

253

Shaved, bathed, sprinkled with aromatic oils and dressed in the rich royal robe and jeweled gold crown of the Sun King, Marukh at last had the air of respectability. The people of Zoar would never respect anyone but a Sun King; and now Marukh owed his life to the Empire, and would never disobey it.

~

Having taken all the great golden ornaments and silver statues from the king's palace, the Imperial legion loaded the loot onto the fleet of ships. Eudora, weakened by hunger and abuse, rested with Numa in the emperor's quarters on the flagship *Imperium's Hand*. In a blanket of silk she rested, and leaned her head on his shoulder. Numa laid his hands around her, shut his eyes, and tried to sleep.

CHAPTER SEVENTY-FIVE:
HISTORY

Appian

Appian and his wife Astarthe sat in their conjugal room in the Imperial Palace, preparing their disembarkation for Haroon and their plans once they reached the City of Issa. It would involve five days at sea, at best, and likely more.

"I hate the water," Astarthe said.

"Do you?" Appian answered. He smiled, and she laughed; it took so little for her to laugh. When he first met her, she had been a grave creature, a woman doomed. But now, the darkness had been replaced with constant joy.

There was a knock on the door.

"Come in," Appian said.

A palace guard with a sword hanging from his belt stood there. "A man has come to the Imperial Palace. He wishes to speak with the emperor, or with you, Appian. He is quite insistent. We had to throw him out twice but he continues coming back. He is a writer of histories… Perhaps if you let him down easy, he would stop bothering us."

Astarthe laughed again, and Appian joined her. "I do believe persistence should be rewarded," Appian said. "Let him in."

~

The man who greeted Appian was thin, a bit frail, and quite old, with more gray hair than brown. In his wrinkled hands he had a pile of books that went up to his chin. "Signor Appian, savior of the Empire… these are the Imperial Chronicles." He let them drop.

Astarthe giggled.

"I have worked for years on these. It begins with the Empire's inception. You are in it, Appian, and you, too, Astarthe. I hope you like it. I am Primo Alleus. I have written where I live on this piece of paper." He walked over to Appian, put the little slip in his hand. "If you are happy with it, Appian, please let me know. I should certainly hope it will be published, but if not, I am happy to write the Empire's tale. A happy new age is beginning, golden and glorious, and you and Astarthe and Numa Adamantus are all responsible for it. I wish you well, and thank you with all my heart."

He turned and left. Astarthe turned to Appian, smiling. "Will you read it?" she asked.

"Of course," he said. "I was Norriva's biggest bookworm, after all."

~

LIKE ALL GREAT THINGS, THE EMPIRE BEGAN WITH AN IDEA: AN IDEA OF FREEDOM FROM TYRANNY, OF A LOVE FOR LIBERTY, OF A HATRED FOR KINGS. IT WAS AN IDEA THAT DID NOT LIMIT ITSELF TO ONE PEOPLE; NAY, IT WELCOMED MEN AND WOMEN FROM THE FOUR WINDS, PAYING NO ATTENTION TO NATIONALITY, SOCIAL STANDING, OR FAVORED GOD. IT WAS AN IDEA THAT BEGAN WITH THE REMOVAL OF KINGS, WITH THE ABOLISHMENT OF TYRANNY; BUT NONETHELESS WE MUST BEGIN THE STORY OF OUR NATION EARLIER, WITH ITS FOUNDATION BY KING PEREGOTHIUS. FOR THOUGH WE REJECTED MONARCHY AND AUTOCRATIC RULE, OUR STORY NONETHELESS BEGINS THERE.

Outside the sky was dark; Astarthe lay in her bed snoring. But Appian had lit candles, and so far he was happy with his choice.

CHAPTER SEVENTY-SIX:
SOLDIERS IN HIGH PLACES

Tertio Araceli, Legate

The orders had come from Numa Adamantus, emperor and god, and Tertio would take great enjoyment in carrying them out. In Thénai, second-largest city of the Empire, most had not yet returned to the site of the great horror that taken place there. Many homes lay empty, and where the black theurges had trafficked in the souls of men, where they had conjured up hellfire and demons before destroying themselves, the remnants of that evil remained. Marching through the gate with the legion, ghosts whispered in Tertio's ear, low strained sobs swirled around him like vapor, and the air was dead, devoid of life, before he reached the city proper, and the Academies of Thénai themselves.

The grand market of Thénai echoed with the noise of buyers and sellers, yet over the grand colonnades and defaced statues of the Academies' campus a grim silence prevailed, a silence borne of great shame. They had orchestrated the Empire's troubles; all their self-professed love of learning and books had been exchanged in an instant, for their hatred of the nation outweighed their love of learning. They had joined hands with barbarians who believed the exact opposite of what the Academies claimed to. Numa's orders were clear and final, yet Tertio wondered if they did not go far enough.

Students still wandered the halls, clutching books as they hurried from one lecture hall to another. Some gawked at them as they entered; most looked down and rushed on.

In a garden courtyard, before the statues of ancient

philosophers—their eyes scratched out to appease the lawgivers—a scholar came rushing out. "War criminals!" he shouted. "Get out of the Academies! You have blood on your hands, the blood of innocent foreigners, the blood of babes and women!"

"Beat him until you cannot recognize his face," Tertio ordered, and the soldiers at once set to work, rushing over to him, pinning him down, and bashing him mercilessly with the pommels of their swords.

"Please! Stop! *Please!*" the scholar cried, but his words fell on deaf ears.

Glaring at him, Tertio announced their purpose. "By order of His Undying Glory, the emperor and god Numa Adamantus, a garrison of soldiers will remain here in the Academies. A soldier will stand guard over every lecture hall and every room, a reminder of Imperial power that the vacuous ideologues of the Academies cannot and will not ever shake."

"Please! *Stop!* I am *sorry!*" the scholar screamed.

"Do not stop," Tertio ordered, "until he is on the very edge of death."

~

The scholar died that night. Other lecturers who resisted were beaten as well, often in front of their students. But before the day was done, a soldier stood guard in every classroom, with full power to read every missive and letter, and Tertio Araceli—general, warrior, and killer of the Empire's enemies—was made the supreme provost.

CHAPTER SEVENTY-SEVEN: PEACE ETERNAL

Emperor Numa Adamantus the God

Back in the Imperial Palace, Numa had returned for a brief visit while preparations for the triumph began. He had brought his future wife Eudora with him and a physician immediately attended to her needs. Yet he had not gotten a moment by himself before the Imperial Council summoned him.

"I am in a hurry," Numa announced to the thirty men as soon as he reached the council chambers.

"And yet our matter is urgent," said Gaius Vorenus, Speaker of the Council. "We are debating whether to ban the faith of the lawgivers. Some have clung to their vile religion. Others were born lawgivers, and remained here, surrendered to the Empire and agreed to live in peace. We are tied… fifteen versus fifteen. By law the emperor casts the final vote."

"Ban the lawgiver faith?" Numa said. "I vote no. To do so is to give in to the same insecurity that upholds their religion. All faiths may be practiced in the Empire. The lawgiver faith will fail the light of scrutiny. There is a worse fate for them; the derision of the Empire, the scorn for every lawgiver man, woman and suckling babe. We will leave up the black *kabakh* that the Theomancer built—and everyone who enters, the people will see."

"A wise choice," said Gaius Vorenus, one of the new men that now filled the August class. Unlike Crispus Servillius and the others, he earned his position and did not inherit it. "The lawgiver faith may be practiced in the Empire. His Undying Glory had spoken.

~

A crowd cheered with deafening volume as the soldiers

proceeded along the Walk of Triumph. Numa rode at the front, and immediately behind him were carts filled with jewel-eyed gold statues, piles of silver and gold, and jewelry, to be thrown to the citizens.

"Empire!" they cheered. "Empire! Empire!"

Numa drew *Imperium's Rebuke,* his priceless sword of adamant, and lifted it high in the bright and joyous sun. At the sound the crowd's cheers grew louder.

"Empire! Empire! Victory!" The despair and fatigue of a beleaguered people had vanished in the light of a new and hopeful day. Their dark sadness had vanished at the sight of Numa; their heaviness of heart had evaporated at the sight of Imperial victory. "Empire!" they shouted. "Empire! Empire! Victory!"

The blue skies had never looked so bright; the sun's warmth had never felt so refreshing.

"Empire! Empire! Victory!"

The statue of Horatio the Citizen-Soldier smiled at him, lifting the eagle banner high. The statue of King Anthans rode on its stone horse, proud of Numa, happy for the Empire's soaring spirit. The statue of Claudio-Valens Adamantus gazed upon Numa, seeing in him a shared soul, a shared self.

"Empire! Empire! Victory!"

The Walk of Triumph opened into Imperial Square, where the crowd was countless, a sea of Imperial citizens. The cheers went from deafening to overpowering. There were even lawgivers in the crowd, dressed in black, their dark sun-bronzed faces inexplicably glowing with joy.

"Empire! Empire!" the sea of voices cried out, and the lawgivers were among them. "Victory!"

Behind him, legionaries had begun throwing gold and silver into the crowd, yet they did not swarm over each other to catch them. A greater treasure was here, the unseen treasure of a new age, of a great and glorious beginning. A treasure of renewed Imperial strength, a new Imperial century, a new Imperial millennium.

"Empire! Empire! Victory!"

On every window in Imperial Square, a red-gold Imperial flag glistened in the sun.

"Empire! Empire! Victory!"

There was not a traitor left; they were all dead, and only patriots remained.

"Empire! Empire! Victory!"

Numa drew near the High Podium; they wanted a speech, an assurance of renewed peace. But peace eternal was self-evident; peace eternal was as visible as the sun, as the blue sky. There were no enemies left, within or without. Fharas had faded in power; the northmen had backed off from their claims. Peace was rising, peace eternal, peace through strength that none could take away.

"Empire! Empire! Victory!"

The Empire's lamp burned brighter than ever before.

"Empire! Empire! Victory!"

A glorious new beginning was at hand.

"Empire! Empire! Victory!"

Seven provinces awaited a prosperous future, seven provinces under one unconquered son.

"Empire! Empire! Victory!"

A glorious beast had broken free from its chains. The shackles that restrained the Empire's strength had been thrown off by Numa's hand. The traitors rotted on crosses. Their days had come to an end.

"Empire! Empire! Victory!"

A glorious beast had arisen, a beast to rule the world, but what better beast than this, what better beast than the Empire? Who else was more deserving?

"Empire! Empire! Victory!"

Numa dismounted and ascended the High Podium. Eudora awaited him there, his beautiful bride, dressed in white and fully recovered from her travails.

"Empire! Empire! Victory!"

In view of the citizens he grabbed her, kissed her. Exhilaration shot through his veins like lightning. A great and glorious beginning was at hand for the Empire, but also for Numa.

"Empire! Empire! Victory!"

None could question the Empire's might.

"Empire! Empire! Victory!"

None could deny the Empire's power.

"Empire! Empire! Victory!"

None could stop the Empire's rise.

"Empire! Empire! Victory!"

An eagle soared overhead, spreading its brown wings. It let out a shrill cry. At the good portent, the crowd let out a wild cheer. Their chant grew more spirited, more deafening, more joyous.

"Empire! Empire! Victory!"

The traitors lay dead, and the Empire is rising.

"Empire! Empire! Victory!"

The Empire is rising. There are more patriots than traitors.

"Empire! Empire! Victory!"

The Empire is rising.

"Empire! Numa! Empire!"

Sketches from a New Empire

A LAST REQUEST

"The coming years would test the courage of citizens and subject peoples, of legionaries and slaves, of the men and women of the Empire; and determine whether the nation chosen by Imperium would fulfill its calling: to rule over all the world. Yet through famine and plague, through shadow and flame, through invasion and dark betrayal, the Empire would overcome its challenges and rise in the light of a new day brighter than any before."

As Appian read the final words of the ten-volume *Imperial Chronicles*, a shiver passed through him. He had never read histories so complete, so detailed yet so concise. He had never read anything that so captured the spirit of the Empire, that so captured its culture and its constitution. Most of all, he had never read a work so patriotic, so unashamedly filled with love for the Empire. The historians he had read before had been cynics, discussing only the dark side of the Empire, discussing its shortcomings rather than its more plentiful strengths. *This has to be published,* Appian thought. *I am not leaving Imperial City until I have Numa's word.*

"Appian, dear." Astarthe had taken a break from her ceaseless packing, and now she had fixed her eyes dead on him. "I know you want to delay our trip, but it is ten days at the very most. And you will love Haroon in peacetime. You will learn to enjoy it, husband."

"I am sure I will, my sweet," Appian said, still lost in thought. "Excuse me one moment." He grabbed the pile of books, allowing it to lean on his chest as he carried it down the hallway. Astarthe's frustrated sigh followed him as he left.

~

"Signor Numa," Appian snapped at the emperor-god in all his glory, as he sat on the White Throne. "If I am to be governor of Haroon, you must do one thing for me."

"Anything," Numa said, and smiled.

He may be an emperor and a god, but he is still my friend. "I want these books published. Send them to Paladium for copying. These are patriotic histories, not the ramblings of cynics. We need an influx of those across the Empire. We must reverse the anti-Imperial sentiment the Academies have instilled in our youth."

"Indeed," Numa said. "You are wise to ask it, and it will be done. Rule well, Governor Appian, and do not forget to enjoy Haroon. I am sure I will see you soon."

"I am sure," Appian answered, and a new energy infused him, a new hope, a new eagerness for life. Surely happiness and prosperity would follow him all his days. His life was just beginning, and it promised to be a good one.

VIGILANTES

"The Empire," the lecturer in the Thenoan Academy of Politics said, "may have prevailed, but we cannot excuse its crimes."

"What kinds of crimes?" Mather snapped. He had not traveled all these hundreds of miles from Paladium, only to hear Empire-hatred.

"We have bullied the world. We have controlled nations that do not wish to be controlled. In a very real sense, the Empire deserved what it got. It deserved to be destroyed."

Mather was the first to run at the lecturer, but he was not the last. With ink jars, with books, with everything they could find, the students beat the helpless man before them.

For though he was helpless, Mather and his fellow students had had enough; the traitors had their time. Now—Mather heard—they lay rotting on crosses all along the Path of Tidus, from Imperial City to the border of Gad. No more would he, or any of his fellow citizens, endure them.

EMPIRE, EMPIRE

Melodia had attended the most prestigious school in the world, the Thenoan Academy of Theiarkos. From the first day she had loved the ways it had taught her to think. She had even listened to Priscilla Marianus give her speech on absolute truth, as opposed to positive and negative truths and how it related to the existence of morality.

On the days she did not lose herself in Haroon spice—alcohol had never been her thing—she had gathered all her fellow students in her upper-story apartment to discuss the wider issues of the day. Some common folk had despised the coup, had wished for things to return to the way they always had been because they hated change. Yet among Melodia and her friends, their decision was final: the Empire deserved it, and whatever came after it could not be worse.

"Now let's discuss the ramifications of it all," Melodia had said. Her friends were gathered in the apartment. Rumors had spread that some rustic from Gad had re-conquered Anthania—impossible, since not a single man from Gad was attending the elite academies— yet to any sane person the Empire's inevitable collapse was clear as day. "We've already established the Empire's fall, and that the lawgivers will be a more just society," she continued. "Now let's not have some ridiculous, ancient discussion that old Imperial men might have—how many gods can fit on the head of a pin, for example. Now given the beliefs of Theiarchus, is the justice of the lawgivers positively true, negatively true, or absolutely true?"

"If we say it is positively true," her friend Samara answered, "then we can exclude the fact, by nature, that it is negatively true. But if it is absolutely true, it can be either. If we establish the truth by negative proofs, then—"

A voice outside the room, in the corridor, interrupted her: "Did you hear, Marco? The lawgivers have been driven out! The Empire's won the war! We've won!"

Melodia's heart sank, and her stomach soured. Her neighbor

Marco was a student at the Academies too, but his heart had never been in the revolution, and his father had been a soldier—by definition, a war criminal.

"Thank the gods!" Marco howled back at his friends.

The gods—imaginary instruments used to bully the world. Melodia cursed them, and cursed Marco, son of a military man. Samara had a stunned look on her face, and the atmosphere in the room had suddenly turned grim.

"It cannot be true," Melodia said. "We have already established the Empire's fall is negatively true… We've already established that the lawgivers' injustice is positively false."

Yet her friends gathered there—male and female both—did not seem as convinced as Melodia. A sense of doubt had crept over them.

Outside a horn blew, followed by marching feet. *The legion.*

Melodia drew back into the corner of the room. "No… No…" It could not be true. It could not possibly be true.

"Empire! Empire!" a crowd began to chant outside. "Empire! Empire! Victory!"

"Impossible!" Melodia cried, but the crowd drowned her out.

"Empire! Empire! Victory!"

"Imperial triumphalism!" Melodia screamed, but even then the crowd's chant was too loud, and growing louder.

"Empire! Empire! Victory!"

"*Imperial triumphalism!*" Melodia howled, but her voice sank into the sea of voices.

"Empire! Empire! Victory!"

"The Empire's evil is negatively true! Its strength is positively false!"

"Empire! Empire! Victory!"

THE SACRED UNION

Numa had proven unpredictable and full of surprises, and yet Eudora did not resist when he announced they would travel down the roads—while Anthania was yet in reconstruction—and visit Mount Hylea.

In the brush, in a high valley, lay the ruins of a temple. When a nude woman appeared with blind eyes and a snake around her body, Eudora was surprised she did not shudder. Yet the sight of her, and of this place, was strangely familiar. She felt like she had been here before—with Numa, before.

"Husband, you are full of surprises." Numa's light brown hair, his warm eyes, his Getan accent, had grown on her.

"Husband?" the woman boomed. "The marriage, the sacred union, is not complete until I say it is. I pronounce you husband and wife… but you must consecrate the union here, before the Temple of Hermas, and before me, Io…"

They made love in the warm air. Claudio's embrace had never felt so sweet; Anthea lost herself in the joy of the moment, in the fullness and richness of a new life, a new beginning.

IMPERIAL CITY, 1125

Decades after the Empire's worst crisis, Numa and Eudora Adamantus stood before the just-completed Temple of Imperium. Their daughters, Claudia and Kyrilla, and their sons, Tidus-Valens and Lucento, stood by them, dressed in the fine purple silks and woolens deserving of the Imperial family. The Temple of Imperium was twice the size of its predecessor. The war eagle statue was twice the size of the one that came before, layered with gold and inset with rubies. And Imperial City had changed… there was more food, more wine, more music and more song than ever before. Their struggle had defined who the Empire was, in opposition to its enemies. In the fires of strife the Imperials had united, even though now, in peace, they had begun to drift apart.

Behind him was Appian, Governor of Khazidea, his wife Astarthe Appenina, and their three sons and two daughters who no doubt had political lives ahead of them. Like the Empire, Appian and Astarthe had their happy ending. And the years ahead looked prosperous. The traitors were gone, and the August class had no resemblance to its former self.

Umar stood there, the former field marshal of the lawgivers, who now was quite a fixture of Imperial life, a welcome presence at dinner parties and a fervent enthusiast of the Imperial Arena. He had forsaken Mazda and his Law, and found a new reverence for life where he had once yearned for death and false hopes of paradise. Others of his kind remained in the Empire, which welcomed them with open arms; yet most had drifted steadily away from their faith.

Once again, free bread was distributed to the poor. Once again, the crowds flocked to the Arena or the theaters throughout Imperial City. Yet the capital—and the nation—was not the same. The reforms of Numa had destroyed and remade the August and Knightly classes. What the oracle had begun in Claudio-Valens Adamantus she had finished in Numa Adamantus, his successor and shared soul.

As the priest of Imperium sprinkled oil on the entrance to the

Temple of Imperium, a familiar chant arose from the crowd, a chant of triumph and victory, a chant of joy and of power: "Empire, Empire! Victory! Empire, Numa, Empire!"

WHERE IT ALL BEGAN

A man like Primo Alleus would never be satisfied with just one book. Years after *The Imperial Chronicles* were copied en masse and sold throughout the Empire, to booksellers and libraries around the Imperial Sea and beyond it, Primo Alleus made the journey north from his villa in Paradise Gardens. The journey would, no doubt, wear severely on his old bones, but he had no doubts it would be worth it.

A week of travel passed in a rickety carriage, and though the inns along every mile of road provided respite at night, Primo Alleus rejoiced when it was over.

~

Before him lay Cipium, the Adamantus family ranch. Long studies of history and reflections on current events had proven two things to Primo Alleus—that Claudio-Valens Adamantus had begun the war on the Empire's noble classes, and that Emperor Numa had finalized their destruction.

Cipium, like the Adamantus family's origins, was humble. The Adamanti had never put an emperor on the White Throne before, nor had anyone truly distinguished himself before Lucento-Valens the great general, Claudio's father. Yet their love for the Empire had always run deep, their patriotism unquestionable, their hatred for treason unfathomable. To a superstitious mystic, it might seem that Claudio and Numa shared a soul.

"Unconquered, he rises," Primo Alleus repeated the Adamantus family motto. It had always been their motto, but in light of history it seemed even more appropriate.

Primo crossed the yard toward the ranch house, where a few idlers stood. Now, it served as a monument to the emperor—by Numa's command it had been restored, refurbished and reopened after long decades of neglect.

What created such a powerful soul? Primo wondered. *What fires was his soul forged in?*

Immediately inside, a wine-rack displayed a hundred bottles, some empty, some full. The tile floor was an earthen red. The wood-paneled ceiling was inviting yet simple. Here, in the entry hall, a picture hung on the wall of the great Lucento-Valens Adamantus, who had driven away the Fharas-aided rebels in Zoar, who had secured the provinces, driven back the Empire's enemies. And yet—though Khazidea was always within grasp of the Empire's reach—the vacuous ideologues of the Imperial Council prevented its capture. They knew full well they could expand the Empire, bring prosperity, lower the price of food, and yet they did not. If ever a mistake could be made, they made it. If ever an ally could be alienated, he was alienated. If ever a hostile enemy could be embraced, the Imperial Council embraced them.

It was a wonder the Empire had survived those thousand years before Claudio-Valens arrived.

Primo passed into the kitchen, where pots and pans hung from the ceiling and a stove lay, unlit. Here, Catalina Adamantus, the revered empress mother, cooked her son's food and poured his wine, not knowing he would one day rule the world, not knowing he would be the first emperor named a living god.

In Claudio's bedchamber, Primo stopped. There was a simple bed and a bare plaster wall, a wooden cabinet and an end table, nothing more. There was no trace of heaven, no mote of divine power that infused Claudio-Valens.

Primo questioned what he would have done if the traitors succeeded, if the Empire fell. He questioned if he would have continued fighting. *Yes,* he thought after a long pause. For as long as his nation lived on in his heart, it would never die; he would live as an Imperial or die as an Imperial. He would fight its enemies to its last breath; he would savage the traitors with all his strength.

The Empire did not deserve its power because it was powerful, because of luck or fortune. Otherwise the lawgivers, or the Fharese, could be deserving, too. The Empire was deserving of power because its liberty, its freedom, its honor, were greater than any other nation in the world.

THE IMPERIAL CHRONICLES

Near the end of his life, Primo Alleus, national historian, writer of the "Imperial Chronicles," traveled to Paladium for the first time. The sea-journey had exhausted him to his core, yet he had soldiered on. In all his life as a historian and a writer, Primo Alleus had never traveled here.

In Sanctum, in a workshop vast and spacious, a thousand slaves copied the latest edition of "The Imperial Chronicles," now with an added reflection on the characters of Claudio-Valens Adamantus and his heir, Numa. Within a month's time, another ten thousand bound books would set sail across the Empire, to the east—Imperiopoli, Korthos, Kersepoli, and Thenoa Appiana; to the south—Carta Mega, Zoar, and the Appian Library in Haroon; to the north—Bregantium and Brilium; and to the west, the heart of the civilized world, the seat of earthly power, Imperial City. Now the seven provinces lay in unending peace and unprecedented prosperity—seven lands ruled one man, seven provinces under the command of a living god, seven nations under one unconquered son.

EPILOGUE

Autumn, 1150 Y.E.

Tertio Septimus, Marshal of the Guard

Outside the Imperial bedchamber, the air had grown chill. The people of Imperial City had donned their masks and costumes for the Feast of Spirits, yet here, a somber crowd had gathered around the sick and dying Numa Adamantus. It was no surprise to anyone; he had grown feeble in his old age, prone to many illnesses and infections. Yet he had never lost his calm spirit, his commanding presence, his shrewd wisdom and his strong self-control.

Around him stood the members of the Imperial Court—Appenina the Younger, daughter of Numa's childhood friend, still astonishingly beautiful even in her middle age. There was Reekee, Maestro of the Treasury, the son of the ratling councilor Shareeka. There was Astarthe, Appenina's mother, old and yet healthy, world-wise yet full of life.

Tertio did not belong here with these people, these great men and women of the emperor's inner circle, these legends of the Empire's past. And yet he was here. As Marshal of the Guard, his duty was nothing less.

"The Empire," Numa began, "is the greatest nation in the world. Its peace must be upheld at all times by the end of a sword. Its enemies must be humiliated; its friends must be rewarded, defended, and instilled with trust. When you are emperor, Marcus Amaranthius, you must serve your nation above all; you must never concern yourself with any other tribe or people. You must punish treason without mercy, sedition without restraint."

Before Numa stood Marcus Amaranthius, a man Tertio hardly knew.

"There is no community of nations, there is only Empire." At

Numa's words a chill spread up Tertio's spine. "There is no peace without strength. There is no power without conquest. Let your name forevermore be Empire; let your goal forevermore be Conquest."

Tertio watched as the savior of the Empire, the rustic from Gad who had become a living god, draw in his last breaths. Popularity, to him, had always been secondary; his governance had never been reactive, but commanding. The coffers of the Empire now overflowed; its possessions stretched further north and south than they ever had. Its enemies had faltered; now no one questioned its position as first in the world.

The traitors had failed. The seditious whispering of the cretins had been drowned out by the cheers of triumphal patriots. The will of the cowardly and vile had been decimated, driven away and burnt to dust by the almighty will of Imperium. The Empire had overcome its trials and arisen, more powerful than ever before.

The Empire is rising. Let no one tell you otherwise.

AND YET, EVEN IN THE LIGHT OF THIS BRIGHT AND GLORIOUS DAY—THIS TIME OF INFINITE PROSPERITY AND PEACE—A SHADOW WAS FALLING OVER THE LAND. IN THE NORTH, A TROUBLED WIND BLEW THROUGH AN AUTUMNAL FOREST. IN ROADSIDE INNS AND IMPERIAL CITY ITSELF, A RUMOR SPREAD THAT THE DARK ONE WAS TAKING PHYSICAL FORM, THAT THE ARMIES OF SHADOW WERE MARSHALLING, THAT THE END WAS COMING SOON...

GLOSSARY

CURRENCY

Aes: A copper coin, the cheapest unit of currency. Also called a copper or an "eagle." Plural aesa.

Denar: A silver coin, worth twelve aesa. Also called a silver or a "moon." Plural denara.

Liber: A gold coin, worth eighty denara or approximately one-thousand aesa. Also called a gold, a "crown," or a "sovereign." Plural libra.

TERMS

Adamant: A metal of light bluish color. Its existence was known, but it could not be shaped until the eleventh century, when the Alchemist Collegium created a flame hot enough. The process of making adamant weapons is so expensive that hardly any can afford one outside of the upper tier of the military.

Amara: The goddess of motherly love.

Amaroth: A small temple city, the center of the priesthood of Amara.

Athra: A god of fire, favored in Fharas and especially by the magi.

Atman: A god of fertility, the male counterpart to Issa. His highest-ranking priests are called the Godlings.

Augusts: The higher of the two ruling classes (the other being Knights). They are the descendants of the original Peregothian families through the male line, and are the only people allowed to serve within the upper tier of the government.

Anthans: (1) Another name for Imperial City. (2) Anthans the Great, the last of the Sea Kings and the first emperor (having achieved the title with the ceding of Anthania).

Barbarians: A general term for non-Imperials, both to the north and to the south.

Brilium: A lumbering town north of Bregantium. In the native tongue of Northern Gad, "Brill."

Carta Mega: A city on the coast of the Imperial Sea, located on the edge of the desert. Dry-farming techniques, deep wells and cisterns, and extensive trade sustain the population of 100,000.

Desolation, the: An area of intense fighting between Fharas and the Empire on the southern part of Khazidea. The constant burning and leveling of towns has turned this once-fertile region into a desert.

Demons: The enemies of the gods.

Eloesus: An ancient land famed for its wealth and rich culture. Since the 500s YE, an Imperial province. Their flag is a laurel-wreath on a green field.

Elders, the: According to legend, a race of mystical beings rumored to live "beyond the reach of the north wind."

Fharas: An ancient empire centered in the plain of Gor Ilán. Their flag is a golden four-pointed star on a purple field.

Feast of Spirits: A celebration honoring the spirits of the dead. Masks and costumes are used to frighten away evil ghosts.

Fingers of Barukh: An elite military order with origins in Kheroe, known for their mystically-conjured explosive arrows. The Empire values them highly, but they command a high price. In general, they are apolitical, claiming to give no preference to the Fharese padisha or the "northern emperor"; and giving only reluctant lip-service to the king of Kheroe. Their name refers to their worship of Barukh, god of entryways.

Gad: The northernmost and least populous province of the Empire, known for its light-featured inhabitants.

Godlings: An elite order of eunuch priests, worshippers of Atman. Their temple is located in Qabash, a region of Khazidea.

Gorgon: A legendary animal, said to resemble a boar with scaled, metallic skin. Its gaze was said to turn an onlooker to stone.

Haroon Spice: An intoxicant, currently banned in the Empire, which causes hallucinations and feelings of euphoria but—over the long term—afflicting the consumer with severe weight loss and, oftentimes, dementia. Crimson eyes are the telltale sign of long-term addicts.

Hieronus: The god of justice and just war.

Imperial City: Also called Anthans. The de facto capital of the Empire, and the largest city in the known world.

Imperial Council: A body of thirty Augusts (see above), given certain governmental powers, including the ability to remove the emperor. They are elected by the people of Imperial City across its thirty districts.

Imperial Cult: A group devoted to the worship of the emperors, especially the Adamanti, located in Imperiopoli.

Imperiopoli: A large city of Eloesus.

Imperium: The god of the Imperial state, represented as an eagle. His cult was founded in the 400s YE. The theologians of the Magisterium consider him a human invention.

Issa: Goddess of fertility. Worshiped mostly in Khazidea and the southlands, she nevertheless has a large temple in Imperiopoli.

Kersepoli: An Eloesian metropolis, in ancient times the home of a militaristic warrior society.

Korthos: An Eloesian metropolis, known for its excellent wine.

Khazidea: A southern land along the Khazan River, surrounded by desert.

Kheroe: An area of greenery and rainfall, west from Khazidea across the desert.

Knight: (1) A mounted warrior, especially one wearing heavy armor; (2) A member of the lower tier of the Imperial upper class— the other being Augusts—officially tasked with the defense of the Empire. In actuality, not all knights serve actively as soldiers.

Mazda: A god mostly unknown to the Imperials. His worshipers consider him the only good god.

Monk: A member of a religious order. Monks Militant go to war, but are generally forbidden to shed blood; some wield clubs or maces to overcome this barrier, while others are sworn to use their fists.

Paradise Gardens: An elite enclave of the wealthy in the foothills of the Goldenhorn Mountains, a summer retreat popular with the August families of Imperial City.

Path of Tidus: A long paved road running from Imperial City to Zarubad far to the north.

Peregoth: The founding city of the Empire, built on an island of the same name.

Peregothius: The first of the Sea Kings.

Pontifex, the: The high priest of Hieronus.

Rite of Spring, the: A festival on the spring equinox marked by offerings to Kernunnos and Seladora, gods of nature, or to Jaine, god of beginnings, endings and open doorways. Festivities include cooking sweet "spring bread," drinking spiced wine, and cleaning homes.

Spice: See Haroon spice.

Theomancer: The religious and political leader of all Mazda's worshippers.

Vestal: Generally, the Imperial equivalent of a nun in the north, a female monk.

Wall, the: A large wall separating the Empire from the northern barbarians. Its origins are a mystery.

Zoar: The capital of Kheroe. Nicknamed "the City of Stone" because its buildings are carved from rock hill. The King of Kheroe and the Council of Elders rule it in name. Its lighthouse is famous across the world.

IMPERIAL CITY MAP KEY

Suburro: An ancient, poor section of town, flanked by the Equine and Aurean Hills. Though widely known for its poverty and shanty homes, many great Imperials found their origins here.

West Side: Arguably part of the Suburro, a poor section of town predominating much of the western two-thirds of the city. It is filled with parks and spice dens.

a. **Armory District:** Once a center for the production of armaments and siege weaponry, this quiet district northeast of the Suburro is known for its charming shops and sprawling apartments.

b. **Kings Terrace:** An ancient enclave near the center of the city, featuring the mansions and homes of rich councilors and government officials. Most of these mansions cannot be bought and are passed down through families.

c. **Maxima:** Shops and theaters abound in this district, a center for drama and entertainment. Named for the war hero Adriano Maximus.

d. **Villa Regis:** A wealthy section of town, built along the shores of the North River.

e. **Bulus Wharf:** A section of town facing Imperial Harbor, a center of fishmongers and the fish trade.

Celsus Heights: A rich section of town built on a steep promontory. It is named for the infamous shipping magnate Celsus, who — rumor has it — burned down the area to build one of his mansions. Beside the rumor for arson, he was known for his unscrupulous business practices, charging exorbitant rents for those who stayed in his apartments, and was rumored to be a Strig, a kind of undead. Today, the mostly sumptuous apartment buildings overlook Imperial Harbor. Shops and music halls can also be found in abundance.

Harbor District: A sprawling district bordering the Imperial Harbor, featuring docks and warehouses.

Cloaca: The sewer district of Imperial City, flushing effluent into the South River. In ancient days, the first Cloaca broke and gushed forth water into the low-lying fields south of the river, creating the Palladian Swamp. The second Cloaca was built, much larger and stronger, after years of construction.

f.   **Market District:** A vast district predominating the center of the city, featuring its eponymous markets as well as slum areas.

g.   **Canyon Row:** Shops, apartments, temples and shrines predominate this central section of town. The Walk of Triumph begins here.

h.   **Newmarket:** A quiet district of shops and apartments.

i.   **Mud Bottom:** A dilapidated, ancient section of town, the most impoverished district.

Avediccus: A section of town facing the Palladian Swamp. Predominated by homes, shops, and small shrines, a concrete stairway into the swamp can be found here.

j.   **Meridia:** A section of town bordering the Palladian Swamp and city bounds, featuring apartment blocks, shops and administrative buildings.

k.   **Mystia:** A large section of town featuring markets, shops and homes, as well as the garrison for the city watch.

l.   **Villa Maris:** A section of town bordering the South River, highly developed, known for its taverns along the river's shore.

Emporia: Markets and shops predominate this central district.

m.   **Loud Surf:** A section of town built along cliffs, featuring often more pleasant weather than the city below. Its inhabitants call this section of town the city's most blessed area.

n.   **Perrine:** Named after the Emperor Perrius, this section of town has a mixture of wealth and poverty. It is a favored home for members of the military, as it connects to a road to Fort Mettius several miles away.

o.   **Gaboline:** Named after the Emperor Gabolus, originally built around a fort then outside of city bounds, this district is known for its quaint stone streets and temples.

p.   **West Limes:** A border area facing Wagontown Settlement, it is nonetheless highly developed and features vast theaters and gladiatorial arenas.

q.   **East Limes:** A border area featuring many gladiatorial arenas. It abuts a section of cemeteries outside city bounds.

r.   **Terrentian:** Named after the legate Terrentius, this section of town is known as a site of public executions. Shops and homes can be found here.

s.   **Majorian Markets:** Named for two sprawling indoor market complexes, it is rumored that anything in Varda can be found here on sale.

The Ricci: A walled-off, closed section of town that houses the city's ratling population.

t.   **The Strand:** A highly developed area of town known for its lighted roads, specialized taverns and bookshops.

u.   **Meletus**: A section of apartments, shops and temples bordering the North River.

v.   **Urubus**: A vast section of town below Celsus Heights, relatively impoverished, where the smoke of the city often settles. City administrators consider it a public health nuisance.

ABOUT THE AUTHOR

Cursed at birth with a wild imagination, Andrew Cooper spent his youth dreaming of worlds more exciting than Earth.

He is a graduate of the Odyssey Writing Workshop. His stories have appeared in Morpheus Tales, Fear and Trembling, Residential Aliens and Mindflights, among others.

Contact the Author

Visit **www.aj-cooper.com** to sign up for the newsletter and stay up-to-date on new releases.

Find him on Facebook at:

www.facebook.com/AJCooperauthor